CAPTIVE SOULS

By R.E. Taylor

ISBN 978-0-9942128-2-5

ISBN 978-0-9942128-3-2 (ebook)
CIP National Library of Australia
Shadowlight Publishing
Redbank Plains, Queensland, Australia
www.shadowlightbooks.com

DEDICATION

There are a lot of people I would like to dedicate this book
to but two in particular the real life Tina and Edward, who
"lived" in an abandoned church which was changed into
a theatre. Tina was a lively spirit who liked to play games
with us while Edward was more aggressive towards us.
Anyway, they inspired this story and I thank them. I would
also like to thank Elizabeth Waterhouse for her all efforts
in editing my work as well as Audrey Van Ryn and Elsbeth
Johnson for their proofreading skills.

CHAPTER 1

At one time, there were a dozen movie theaters scattered throughout the city of Akron, Ohio. Some offered live shows, but most showed movies ranging from the old silent films to movies made just a few years ago.

The thing was, the movie palaces were slowly replaced with multiplexes that had less than one hundred seats per screen and sixteen or more theaters under one roof. That was the reason the Strand Theater on West 11th St, just a bit down the block from State Street, died. It wasn't lost because of its age... it just wasn't in a mall, and that was where the people were.

For more than twenty-five years after the last movie was shown, sadly the Strand sat empty and neglected. Oh yes, people talked about her and the memories they had shared there, but not one person looked in through the dirty doors, much less went in to see what the theater was like.

That was truly a shame. The red velvet curtain that lined the stage was still there, as bright and as red as ever. Unfortunately, it was now covered with spider webs, but it was still there. All seven hundred seats were still there, seats raised as if saluting, and not one was torn. The concession stand was still there, and there were even a couple of petrified Mars Bars in the glass case. They were half eaten by the mice that freely roamed around the lobby, but enough was there to tell what they were. There were even discarded ticket stubs thrown around the floor, all now faded and barely readable, but they were still there. It was as if the people who were there for the last show had just disappeared.

Several times developers wanted to buy up the land and tear the theater down, but something always happened at the last minute to stop it. Sometimes the city wouldn't grant the necessary permits. Other times the developer would suddenly have a change of heart, or maybe they'd find another location, but there was always something that kept this particular theater intact.

Finally, a young man named Stephen Baker, who had always dreamt of owning a theater that didn't only just show movies, but also had live plays, walked by the old Strand. He didn't see the old discarded Strand that was right in front of him; instead he looked and saw a marquee with its bright lights announcing a new show. He also saw the ticket booth alive with action; he saw ticket takers and usherettes dressed in the uniforms they would have worn forty years before. He didn't see an abandoned building. He saw a theater as grand and beautiful as it was that day in 1922 when it first opened its doors. At that moment his heart was set on purchasing the Strand Theater and to restoring it to the showplace it had once been.

It took him a little while to work out the details, but after many months of haggling and negotiations, he finally opened the doors of the Strand Movie Theater, and saw exactly what he had hoped for: a theater that he owned and that he could now happily bring back to life.

He started his efforts alone, hauling out decades-old garbage and papers. The rest of the time he spent chasing out the mice and roaches that scurried across the floor in nearly every corner of the building. Then came the wallpaper and paint. He was very, very careful to match as closely as possible the original look of the walls, ceiling, and floors. The white granite statues that lined the lobby were cleaned and polished; the brass was shined until it reflected the sunlight enough to light the whole lobby. Even the toilets were worked on for days at a time to get them to look brand new.

When he slept, which was less than four hours a night, he dreamt about the theater, the way it was when he was a kid, and the way he wanted it to be again.

As the days, weeks, and finally months became longer and longer, some of the neighborhood people started stopping by to help paint, clean, or just give some encouragement to this young man... the man who was taking something that they had once ignored, and, through his tireless dedication, rekindled their interest again. However, along with the well-wishers there were a few who told stories of things happening in the building just before they closed the doors. It was nothing serious. No one got killed, or anything like that, but what they said was disturbing all the same.

One man, Stephen guessed he was somewhere around seventy-five or eighty years old, told of a young woman who liked to walk around the theater. She never spoke to anyone, but she liked to play jokes on people, like turning the lights on and off, shutting off the singer's microphones, and tilting the dozens of old photographs that lined the lobby and hallways of the building.

Stephen listened intently to every story that was told to him. He remembered, as a kid, that he had seen a lot of things he couldn't explain, but this was the first time that he had heard a large number of stories about a building with an entire history of spirits hanging around. However, just like he did when he was a kid, he dismissed everything as a bunch of old people just keeping something they heard alive by sharing all their stories with him.

One night, though, about two months after he bought the building, Stephen was just getting ready to lock the doors when he looked back and saw a young woman standing at the concession stand. He walked back into the theater and stood about twenty feet away from her. He could see her mouth moving and her hands move, as if she was asking for some of the candy that used to be in the glass case. He could not hear her voice, but it looked as if she was talking to someone who wasn't there. She had a lovely face and sad blue eyes; her hair was quite beautiful long and auburn. She was wearing a long black cotton dress, with white flowers around the sleeves and neck. The bottom half of the dress also had the white flowers, but they were a lot larger and a lot more noticeable. She had on a string of grayish, white pearls centered with a very large, red stone. Suddenly she reached into her purse as if she was paying for something, then she turned and walked back into the theater without even acknowledging that he was standing there. He watched as the curtains hanging in the doorway opened around her and then swung shut.

"Hello?" he called out, as he followed her through the doorway, but then he only found a dark and empty theater. "Hello?" he called out a second time, a little bit louder than before. His voice echoed through the empty room, but there was no response. He walked row by row, checking the seats. He knew that every seat was up when he left. He was kind of obsessive and compulsive about things like that, and despite the fact that his friends and employees joked around about it, that was something Stephen was actually very proud of.

Finally, after checking every row, he found one seat in the twelfth row that was down. He touched the cushion and it felt cold, colder than the surrounding room, and he saw in the dim light that there was an impression which looked as if someone had been sitting there rather recently.

"What the heck?" he said in an irritated voice. He didn't say anything else. He just smoothed the velvet on the seat, put it back up where it belonged, and walked back up the aisle. Suddenly he heard something, and, as he turned, he saw the same young woman with the auburn hair walking across the back of the theater and toward the front doors.

"Wait a minute!" he yelled, as he rushed back up the aisle. "Hold it right there," he said with more authority, as he stepped into the hallway at the back of the theater. He looked for her once again, but she was gone. After checking the doors, he found they were locked. He checked the entire theater again and found nothing. The lights were off, the seats were all up, and even the Coke cup he had drunk from earlier had been thrown away. He let himself out, double checked that he had relocked the doors, and went home for the night.

He spent the night thinking about that young woman in his theater and what had happened. In fact, he didn't get much sleep during the night at all. Every time he tried, another vision he could not understand came to him and he was awakened again and again.

The morning couldn't have come soon enough for Stephen Baker. The sun shone through the window and he crawled out of bed, dragging himself to the bathroom. He looked at the shower. It was inviting, but he whispered to himself, "Oh, damn it. I'll take one when I get home." It wasn't as if he was dirty or anything like that, he was just too tired to give a damn about anything other than trying to force his eyes open with some strong, very strong coffee.

Stephen had a couple of meetings before he got to the theater. The first was to arrange the order of some of the older vintage films he wanted to show. The other was at the bank, to try to arrange an additional loan in order to make a couple more improvements to the building before it opened.

The meetings took a little over an hour each, and after stopping at Hamburger Haven, he finally made it to the theater.

The doors were still locked, but once again he could see through the windows the same young woman at the concession stand. As he opened the door, he could see she appeared to be talking to someone, but there was still no one there. He didn't walk further into the theater lobby; he decided that he would just stand there and watch to see what was going to happen.

She was wearing the same dress she was wearing the night before.

As he watched, Stephen saw her point to several different places in the glass case, smiling at whoever she was talking to. A couple of times he saw the sweetest blush come across her cheeks, as if someone said something to her that either flattered or embarrassed her. From the smile, he guessed that her color didn't come from embarrassment. Finally, it looked as if she gathered up some things he could not see, holding them in a way one would hold a present. Once again she smiled and turned, walking through the curtains and into the theater.

"Hold it right there!" he said with authority, as he stepped further into the hallway at the back of the theater, but when he opened up the theater entrance curtains to look for her, once again she was gone.

"Who in the hell was that young woman?" he asked out loud.

"That was Tina," a voice said from behind him. "She has been around here since the mid 1930's. No one knows anything about her. She just goes to the concession stand, buys something, and goes in to watch the movie."

"What are you doing here, and what are you talking about?" Stephen asked the man.

"I don't remember exactly what the movie was, but the first time she was seen here was way back in 1933… at least, that is what my grandmother always told me."

"I do not understand. What are you doing here and who the hell are you?" Stephen asked, as he turned in puzzlement to look at the man standing behind him.

The man, who was obviously in his mid-seventies, said that his name was Edward Harold Lloyd and that he had worked behind the concession stand when he was a teenager. "I spent a lot of my younger years here," he said. "It was nothing to see her come up to me. I never heard what she was saying and she never took anything I offered her, but to tell the truth, it kind of got to be sort of calming whenever she showed up. At least to me… the universe was in order when I saw her. I knew everything was okay."

"What happened when she didn't show up?" Stephen asked.

"There were only four times she didn't make an appearance and the theater closed a couple weeks after that," Edward stated, as he walked with Stephen back into the lobby. "The last time was back in 1963. It was a few weeks after Kennedy got shot. Naturally business had been lousy, as people just didn't feel like going to the movies, so it was decided to close the Strand. I remember that final day, we were all very upset. Now, if I remember right, there were five showings that day, but don't hold me to that, and they were all sold out. The movie was a comedy, but, believe me, the place was like a funeral. No one was laughing and I even saw a couple of people crying; they just didn't want the old Strand to close. But the owners weren't making the money they wanted, so the doors finally shut after the Saturday night show. Everyone who worked there and knew about Tina was very concerned about her and kept looking for her, calling for her, but she never showed up, and this beautiful theater died that night."

Stephen looked at Edward, half with disbelief, and half with curiosity, wondering why this man had suddenly appeared in his theater. He asked if there had been anyone since then who was in the building or saw 'Tina' walking around anywhere around the building.

"No," Edward replied. "There may have been some people, maybe a few, who looked through the doors, but I don't recall anyone saying that they have seen her hanging around. As far I know, you're the first person who's been in there since 1963. I guess it's just been those rats and roaches living on that petrified candy and popcorn. I imagine it was pretty hard after all those years."

Stephen didn't say a word. He just stood there, watching the concession stand to see if 'Tina' would come back, and listening to this old man rambling on. Finally, he told the old man that he had a lot to do and not a lot of time to finish it in.

The old man turned and started walking out of the theater, but before he did, he looked at Stephen straight in the eyes. "Tina is a friendly little girl. You be nice to her. Let her do what she does and they won't cause you any trouble," he said cryptically, as he started walking away. As he left the theater and walked away, he kept turning back and locking his eyes on the Strand Movie Theater's new owner.

"Wait a minute!" Stephen called out in shocked disbelief to the man as he walked out of the theater. "Did you say, *they?*" The old man kept walking away, mumbling as he walked. Once again, Stephen tried to ask, but he couldn't get through to him and suddenly, softly through the mumbles, he heard him say, "Tina is a friendly little girl. You be nice to her. Let her do what she does, and they won't cause you any trouble."

"Who are they?" he yelled. The man didn't say another word. He turned the corner and was gone.

Stephen walked back into the theater and locked the door. His first stop was the concession stand. There was a fresh layer of dust across the glass and in the middle were two, very slight handprints. The dust was barely moved, but he could see the outline of a hand. He placed his hand on the glass and saw that the handprints were about half the size of his. He also noticed that the fingers were slim and tapered like those of a teenage girl. Other than that, he made sure that the concession stand was untouched.

As he was checking, his thoughts returned to the young woman he had seen a few minutes before. What if she was the 'Tina' that the old man had talked about? What could he do to keep her happy, and was there any way to talk to her? The last question he didn't just think about, he said it out loud and not in a whisper.

As he walked toward the theater itself, he started to become apprehensive about the building, everything that he had seen, and the stories he had been told.

The deep red velvet curtain hung nearly to the floor. It was old and ratty in some spots, but other than that it was as good as the day they hung it, back when the theater first opened. His movement made it move slightly as he approached. He opened it and stepped through. The theater was as dark as night, but usually the exit signs gave him enough light to travel up and down the aisles, however, somehow they had gotten turned off during the night. There was one extremely small light at the edge of the stage, but it was like looking at a single star in the midnight sky… a mere point of light but nothing more.

He reached over and threw the switch that was located behind the curtains at the entrance. The exit lights flickered as if they were candles instead of bulbs, but they finally kicked on and the theater was filled with a red glow.

Then, there in the twelfth row, he saw her. She just sat there, as if she was watching a movie, eating some popcorn and taking sips from a cup of Coca-Cola. The more he watched, the more he swore that a couple of times he saw her whisper to someone seated next to her, but all of the seats beside hers were empty.

Quietly he made his way down the theater steps. A couple of the steps creaked under his weight as he thought to himself, there was another thing that had to be fixed. As he moved, he kept his eyes on the young woman, but she was too entranced in the movie and whoever she was talking to, to pay any attention to him. He finally got to the twelfth row. She was in seat fifteen, which was towards the middle of the row, so he took the seat directly behind her in row thirteen.

"Hello," he said. She ignored him, but although he couldn't hear it, she appeared to be laughing at something on the screen.

"Hello," he said again, in a slightly louder voice. As with the first time she didn't look over, didn't say anything, and acted as if he wasn't there.

"She either can't hear you, or she doesn't want to hear you," said a voice from the back of the theater.

Stephen looked back and saw it was Edward Harold Lloyd, the same old man from earlier, standing inside the entrance curtain. Stephen quickly stood up, moved back to the aisle, and started walking up the stairs to talk to the intruder. "Mr. Lloyd, how did you get in here?" he asked.

"I didn't think you'd remember my name," Edward replied.

"I have a good memory for names," Stephen replied. "Now, Mr. Lloyd, how did you get in here?"

"You left the keys in the door, so I thought I'd do you a favor and return them to you before someone stole them."

Stephen checked his pockets, and, sure enough, the keys were gone. He thought he remembered taking them out of the door and putting them in his pocket after relocking the door, but he could have been wrong. With everything that had been going on, how could he be sure of anything?

Edward Lloyd handed him the keys and looked at Stephen straight in the face. "She didn't answer you, did she?" he asked.

"No."

"As I told you, just let her be. She'll be happy and the theater will stay open as long as she remains happy."

"I just wanted to see…" Stephen started to say before he was interrupted.

"Mr. Baker, just let her be and I assure you they will leave you alone. If she wants to talk to you she will, but then she never has spoken to anyone before, so don't be disappointed if she doesn't. But of course, there is always a chance…"

Stephen's attention was then drawn back down the aisle because it was as if a movie had just ended. The young woman, whom Edward Lloyd had referred to as Tina, got up and walked to the stage door at the bottom of the screen and disappeared. The door never opened, but Stephen could have sworn that he heard the door open and close.

"Where does she go?" he asked. Edward responded that he never knew, and, quite honestly, everyone was too afraid to ever find out.

"All we know is that she does the same thing every time she appears and has for nearly eighty years. I do know that there is a staircase back there, but no one has used it for as long as I can remember. I'm not even sure if it will hold someone's weight anymore."

That gave Stephen something to think about, as the rest of the workers who had been helping out at the theater began to show up. As the first of the people came through the door, Edward Lloyd walked out without saying another word. Stephen did think of stopping him, but then he didn't want to have to say anything to the people helping out, much less try to go into any details about what was going on.

Stephen, his new staff, and some of the helpers spent the day talking and getting the final things done for the opening, which was scheduled for that Friday night. One of the older women did ask about the handprints, so Stephen, thinking furiously for a moment, had to tell her that he met a new girl the night before and brought her to the theater, since she was a kind of movie freak. The volunteer then had a look on her face that was a mixture of confusion and embarrassment, but that was good, as fortunately she didn't ask any more questions and he didn't have to come up with any more answers. Finally, sometime around 7:00pm he bought them all a pizza and got them together in what he called a 'magic circle,' to share a shot of Jack Daniels with him for good luck.

As he put the shot glass down he looked over the shoulder of Miss Greene, a woman who wanted to be the head of the concession stand, and he saw Tina standing there ordering her usual treats for the movie. He started talking to keep everyone's attention on him and not on what was going on behind them.

Suddenly he saw something that he never expected… Tina got her 'order' and was just standing there. She was not going into the theater like she usually did. She was standing still and looking at him, with a very faint smile on her face.

As their eyes met, she turned and walked into the theater. He followed, but once he made it through the curtain… she was gone.

"You guys do what you have to do tomorrow," Stephen said to the staff. "I have to take the day off and check some things out. I'll stop back later tomorrow night to lock up. Thanks for all your help today, it has been greatly appreciated." With that said he immediately departed, leaving the small group of people standing in the empty theater wondering what in the hell was going on and why their boss had left in such a hurry.

CHAPTER 2

Stephen Baker's 'important' plans were just to drive around and try to figure out what to do next. He did, as usual, stop at the Hamburger Haven out on old State Route 8 on his way home. It wasn't much of a place; he always thought of it as a hole in the wall, a dive actually, but they did serve the best little hamburgers he had ever found, and he was very hungry, so he polished off quite a few that night.

Once again, he did not sleep very well; he kept tossing and turning. But it was not so much what he had eaten, it was more that he could not stop thinking about Tina and all he had been told.

Stephen had never really caught up on his sleep and was exhausted from all the manual labor he had been doing, so when he finally did fall asleep, he slept till past noon, which was certainly not his usual routine. Once awake, aware of all he had to do, he quickly showered and headed into town. He stopped at the Cascade Plaza to eat his lunch. It was just a couple blocks from the theater, but it was hot out and the cool mist from a small fountain was just enough to let him relax.

He still could not get his mind off Tina. "Why did she look at me?" he said to himself in a voice just a little above a whisper. "That man Edward, didn't he say she never looked at anybody, that it was usually just the same routine... day after day after day?" Some guy sitting on the bench next to him was sort of listening, but trying hard not to look like he was listening. He took a bite of his McChicken sandwich and looked at Stephen with a kind of bemused look on his face.

"Hey, dude," he said, "I take it you've been watching a girl, and now that she's looked at you, it feels weird... right?"

"What?" Stephen asked.

"You like her, and now she is showing an interest in you and it freaks you out, right, dude?"

"No, it isn't like that at all, dude!" replied Stephen in annoyance at this man who seemed to be reading his thoughts. "To tell the truth, I have only seen her a couple times. Oh hell, you aren't ever going to understand and I don't have time to explain it to you."

The guy then had a confused look on his face and asked Stephen to try and explain it.

"Dude, it is really complicated," Stephen explained. "It is just something that is going to have to play itself out. That's it!" With that, before the guy had a chance to ask anything else, or make another 'knowing' comment, Stephen got up and started walking back to the theater.

"Hey, dude! Wait!" the guy yelled.

Stephen just kept on walking. It didn't matter what the guy had to say. In his mind, if that annoying man was yelling that the street was caving in he couldn't care less! He wanted done with him and the conversation, and that was that.

After taking a couple more detours on the way, picking up some groceries, he finally made it to the theater. The doors were unlocked, although there didn't seem to be anyone there. It was then that he realized he had the only set of keys, so there was no way anyone else could have unlocked the doors, even if they wanted to.

There on the concession stand was a note left by one of the people who had been working earlier. It was folded nice and neat, like the way you did it in grade school, and you were passing a note to that cute little blonde who sat next to you in every grade and every class you had. "I wonder whatever happened to her?" Stephen said out loud, as the cute blonde's face flashed through his mind, and then just as quickly his attention went back to the note.

"We left sometime around two o'clock," it said. "We got the carpets and the curtains all done, but Lindsey found something in the back. You might want to talk to her about it." It was signed by one of the women in the group. He wasn't exactly sure who it was, but he knew that the writing was unmistakably that of a woman.

He spent the next fifteen to twenty minutes just looking around. It was almost as if he was in some kind of a daze. He was mumbling to himself. What he was saying wasn't important and it probably wouldn't have made sense to anyone other than himself. Hell, he thought, there isn't anyone around, so he could say and do anything he wanted. After all, this was now his theater and if he wanted to shout from the rafters, so be it!

Now, it wasn't like Stephen to be so flippant. A few of his friends actually asked him on several occasions, when was he going to have the surgery to get the stick pulled out of his ass? He usually just laughed them off, but for some reason right now he was feeling relaxed, for the first time in months, so he decided to let his hair down and just chill.

After all, it was his building and he did love movies. So he went into it, threaded the projector with an old print of something or other, turned it on, and then went back into the theater to watch the movie. He wasn't sure what the movie was and he didn't recognize the actors, but it was funny and somehow it managed to take his mind off of everything that was going on.

Stephen must have sat there ten minutes watching the movie. It was hard to watch, as the film must have been sitting in that metal case since the theater opened so many years before. It was grainy and some of the scenes had turned sepia instead of the black and white it was originally shot in.

"You know... I always liked Roscoe Ates; he was a good actor," a woman's voice said from behind him.

He turned and saw Tina, the young woman from the concession stand, sitting behind him. Although he felt the blood rush from his face, he remained calm. If this young woman was who he thought she was, he sure didn't want to anger or scare her.

"Do you know this movie?" he asked.

"Sure," she said with a smile on her face. "It's 'The Grand Parade.' It's only very short, but I have seen it five or six times." Still not trying to upset her in any way, he asked her more about the movie. "Like I said, that man there is Roscoe Ates. The woman in the white dress is Catherine Hayes. I never did like her; she only made a couple of movies, but she is okay in this one…"

He leaned back to get a better look at Tina. She looked exactly as she did the other times he had seen her, except she appeared happy to be talking to him.

"You know what?" he said. "I must admit, I have never seen her before, but I think Myrtle Steadman would have done a much better job." He wasn't sure what he was saying, but it sounded good and his memory of movies, especially the old films, might just work for him. She looked at him and just smiled.

"My name is Stephen… Stephen Baker," he said.

Her smile got bigger, so big that it made her cheeks appear a deep, almost apple red. "My name is Tina. I come here all the time. It makes me feel happy."

"I am here most of the time," he said. He didn't want to tell her more than that. He thought that if he let her know that he owned the building it may shock her, and she may disappear before he got to find out more.

Just then the movie ended the screen turned to a very bright white. After his eyes adjusted to the light, he looked back and saw that she was gone. The seat looked as if it hadn't been touched.

"Tina?" he said in a soft yet controlled voice. Again and again he called out her name and every time he got the same thing… nothing but silence. He walked around the theater and out into the lobby, but all he found was another handprint in the fresh dust on the concession stand glass. He took a towel from the back shelf and wiped it clean, but no matter how hard he wiped he could still see the faded image of her tiny hands as she rested on the glass.

He spent the rest of the day watching movie after movie, hoping for her return. A few people knocked on the door and the phone rang more than a few times, but he ignored everything except what was on the screen. In the background he could hear the faint but constant click, click, click, of the aging projector. He thought about all of the movies that were shown on that screen, how many miles of film went through the sprockets, and he smiled. Instead of being annoyed by the sound, he found it strangely comforting as it echoed through the theater. The sounds were almost as if it was being projected in surround, with the way they bounced off one wall and then the other before they faded away.

This was the way movies were shown when he was a kid. None of this digital crap he saw at the multiplexes. This was real film, with all the scratches, static, and that clicking. Stephen Baker was a romantic at heart, so he had many fond memories of the movies he had seen, the girls he had dated, and the popcorn he had eaten.

There was this one special girl, Maryanne. He remembered he took her to the movies on their first date. In fact, it was at a theater just down the block from where he was standing. They dated for almost five years, until he finally got up the nerve to ask her to marry him.

Of course, it would have to be in the same seats, in the same theater, but it never happened. Maryanne just never showed up. She never answered his calls and was never seen again. That was back in 1975, but the memories were as clear and crisp as if it happened the day before. He always wondered what had happened to her, but he never did find out, and it always deeply bothered him.

Those clicks brought back the memories in vivid detail, making him as depressed as he was all those years ago. Tina also did not appear again, and as he sat there with his own memories of Maryanne and other lost dreams, the last movie finally ended. He just sat and stared at the white screen. Finally he 'woke up' from his trance, and, without any hesitation, walked out of the theater, through the lobby, and out of the door.

The noontime sun was long gone and there was no moonrise to speak of in the mid-evening sky either. There was still the slightest tint of red out behind the towers of the Cascade Plaza. Jupiter and Venus were next to each other, glowing like distant torches. The streetlights on Main Street were casting an amber tint on everything. Stephen just looked around and took in everything he saw as he started walking to his car.

He didn't see anyone and he probably wouldn't have talked to them if he had. For some reason… he felt cleansed of the past and instead thought of all he was achieving. Suddenly he felt content and nothing was going to ruin that rare feeling for him.

CHAPTER 3

Finally, the day came when the theater was going to open its doors. The movie wasn't supposed to start until sometime around 7:00pm, maybe 7:15, but there were already dozens of people waiting in line. Some had been there a couple of hours before the doors were even set to open.

Inside, the few people Stephen had hired were scrambling around, trying to make sure that everything was in its proper place. Stephen ran around making sure that every piece of paper was exactly where it was supposed to be, spending more than ninety minutes making sure that the cloths on the concession stand were perfect, and the chairs and tables were just right. They were not allowed to be even a half an inch off, or he would yell some vague threat that never really had any real purpose other than hearing his own voice, as he set about making everything perfect.

By the time everything was ready, there were almost three hundred people standing in line to buy a ticket. Now, it wasn't as if he was showing a new blockbuster; the movie he was showing was made more than forty-five years ago. Yet, for some reason there was a real interest in what he had to offer. Stephen could not quite understand why the people of this major city were looking for this type of old-fashioned entertainment, but apparently nostalgia was the current mood, and luckily, he, Stephen Baker, had hit on it.

As he opened the door and the crowd passed by him, he tried to greet each one as he took their tickets. There were a few he knew from the time he had been fixing the place up and others who had said hi to him on the streets, but the majority were strangers, and he actually liked that! The great highlight was when he looked at the concession stand and saw Tina walking toward it.

The crowd did not part, yet neither did she wait. She walked through them as if it they were not there. Once again, she ordered without anyone hearing or seeing her, and, as she usually did, she picked up her purchases and walked into the theater. Stephen immediately grabbed one of the girls from the ticket booth and told her to take tickets for a while, as he had something he had to check on before the movie started.

The movie started right on time, but as the last few people were shutting off their cell phones, there was the sound of shattering glass over by the restrooms. There were no windows or any glass anywhere in the area, as Stephen Baker was way too smart to use glass or china coffee cups. Everything he sold was in recycled paper. It made for a lot of garbage, but it was safer and it looked good to the customers. No sooner had the sound faded, Stephen was seen running through the darkened hallway to what he saw was a large vase shattered all over the floor.

The vase was extremely large with ornamental designs glazed on the side. It didn't really match the rest of the theater, but according to a couple of the women who worked there, it was the only piece of anything left over from the day the Strand Theater first opened. Stephen had kept it in a place of honor out of respect for the long history of the building.

There was no one around the area where the vase had been placed: the staff were all in their respective places, and the customers were all in the theater watching the movie.

A few seconds after he got to the shattered vase, one of the girls from the concession stand came over and started helping clean up the broken fragments of glass.

"Steve..." she said, as she bent over. "... look at this." She moved a couple of the larger pieces of the vase and lifted up a plant hanger from the debris.

"Laura, where did that come from?" he asked, while he got a few of the bigger pieces and put them in the garbage can in front of the restrooms.

She thought about it for a minute and pointed about ten feet down the hallway. Stephen looked where she pointed. A large fern was sitting upright on the floor as if someone had set it there, and about seven feet above the fern, two holes with tattered edges were shining like stars against the dark blue paint on the walls.

His eyes glanced back and forth between the holes in the wall and the plant hanger the young girl was holding. Again and again, his eyes darted back and forth as if he was trying to see something that wasn't there, or, most likely, he was trying not to see something that was right in front of him. After a few seconds, he got his senses back and once again he looked at the black piece of metal she was holding.

"How the hell?" Stephen asked, with a strong look of confusion. "How did that get here?"

He took it from her hand and moved it around between his fingers, before he allowed it to settle in the palm of his hand. It couldn't have weighed more than eight ounces, he guessed. How could something that light smash a vase the size of the one that lay in pieces before him? He pretended he had no idea, yet, actually, he did. It was in the back of his mind, but he would not let it come out. He would not allow himself to think about it.

It was then that he heard a ruckus coming from inside the theater. He knew that the movie was a comedy. He had watched it a couple of times to make sure that it was suitable for families, but this wasn't laughter or anything like that. Some of the voices sounded disgusted and others sounded slightly angry.

"Laura," he said. "I have got to go see what is going on. Can you get this cleaned up before someone gets hurt?" Before she could even answer, he turned and started walking extremely fast... not running, but kind of close... down the hall to where the sounds coming from the auditorium were getting louder and louder.

As he turned the corner, he saw what was happening and why the audience was sounding the way it was sounding.

The movie, which was half way through by now, had started running backward, and the lights at the front of the stage had been turned on.

"I'll have this fixed in a minute," he yelled into the theater. "For the inconvenience, I'd like to offer everyone a free coke while I get this straightened out."

Suddenly the crowd was quiet, and they all seemed to be very polite as they filed out to get their free drink. Of course, he still made money even with the free drinks, because the people were more than happy to buy some popcorn or candy to go with their refreshments.

Then Stephen ran up to the projection booth to find out what was going on with the movie. The minute he opened the door, he saw the young man he hired as projectionist lying on the floor, unconscious. Shoving the door open, he went in, just as the projectionist opened his eyes and tried to sit up.

"William, are you okay?" he asked. Once Stephen got an answer in the affirmative, he then asked the next important question... why was the movie running backwards?

"I have no idea," young William replied. "I was just sitting there, reading a book and waiting for the reel change, when suddenly the book flew from my hands. The next thing I knew, I was waking up and you were standing over the top of me." He reached down and picked up the book and showed it to his boss. It was still open to page one hundred and forty-seven and somehow the page was dog eared at the corner, as if to show where he had been reading if he lost his page. "Mr. Baker," I do not know what happened, but I tell you that I certainly don't like this feeling I am having."

Stephen asked him what feeling he was talking about. The young projectionist replied that he didn't like not knowing what had happened, and just a general feeling of confusion.

"You didn't have anyone up here with you, did you?" Stephen asked, as he noticed a bruise starting to form on the tip of William's chin. William assured him that he had been all alone, except for the time when one of the girls from downstairs brought him up a bag of popcorn and something to drink.

"You know, it gets awful hot up here, Mr. Baker. It's nice when the staff have the courtesy to remember we're here, once in a while."

Stephen agreed, and told young William to take a minute and then get the film running the way it should.

William checked the projector and immediately found the problem. Relieved that it wasn't anything serious at all, he said it would only take a minute to fix. He reached down next to the frame timer on the side of the machine and lifted a small clear glass lid and flipped a switch.

"What was that?" Stephen asked as he got to the door.

"It's a kind of a safety switch," William answered. "You use it if the film gets jammed in the projector. It rewinds it and gets the jam out so you can fix it." The tone of voice William was using was, unintentionally, making his boss feel as if William was trying to show off. He wasn't, but that was the way he sounded. "The switch works as long as you hold it. It isn't supposed to lock in the on position." William did go on with his explanation, not that it would have done any good, since Stephen had already left the room, making sure that he closed the door behind him.

Once he got into the lobby, he checked out the fuse box to see what was going on with the lights. He opened the box and found a penny stuck in one of the switches. The second he pulled the penny out and placed it in his hand, the lights down at the stage flickered for a second and then turned off. As the lights faded, the movie started again at the same point where it began running backwards.

The audience went back to watching the film, and even Tina was sitting in her regular seat. Stephen wasn't sure if she was watching the same movie as everyone else in the building, but at least to him, it looked as if she was having fun and was even talking to some of the people sitting beside her. Of course, they were not answering her. They weren't even looking at her, but she just kept on talking the whole time.

"How the fuck did that get in there?" he asked himself, as he finally looked at what he was holding in his hand and saw a copper image of an Indian looking back at him. "I haven't seen one of these in years." He muttered to himself again. He looked more closely at the coin and saw the date; it read 1907. "How the hell…" he started saying before the lights flickered and went off and the movie continued without as much as a popcorn bag crinkling too loudly.

As soon as the movie ended, the people started walking up the aisles. A few of them sat in their seats for a few extra minutes to watch the end credits, but for the most part, the majority of the audience left immediately and they all seemed happy.

Stephen told his staff later that he heard some of them saying how much coming back to the Strand brought back memories of what it was like when they were teenagers. He made sure he spoke to as many customers as he could as they walked out. He felt a kind of pride every time someone walked past him, either talking about the movie or the theater or even if they just had a smile across their face. He was happy.

As the credits ended, he walked back into the theater. There was, of course, the normal mess to be cleaned up, but it wasn't out of the ordinary. He looked around. The seats were all up, just as they should be, the curtains hung straight, and the screen didn't have a mark on it. He remembered back when he was a kid. They, or rather his friends, would always throw chocolate or pop at the screen. Every couple of weeks or so, the owners would have to remove the screen after the last showing and clean it. From what he saw… he wasn't going to have that same problem, thank goodness.

Then in the twelfth row, seat seven, there she was. Tina was just sitting there, watching what Stephen could only assume was a second feature. Although no theaters today could ever afford to do a double feature, he remembered that back in his parents' day it wasn't uncommon to show two or three features. It was obvious to see that young Tina was apparently from that era.

He motioned to one of the usherettes to stop what she was doing to come over to him. She was a young girl, maybe sixteen years old, although she looked younger.

"Do you see anyone in the theater?" he asked her.

Without looking, she just shrugged her shoulders, and other than that, she didn't say anything, other than to give a slight giggle, thinking that this may have been some kind of test.

"I am serious," Stephen inquired. "Do you see anyone in the theater?"

She looked again, shrugged her shoulders and told him that the theater was definitely empty.

"Mr. Baker, the last person left twenty minutes ago," she finally said. "The only ones here are me, Laura, and whatever that one boy's name is. We're supposed to stay to clean up... right?"

Stephen told her that she was right, and that they were all doing a great job and he was very pleased with the staff he had chosen. As he finished the sentence, he looked up again and Tina had disappeared. There were no popcorn bags or Coca-Cola cups where she sat, and the seat was raised to where it should be.

Once again, he signalled for the young usherette to come over, which she did as quickly as she did the first time.

"Did you see that young woman leave?" he asked.

The girl, who was obviously getting confused, asked what young woman. Stephen didn't answer. He just told her to get a sign and mark on it in large black letters that "THIS SEAT IS RESERVED" and hang it on row twelve – seat seven.

Later on, when he was with the three remaining staff in the lobby helping them clean up, Stephen repeated again that seat seven in row twelve was a reserved, private seat and that no one ever would be allowed to sit there.

"I don't care even if we sell out," he said. "No one is to ever sit in that seat. If someone does, you come and get me, and if they won't move they'll have to leave. That is the way it is going to be and I do not want any questions or discussions about it." He wasn't angry, but his voice did take on a tone that was almost dictatorial in nature.

Laura immediately went over to the box office, took a piece of paper and did exactly what her boss had requested her young assistant to do. She didn't understand it, just as her assistant had not, but she did it anyway, since he was the boss and it was his theater. While she was putting the sign on the seat, the other two started picking up the few candy wrappers and popcorn bags that were lying around.

When Laura finished, she finally got up the nerve to ask her boss what was going on. Stephen didn't go into detail about why the seat was being left empty, except to say that there was a VIP who liked the movies and that seat was always to be kept open just in case she showed up. Of course, he knew that she was going to be there for every show; at least he hoped she would be, but he wasn't going to say anything about that right then, if ever.

It took about an hour before they were all finally ready to leave. It always took some time. The theater was actually quite easy to clean, but Stephen's obsessive behavior caused him to insist that the staff never leave until everything was checked and checked again by every employee, and then finally checked by himself. Eventually, Stephen did get to lock the door and head for home, but not before he looked back to see if Tina was going to watch another movie. The lobby and concession stand were empty, as he turned and started walking away.

He soon caught up with Laura and young William and they walked together to their respective cars. No more than a half a block away from the theater, his cell phone rang. He always allowed it to ring three times before he answered it.

"Hello?" he said, as he put the phone up to his ear. He didn't say another word while he had the phone in his hand, but he did get a confused look across his face. The call lasted about thirty seconds, and both Laura and William observed the expression on his face, and knew that someone had said something that had really surprised their boss.

"What was it? I hope nothing's wrong?" Laura asked, as he hung up the phone with a perplexed look on his face.

"No, nothing really wrong," Stephen replied. "It was just very weird. Someone called, and the only thing they said was to check out the history of the theater." He stopped to ask Laura and William. "Do either of you know anything that I don't about the place?"

Both Laura and William shook their heads.

"Well, I guess in that case I am going to have to find out what that call was all about," he said. Stephen inquired if there was a library or historical society somewhere nearby.

William pointed down West 11th and told him to go down to State Street, turn left and go down to the end of the street. "The main library is on the right-hand corner," he said, adding that there was no way that his boss could miss it.

Stephen checked his watch. It was a little after 11:00pm. The library would be closed, so he invited William and Laura to McDonald's for a cup of coffee or a coke before they went home. Both were tired, so they politely declined the offer and went on their way.

Stephen thought about it for a minute or two and decided that going home may be the smart thing to do. After all, coffee would do to him what it had done so many times: it would keep him awake and give him time to think about that very strange phone call, and then he would never get to sleep.

CHAPTER 4

Stephen got home sometime around 11:30pm and after a couple of his normal Jack and cokes, went straight to bed. He usually had a Jack and coke before he went to bed. Someone asked him about it once, so he explained that it helped him relax and not have the bad dreams he constantly had when he was a kid. That night, though, he didn't get to relax; his muscles were hurting and so he twisted and turned for a couple of hours before he managed to finally drift off.

He convulsed a couple of times after that, but eventually slept soundly, until something in his bedroom disturbed him. It sounded like someone was moving a chair in the room, but when he opened his eyes, everything was in its proper place.

Once his eyes closed again, he heard a man's voice calling his name, yet it didn't sound like it was in the room with him. To Stephen it sounded like it was outside, maybe in his yard. This time he got up and looked around, walking to the window. His eyes were still half closed with sleep and it was dark out since it was barely a crescent moonrise. There was still enough light from a street lamp down the road to see. There was nothing... nothing at all. Then he distinctly heard his name called and again he looked around, but there was nothing to be found anywhere.

"What the fuck is going on?" he asked himself.

"I am here, Stephen, to talk to you," the voice said.

"Who are you?"

"I am here, suggesting again, that you find out about the theater you own. There are things that you do not know that you should."

"Like what?"

"That is not for me to tell you. Just look for the things that are hidden from your eyes and you will find the answers to all of your questions."

Stephen then looked around again and still didn't see anything.

"Where are you? Why can't I see you?" he asked, but there was no reply. The room was as silent as a tomb. He couldn't even hear the music from the shit-kicker redneck bar down the street.

Once again, he lay down, drifted off to sleep, and for the first time in a very long time was able to dream.

The mist of his dream cleared and he was somewhere he didn't recognize. It looked like Akron, but everything was wrong. The people looked so different; their clothes were the kind of stuff you might find in an antique store. All of the men wore suits and the women wore only dresses instead of shorts or trousers. They also weren't the bright colors he had been used to, but, rather, they were dull, flat tones.

He looked around and saw a few cars, but they were old... really old. Yet the buildings looked brand new. The bricks were bright red and some of the buildings had white marble on their fronts. Stephen was surprised at just how beautiful they looked. He never did like the big, modern, glass boxes he now saw every day. Finally a man walked by and Stephen stopped him.

"Excuse me, sir," he started to say.

The man looked at him and said hello without a second's hesitation.

"I got turned around somehow. I was wondering, could you tell me where I am?"

The man pointed up at a street sign and told Stephen that he was at the intersection of State and 11th Streets.

Stephen looked around again and about a block away was a streetcar passing through the carts of vendors that lined the street.

"This is so cool," Stephen said to the man, as he struggled to take everything in.

"I beg your pardon?" the man said.

"Nothing," Stephen said. "I have just never seen anything like this before. I do have another stupid question for you."

The man agreed to answer and Stephen asked him what the date was.

"You don't know the date?" the man asked with a somewhat surprised look on his face.

Stephen said that he didn't. Then he made up some excuse about being sick for a long time and not being able to get out of the house. The guy bought it because he didn't laugh and he told Stephen the date… May 14th 1907. He shook his head in confusion, thanked the man, and started walking toward Sassafras Street.

It was no more than a block and a half before he saw the property that his theater sat on. The building that he knew wasn't there. There were large elm trees next to a rather ragged sidewalk. As he walked beneath the elm trees, he could hear hundreds of baby birds chirping for their mothers to bring them a little something to eat.

Shaded by the trees was a set of marble steps that led up to a black wrought iron door. It was open and he could see the faint flicker of candlelight through the opening. He also heard singing. It was not the upbeat music he'd heard coming from some of the other places he had passed earlier. It was more spiritual than that.

There was a sign beside the door. He could see it, but he couldn't make out what the words were. As he stood looking at the sign, a man with a long grey and brown beard walked out and started walking past him.

"Sir, may I bother you for a moment?" Stephen asked.

The man stopped, smiled and nodded his head without saying a word.

"What is this place?"

"It is called L'église du Sacré Féminin… The Church of the Sacred Feminine. It has been here since 1845," the man said.

Stephen stood there not speaking as he looked at the building. He noticed that it had six white pillars holding a front portico. They looked familiar; he was sure of it. He thought for a minute and realized that they were the ones he had seen next to the walls in the lobby of the theater. He noticed them, because in all of the art deco of the building, they seemed to be out of place, as if someone had just thrown them in there for the hell of it.

Stephen didn't have the chance to ask anything else, as he heard a series of blood-curdling screams coming from inside the building. He tried not to listen, but it was too loud and too continuous to ignore. The last one sounded like the screams of a young girl and nearly ripped his heart right out of his chest.

At that moment, his eyes opened. His face and head were covered with flowing streams of sweat and his bed was so soaked that he could no longer take being there.

"What the fuck was that?" he asked. He was still shaking and his eyes looked like big black saucers as he tried to look around and make sure that he was back in his own bedroom. He was, and once he realized it, he started to relax just a bit, although the shaking was still present.

The voice came back and spoke to him again from nowhere.

"I told you that there is a lot to know and a lot for you to learn and then you will understand," it said.

Stephen looked at the clock. It said that it was 5:30am, but he felt like it was a lot earlier. He did not want to think and he didn't want to talk to a voice that wasn't there. Not that he believed what was going on anyway; he just wanted to get back to sleep. He took the time to change his underwear and change the sheets, then climbed back into bed. He fell asleep as soon as his head hit the pillow… which was still wet but it didn't matter. He just wanted to sleep.

He usually set the alarm for 7:00am and he knew that he set it before he fell asleep, but either he didn't hear it or it didn't go off because when he finally did wake up it was almost 11:30am. He then realized he hadn't eaten anything since sometime around two o'clock in the afternoon the day before. It wasn't that he wasn't hungry. His nerves from opening the theater and the dream that he had been part of that night had kept him from thinking about food, much less about eating anything. Still, he knew he must eat so he microwaved a couple of small breakfast sandwiches and took off down to the library to see what he could find out.

He got there sometime around 1:00pm. The library was full of senior citizens, who, after spending the morning riding the buses around town, spent the rest of their day reading books they found on the shelves. He recognized a few of them from the night before, so he politely said hello to them, but moved quickly past them, as he was not in the mood for conversation.

The first thing he did then was to head towards the inquiry desk, which was up on the second floor. As he got out of the elevator, there was a sign hanging from two bronze wires that told him where the research department was, so he figured it best he look there first.

There was no door, so he just walked in. Glancing around, he saw thousands of old books that looked as if they had been stored in someone's attic and forgotten about. There were a few new ones, but most of them looked old… really old.

"How may I help you?" a woman asked, as she walked out of an office at the back of the room. She was not the type of woman he expected to be working in a library. She wasn't old. He guessed her to be somewhere around thirty or thirty-five at the most and she wasn't wearing the office clothes he thought a librarian would wear. Instead she had on an ankle length skirt… denim, he thought, and a paisley blouse. Actually, she kind of reminded him of the hippies he saw when he was a kid… even to the point of having a big white flower tucked over her ear.

"I am trying to find the history of a property I own, the theater over at 145 West 11ᵗʰ Street," he said.

"The old Strand Theater, right?"

He replied that, yes, it used to be the Strand, but now it will be called the 11ᵗʰ Street Theater. Well, at least it would be after the new marquee showed up. Actually, that was a rather sore point with Stephen. Part of the deal he had made when he bought the place was that the previous owners were supposed to change the marquee, but they never did and now it was going to take about a month until the company could send a replacement. He had wanted to start afresh, to put his own signature on this beautiful old theater, and also there was a coffee shop down the street called "The Strand". It was a bit of a dive and he didn't want his theater associated with it.

"You know," she started, "I wonder if it is a good idea to change the name of something so many people are so used to?"

In his heart he was possibly beginning to agree with her, but he ignored the statement... as he tried to get the conversation back on track.

"There have been some stories going around about the building and I want to see if any of them are true," he said, as he glanced around the book shelves.

She walked over to a stack of books that looked as if they hadn't been touched in years, pulled out a few that she believed might be of interest, then took one from the middle of the stack. He watched as she dusted off the edges and handed it to him. It was entitled, "The Unknown and Dark Legends of Akron."

"Here, look at this for a while," she said. Stephen took it, started looking at the table of contents, and almost immediately saw what he was looking for. Out of the fifteen chapters, there it was. Chapter three under the title "L'église du Sacré Féminin: The Witches Church".

He leafed through the first few pages of the book and saw stuff about tunnels that ran between the old train station and the main post office. He saw other stories about several of the cemeteries in the area, and then finally there it was. Chapter three, with all the information he had been looking for.

There was a very old looking engraving on the first page. It was the building he had seen the night before. The lines were very thin, making the picture look more detailed that it really should have. The detail was amazing. It even showed the slight cracks he had noticed in the pillars. He hadn't seen the cracks in his dream, but he did remember them from seeing them in the theater's lobby.

Beneath the picture was some fancy lettering that said, "L'église du Sacré Féminin – 1845 – 1907". The writings about the church didn't start until the next page, so he took the book and walked to a cubicle in the corner of the room. Sitting down, he opened the book and flipped through the pages to see how much information there was, before finally starting to read.

"L'église du Sacré Féminin was formed by fundamentalist Catholic priests and monks from a church in Besançon in the Franche-Comté region of France. The original church was formed in 1375 and was maintained throughout the 18th century, when the French Government dissolved the church and sent the church to the Americas to end their influence with the local population."

He continued to read, taking more and more interest in the information. When the librarian walked over and offered him another two books to look at, he simply waved her off without saying a word. Smiling, she placed the books beside him. Stephen observed none of this; his eyes never left the pages in front of him.

"Their priests and monks settled in the British colonies, keeping to themselves. They developed a conviction that everything other than puritanical, Christian belief was evil and must be dealt with without mercy or patience. Once the colonies, later the United States, began to grow, the members of the church spread out across the new territories, finally settling in the western territory of New York. In 1845, the church members came out of hiding and settled in Erie, Pennsylvania, setting up their church.

"L'église du Sacré Féminin lasted until 1907, when rumors surfaced of the priests torturing and murdering local citizens whom they felt were practitioners of witchcraft and other black arts. It was rumored that twelve people were killed for their infidelity. Although there were no written records or any other evidence of any such acts, the church was burned to the ground by the citizens of the Erie area on Friday, March 15th, 1907. The priests and church members fled to the west and were never heard from again."

Stephen finally looked at the librarian and asked her what she knew of the property where the Strand Theater now stood.

"From what I heard…" she said. "In fact, quite a few years back, after the theater closed, several people tried having a small business there, but no matter what they tried, everything failed. A couple of them even reported seeing ghosts, as if there is really such a thing." She kind of snickered when she said that, mainly because she had heard all the stories over and over all her life. She never believed them, since most accounts came from people who had seen the other side of sixty and she thought, possibly they were all a little senile.

"What, you don't believe in ghosts?" Stephen asked. Then he just shook his head as she replied she thought that anyone would have to be crazy to believe anything like that. Stephen smiled, picked up the book he had found so interesting, as well as the two others she had also set down on the table beside him. He thanked the librarian, and went to check the books out. Before he left, he made his way over to the librarian and told her not to always doubt something that she could not see.

The woman shrugged her shoulders and just rolled her eyes. It was obvious that she thought Stephen was a little… not much… but just a little crazy.

CHAPTER 5

It took Stephen about an hour to make it from the library back to his house and then finally down to the theater. A couple of the workers were hanging around out front, waiting for him to arrive. He could also hear the phone ringing inside, but he just slowly reached into his pocket, took the key out, and held it in the lock, hesitating for quite some time. He knew that he had to go in, but for just a moment, he was going to do everything he could not to open the door and go inside.

His behavior was so strange that Laura asked, "What's wrong?"

"Nothing," he replied. "I've just had a big day and I haven't had anything to eat yet." As soon as the door opened, the workers walked in, and he took a $20 bill out of his pocket to give to Laura. "Could you do me a favor? Do you think you could run over to Subway and pick me up a sub? I don't care what kind; anything will do, just with a lot of shit on it."

She nodded and took the money he handed her before heading over to Subway. It took her a while to get back, since she stopped and talked to some friends on the return trip. When she arrived back, the boss was nowhere to be found. She asked a couple of people and found out that he was in his office and didn't want to be disturbed. She didn't pay much attention, and, as she got to his door, it was open a crack. She could see Stephen picking glass shards off of the floor.

"What happened?" she asked as she walked in after a very feeble attempt at knocking.

Stephen didn't look up; he just kept picking up the glass. "I don't know what happened," he said. "I walked into the office and my lamp just flew off the shelf. I actually watched it. It was almost as if it was thrown down and purposely broken."

She asked where he was when it fell and he pointed at a chair across the room. She looked around and saw the book that Stephen was reading. He was at a page that told of the supposed deaths that occurred on the property. Laura picked it up and glanced at the cover.

"Wow, is that about this place?" she asked.

He replied that it was, and just as the last word came from his mouth, a picture frame, one that was there from the previous owners, suddenly fell and smashed on the floor. Neither he nor Laura were anywhere near it, and, like the lamp, it seemed to have moved all by itself.

"What the hell!" he yelled with a touch of anger in his voice. "What the fuck is going on?"

Laura was so stunned she didn't say anything. All she did was start picking up the pieces of the picture frame and set them on his desk.

Suddenly one of the ticket booth workers, Meghyn, walked in and asked what time the doors were supposed to open. She also informed her boss that customers were already starting to gather outside the theater.

"What time is it now?" Stephen asked. Both Laura and Meghyn answered as if they had one voice, that it was about twenty minutes to one. Stephen thought about it for a minute and then said to give it ten minutes and start letting the people in. Meghyn happily said that she would do that. As she started walking back to the ticket booth, she hesitated; she then turned and went back into Stephen's office.

"Mr. Baker, sorry to..." she said.

"Please, Meghyn, let's not be so formal. My name is Stephen, but I'd really like it if all the staff just called me Steve," he said.

She looked at him and smiled. "Okay, Steve. What should I do about the girl at the concession stand?"

Both Stephen and Laura got up off the floor and looked at her. Immediately Stephen headed out towards the lobby, followed by Laura.

"What girl?" Laura asked.

"The one standing right there by the concession stand," said Meghyn.

"What girl?" Laura asked again.

"What, are you blind?" Meghyn asked in frustration.

"Meghyn, it's okay; that is Tina," Stephen said. "Whenever you see her, just leave her alone. She can be here anytime she wants. She never pays for anything, so don't even think about asking her, and she has a special seat reserved for her. To put it simply, she isn't really here."

"I understand," Meghyn said, as she turned and started walking back toward the lobby.

Laura looked somewhat confused as she went back into the office and finished picking up the pieces of the frame. Stephen soon came back into his office to help her. Laura looked at her boss with a very puzzled look on her face. "If I may ask... who is Tina?" she inquired.

"Laura, let's just say that she is a VIP and just let it lie at that," Stephen said politely while he put his hand on her shoulder, trying to calm her.

Stephen thought it was strange that he would care at all about how she was feeling, or what she even thought. He knew that he was the boss and she really didn't need an explanation, but he wanted to give her something to keep the inevitable questions down to a minimum. "Every theater has one special person who has a history with the building and here in this theater, that person is Tina. I have talked to her and she is a very nice girl so..." He didn't finish the sentence, but he knew, well, at least he figured, that she understood exactly what he was saying. A few second later, Laura was done with picking up all the pieces, and was standing at the office door. "Thank you, Laura," he said.

"You're very welcome," she replied. He didn't see it, but there was a sparkle in Laura's eyes; maybe she didn't even realize it, but it was there. "I'm going to return to the box office now, if that is okay with you?" Stephen said okay and asked her to make sure that the rest of the staff were ready to open. She said okay once again and then immediately headed down the hall back to her work.

Stephen watched her as she walked away. For the first time he actually saw her for the first time, and at that moment, he realized how attractive she was. He also realized that he was a lot older and she did work for him, and so that alone made her off limits.

The doors opened and once again a large crowd of people crammed into the theater to watch another old movie. Stephen Baker was pleased, but also actually surprised that he and his theater were getting such a reaction. Outside of a few strange sounding footsteps across the floor in front of the screen, nothing really happened that afternoon. He did look through the black curtains a few times and each time he saw Tina sitting there watching the movie.

They had three showings that day and every one was as successful as the one before it. Not once did anyone complain or say anything negative about their time at the theater. Stephen went back to his office as the last name rolled across the credits. He just sat back, had a shot of Jack, and chilled. Never once did the thought of L'église du Sacré Féminin cross his mind. He was happy at all he had achieved and nothing was going to ruin that for him.

CHAPTER 6

Stephen went home and did some more reading from the book he had borrowed from the library. This time, at first he didn't look at the chapter about L'église du Sacré Féminin. Rather, he read about those tunnels under the train station. According to the book, they were used as part of the underground railroad during the Civil War. Unfortunately, it was discovered sometime at the beginning of 1865 and during that period, more than one hundred former slaves were beaten and shot. Their bodies were left to rot in those tunnels and both ends were sealed off.

"The tunnels are supposedly the most haunted place in the city of Akron," the book said, but Stephen thought about it for a minute and realized that with all the things that had happened to him in the last couple of days, he figured that his theater was probably going to be taking that title very soon.

He read for most of the night and saw the golden tint of morning shine through his window before he finally managed to shut his eyes and get some sleep.

When he awoke, it was sometime around noon. Once again, he either didn't hear the alarm clock, or he didn't set it. Either way, he was running late. Grabbing a shower and shaving wasn't much of a problem... a total of fifteen minutes... but trying to figure out what to wear was more difficult. He liked to wear suits to work, but he didn't have any clean ones; they all needed a trip to the dry cleaners. Instead, he decided to make it a casual Sunday and just wear a t-shirt and jeans.

He made it down to the theater about 1:00pm and went in. Someone followed him through the door, someone he didn't see, but he knew that they were there and it startled him when he heard a voice.

"Stephen," the voice said. "How are you and Tina getting along?"

Stephen turned around. He was sure he had locked the door behind him, but there he was, the old man standing there, as plain as day.

"Mr. Lloyd, how are you doing today?" he asked, putting his hand out. Now, this was very unusual for Stephen. He was not the kind of person who liked to touch or be touched, except, of course, if it was a female; then he was more than happy to touch.

"I am fine," he replied. "How is Tina?"

"She's doing well," Stephen replied. "How did you get in here?"

"I walked in as the door was closing. I guess you didn't hear me," Edward Lloyd replied.

Stephen told Edward about the conversation that he and Tina had that one day and about how he thought that she was a nice girl. "But," he added, "There have also been some strange things going on around here that I can't quite figure out."

Stephen then took a few minutes to explain about the lights, the vase, and everything else that had happened. He made sure to go into a little extra detail about the things that had smashed in his office. "The thing was, Mr. Lloyd, there was no one around them. It was just as if they were shoved or thrown," he said.

"Stephen…" Lloyd said, "… you DO know that there has been talk of five spirits who live here, don't you?"

"No, I didn't know that," Stephen said. The thing was, neither his face nor his reaction reflected anything at all. It was almost as if it was just an everyday occurrence that he expected to happen and would be disappointed if it didn't. "I take it that they all aren't like Tina?"

"I only know a lot about Tina. She can be a little bit of a prankster, but she never gets violent," Lloyd replied. "Actually, I haven't ever seen any of the others. They are just rumors."

As the old man was talking, Stephen looked around carefully to see if there was anyone else around, but since he had just got there himself, it was going to be a while before anyone else was even scheduled to show up.

"I have heard," continued Lloyd, "some really nasty stories about them, especially the one named Edward. He just doesn't like people around. It is too bad that we share that name. People always think that he is me."

"So what kind of things does he do?" asked Stephen, trying not to sound bothered by what he was hearing.

"Well, I have never seen him myself, but I hear he likes to break things, play with the electricity, and a lot of other stuff." Edward Lloyd then looked at Stephen and said that he had to leave, and, without another word, he just turned and walked out the door. Stephen tried calling out to him, but it was no good; he just walked down the hall, opened the door and left without even a goodbye.

Stephen Baker stood there totally bewildered, but still was enough on the ball not to let it shake him too much. He walked over and checked out the register at the concession stand, and saw that they had sold a little over $500 worth of pop, candy, and popcorn. He thought for a second and added up the money he made from tickets and concessions, and he realized that he had made something like $1,100 for the evening.

"That was a good evening," he said out loud to himself. He gathered up all the paperwork and walked into his office. The lights were on as he opened the door; he definitely remembered turning them off the night before. Looking around, he noticed that there was nothing broken and everything was in its place. The only strange thing was the light, but he decided that it was better to just accept it and thank whoever was responsible.

Just then, he did notice that there was something out of place, but it just wasn't broken or damaged in any way. He walked over to his desk. It was one of the books he had checked out of the library, "The Spirit Book". Looking closer, he saw it was open to a section on something called "Summerland," on page 394. Stephen didn't know what that was. He'd never heard of it, so he sat down and started reading.

The book said that Summerland, or The Summerland as it is sometimes called, is "quite real, and objective to its inmates as our world is to us". It added that, "it is a 'plane of illusion' which appears to be a blissful land of rest and harmony, partly a creation of the inhabitants' own desires and the pleasures of earth-life minus its drawbacks".

Stephen was still by himself in the theater. There were some of the usual creaks and moans that he had gotten used to in the last few weeks, but the more he read about "Summerland," the more he started to notice the sounds all around him. His mind wandered ever so slightly. What did this "Summerland" have to do with the theater and the way things had been happening? Of course, his thoughts didn't elicit a response, but then he didn't really expect them to.

It was now nearly 4:00pm and the first of the employees was knocking at the side door to get in. William was always the first to arrive, soon followed by Meghyn and Laura. Stephen guessed that they were friends outside of work, since he never saw one without the other. Lastly, through the door came Steph and Kelly. This was the first day Steph and Kelly were going to be working. They had been in training the last couple of weeks in front of house management, so Stephen had hardly ever seen them. He put the books into one of the desk drawers and went out to let in his staff.

After he had greeted and let them all in, he started back down the hallway to his office. He didn't realize it, but he must have left his computer on. He heard the keyboard clicking but it took him a second to realize what it was and where it was coming from. He rushed into his office to find his computer on, the monitor on, and Microsoft Word open. Across the screen was a message, "*Summerland will never open for the condemned*," it said. The message was cryptic, to say the least, and Stephen didn't understand who "the condemned" were. By this time, young Meghyn was standing beside him, staring at his computer.

"What the heck is Summerland?" she asked, in her little innocent voice.

"Nothing for you to concern yourself with," he said as he turned off the monitor and guided her gently to the door. "It's time to get ready to open." He walked the rest of the way with her. She kept talking and talking, but anytime she got close to asking about Summerland again, he did his best to change the subject.

Once he got up to the concession stand, he called everyone together and told them that the previous couple of days had been very successful, and thankfully he had a feeling that it was going to continue just as strongly.

As he finished talking, he looked over and saw Tina at the concession stand. She was doing her regular routine, but once again she looked at him and smiled. He smiled back, just before he told everyone that Tina was going to be in the theater that day, and if anyone saw her there once again, she was to be given VIP treatment.

That night there were only about seventy-five people who showed up for the movie. True, it wasn't as good as the previous two nights, but it could have been worse! Nothing major happened during the showings except for the lights flickering a couple of times... However, for some reason that night, the ticket booth, Steph informed him, showed over five hundred seats being sold at fifteen cents apiece. Stephen thought a minute and then remembered that was what a movie cost when he was a kid.

After he heard about the enormous crowd that wasn't there, he went back up to the ticket booth to find out what was going on. He asked Steph what had happened.

"I have no idea, Steve," she stated, not bothering to hide her confusion. "All of a sudden the thing just started running and it wouldn't quit. I even tried unplugging it, but it just wouldn't stop." By the time Steph was done talking, there were tears in her eyes and the poor woman was even shaking, afraid that she was going to be suspended or worse... fired.

"Steph," Stephen gently said. "It is okay. There is a lot of strange... very strange... stuff happening in this place. It is not your fault. Can you tell me how many people actually came in tonight?"

"I'm not sure," she said. "I just take the tickets. Kelly keeps count of who goes in or out."

He turned to Kelly, who was standing on the other side of the theater doors. "Well, Kelly, exactly how many people came in tonight?"

Kelly raised her hand from her side, looking at a tiny counter she had in her palm. She didn't want people to know that they were being counted, so she kept it in a small pouch she hung from her belt.

"I counted seventy-seven," she said, after checking the small numbers.

"How many does the booth say?" he said.

Steph checked her numbers. "It shows five hundred and eighty-two," she said. "There were seventy-seven at the regular price and five hundred and five at fifteen cents. Steve, what the hell is going on?"

He looked at her, and it wasn't hard to see that she was still scared she was going to get into trouble. Stephen couldn't tell if she was afraid for her job, or just what had gone on that evening.

"I guess I have to tell you something," he said. He thought for a minute, trying to figure out what to say and how to say it without scaring the fuck out these good people, or making them think he was totally out of his mind. "This building, hell, this property has a long... very long history, and sadly it was not a good one. People were tortured and killed here back in the late 1800's. They were killed for being what the pious bastards who owned this land considered witches. Tina, who I have talked about before, is one of them, but I was told that as long as she comes in, we will be able to stay open. According to the way people talk, there are five spirits who live here. From what I understand, they like to play jokes, but so far they haven't hurt anyone."

"Are they the ones who…?" Laura asked.

"Yes," Stephen answered. "They are the ones who keep turning the lights on and off, sending me messages on my computer, and they busted the vase."

Suddenly, Steph looked really perturbed, and a look of sheer terror came into her eyes. She came up to him and whispered softly, "Sorry, Steve. Stuff like this scares the hell out of me. I am sorry if I am letting you down, but I cannot work here any longer. I have to get out of here." Then she just turned and walked out of the theater without saying another word.

"Anyone else want to leave?" Stephen asked. No one else stood up, much less walked out the door. There was a lot more discussion, that was for sure, but no one seemed afraid enough to leave. Stephen Baker hoped Steph would return, but that was really up to her. At least the rest of his staff remained.

CHAPTER 7

It was about a week before anything else major happened at the old Strand Movie Theater, not that it was boring! There were the usual flickering lights, and for some reason, all of the change in the concession stand cash drawer disappeared and was replaced with money out of the 19th century.

Stephen actually found amongst this strange collection a couple of Morgan silver dollars and a single gold $10 coin. He quickly took the gold coin and sold it a local coin store for $648.50, quite a gift for letting a ghost hang out at the theater… at least, that was the thought that went through Stephen's mind as he counted out the money.

The strangest thing, though, was that the spirits took a liking to Laura. It, or they, would leave little gifts for her whenever she worked at the concession stand. One time it was an old coin. Another time it was a diamond ring… it wasn't pretty or big, but it was easy to see that it was old, very old. Laura just smiled when she found it and Stephen thought he saw her whisper, "Thank you," but he wasn't sure. She put it on, and, as far as he knew, she never took it off.

It was the Wednesday of that week that Stephen received a phone call from a group of local ghost hunters, who had heard about "the supernatural activities"… to use their words… that had been going on in the theater.

Stephen agreed strange things had occurred, but would not go into details about what he or his staff had experienced. They kept asking questions, and he just kept the answers as vague as possible, until he finally suggested that they come into the theater one night and see for themselves what exactly was going on.

He didn't have to suggest twice. They jumped at the chance, so both they and Stephen agreed that they would come in after the last showing the following night and do their investigation.

As soon as he hung up the phone, Stephen looked around to check there was no one there, and then he said in a loud voice, "Tina, Edward, guys? Some people are coming in here tomorrow night. I want you to behave and not show them anything."

Suddenly he heard a loud crash come from the lobby. He ran up the hallway and saw the glass on the concession stand smashed to pieces. He looked, but there was nothing amongst the pieces of glass that could have fallen down to break the case.

Finally, he looked around the case itself and found the bell that they used up at the ticket booth, when they had to turn money into him. The bell wasn't mixed in with the glass. As a matter of fact, it was nowhere near the concession stand. It was nearly fifteen feet away in a pile of papers, but Stephen reckoned it was the only thing around that could have broken the glass. He picked it up and put it on a nearby shelf and then began picking up all the broken glass.

Laura, Meghyn, and Kelly all walked in together, just a second or two after Stephen had picked up the last piece of glass. They all looked happy until they saw the shattered concession stand. "Did someone break in?" Kelly asked.

"No," Stephen answered. "It just happened a couple minutes ago." He instructed them to pull all of the candy out of the concession stand and throw it away, to make sure there was no broken glass left in the case, and then to restock it with all new snacks.

It was at the moment they started taking the candy out and throwing it away that young William showed up.

"What's going on?" he asked. Kelly and the others told him about the case being broken, just as the boss got there, and how he was throwing all the food away to make sure no one ate a piece of glass. William stood and watched as they put the last candy bar into the white trash bag, and then he followed them out to the dumpster.

The girls took the bag and set it on the ground next to the dumpster, just as if they knew what he was going to do. The minute the bag hit the ground, he rushed over and started filling his pockets with Raisinets, Hershey Bars, and caramel drops.

"You know, that could be dangerous," Laura warned.

William didn't answer. Suddenly he didn't look like himself. He looked as if he was one of those evil assistants in a bad horror film, and he walked as if he had a severely disabled leg. However, it was not disabled, in fact, it was just full of candy.

"C'mon, we have to get back to work," Laura said. "Steve is going to know we're up to something back here, if we don't get back."

"William, get your ass in here," Kelly said, partly under Laura's words, but she was still loud enough to get her point across.

William finally straightened out and he started walking into the building. He wasn't walking as fast as he normally did, but at least he was moving in the right direction. Slowly, he made it up the steps and through the door.

By now the girls had already started back toward the front door, leaving William on his own. There was candy dropping out of his pants, as he was still walking weirdly, but he didn't notice. Suddenly, as he walked down the hallway past Steve's office, he felt a sharp pain across the right side of his head.

Stephen was coming out of his office and stood there watching and actually saw William's head snap sharply to the left as he walked by. It wasn't like anything he had ever seen before. To Stephen it looked as if William had been hit with an object like a two by four, but there was nothing like that around. William's head snapped again, nearly landing on his shoulder, and blood started pouring from his left ear and from the corner of his mouth.

"Steve!" William called out in a nearly inaudible voice, but then his eyes rolled into the back of his head even though he was still standing perfectly straight.

From the moment he had observed all this happening to his young projectionist, Stephen had tried to rush over to help William. But Stephen could not move; it was as if there was an invisible barrier holding him back. He couldn't move, so instead of running to help William, all he could do was stand there and observe all that was happening.

Again and again, it looked as if William was being hit… No, not hit… beaten severely by something that wasn't there. Also something was holding Stephen prisoner and only allowing him to observe this bizarre attack, but it would not let him move so he could go to William's assistance. Finally, Stephen saw William's chest stop moving and his arms started shaking without any control. Then, as suddenly, as it had started, William fell to the floor and didn't move again.

Immediately Stephen was released from what was holding him, and was able to run over to William and do what he could to help him. He took his young projectionist in his arms. William's eyes were black and there wasn't a breath to tell of… well, at least, not one Stephen could hear.

"Steve, what the hell happened to me?" William asked so softly that Stephen had to put his ear right next to William's mouth.

"I have no idea," Stephen answered. He knew better, but he wouldn't, rather, he couldn't tell this young man the truth. But it really didn't matter. While Stephen was talking, William seized up and dark blackish blood flowed from his mouth, nose, eyes, and ears. His body stiffened, his mouth opened and a loud unearthly scream pierced the air. Then, after the sounds echoed off every wall in the building, William let loose one more breath and fell dead in Stephen's arms.

The police, ambulance, and coroner showed up within 15 minutes, and after they loaded William onto the gurney, he was wheeled out and loaded into a black van and driven away.

After William's body was driven away, the police informed Stephen they would be back to investigate the death further, and to question all the staff. After they had gone, Stephen closed the theater for a three-day mourning period. Laura, Meghyn, and Kelly went to the bar down the block and got plastered… spending the night drinking all they could at a local flea bag hotel. Stephen went to his office to shut everything down and saw a message on his computer. He looked at it and looked at it again before he realized what it said. It wasn't in a font that he recognized and it gave an eerily strange message that Stephen would never forget.

It said, "*J'ai vu un voleur, il a été jugé, condamné et exécuté par les lois de Dieu, Jésus-Christ et l'Eglise. Je suis le juge, gardien et bourreau et mon mot est définitive.*"

"What the fuck?" he said as he just stood there and stared at the screen. The only sound he could hear was the ticking of the clock, and somehow he was even putting that aside as he stared at the screen. "Who the hell wrote this?" he asked. He had no idea, but at least vocalizing the question seemed to make it like someone, anyone would answer it. Unfortunately, or fortunately, he was the only one in the building.

He then immediately opened the web browser on his computer and went to the Google.com translation program. After copying and pasting the text, he hit the translate button and what came up shocked him.

He strained his eyes and saw that what was written on the screen translated to, "*I have seen a thief; he has been judged, sentenced, and executed by the laws of God, Jesus Christ, and the Church. I am the judge, warden, and executioner and my word is final.*" Stephen thought about it for a minute and looked a second time to make sure of what it said.

Suddenly the computer turned itself off, then on again, and another message started to appear. It repeated the original message, but this time it was signed *"Father Jacques Marie DuMond"*.

Then the message totally disappeared off his screen. Stephen even searched for it in his recycle bin, but it was not there, so unfortunately he had nothing to show the police, and no doubt they would think he was mad if he insisted William's death was due to an insane dead priest!

Stephen decided that it was too stressful and depressing to think about this DuMond character anymore, or about anything else that had happened that day. He shut off the computer once again, left his office, left the theater, and went and joined the girls to help them finish off a couple bottles of Jack Daniels. That went on to something like five o'clock in the morning. Yeah, the bar closed at two o'clock, but he talked the owner into letting them hang out and drink.

Then Meghyn and Kelly went to their respective homes and crashed. Laura felt as if she could not stand the thought of being alone, so she took a taxi with Stephen back to his house. He brought some bedding out to the couch and got it ready. After a kiss on the cheek, Laura went into Stephen's bed, still crying, while Stephen curled up on the couch. They both slept, thankfully, without dreams, but with the comfort of knowing that the other one was there.

In the morning, Stephen woke up early and went immediately down to the police station. He knew that there were going to be many questions asked and he wanted to get it over with sooner, rather than waiting and having to take care of it at a later date.

He explained in the best way that he could, the events of the previous day. He wasn't sure if the cops believed him or not, and, quite honestly, he really didn't care. The whole thing took about an hour, so Stephen then went back home and crawled back onto the couch. He certainly was not bothered that the door was unlocked when he got back; he just thought Laura had left it like that for him and that she was still sleeping in his bedroom. Actually, Laura had woken up and had gone home about fifteen minutes earlier. Of course, she did leave a note for Stephen, but he was so beat he never found it. He also didn't realize that she was no longer there until sometime around 5:00pm.

CHAPTER 8

That night Stephen did keep his appointment with the ghost hunters, but he didn't want to stick around and have to answer a lot of questions. He especially did not want to get into a discussion about William, so he left them the keys with a request that they return them to him in the morning.

The ghost hunters came in and set up a night-vision video camera in one of the hallways behind the stage that was usually locked to the public. In fact, not even Stephen or any of his staff had gone back in there. Well, Stephen had glanced at it once and had always intended to fix it up a little, make it like a gallery of the theater's history, but he had been so busy with everything else he had certainly never investigated the area thoroughly.

The hall was lined with paintings of angels and demons, women, children, and all types of landscapes. The thing was, no matter what the subject, the painting was always on the dark side… never using bright colors. One strange thing that the ghost hunters noticed was that the sides of the hallway had theater seats from one end of the hall to the other.

Three of them, a woman and two men, were assigned to investigate in that particular hallway. They set up a video camera, using infrared motion sensors and a couple of voice recorders, and, after taking seats, they started inquiring of the spirits.

"We know that you are here," one started. "We don't want to hurt you or scare you. We just want to find out who you are, and we'd like to get to know you."

There was no answer, not even a knock or anything else, just silence. Suddenly, one of the people noticed that the end of the hallway had a shadow pass by the darkened end of the hall. It also sent a cool breeze towards them.

"Look at that!" the woman called out. The two men turned and looked, but by that time the shadow was long gone, although the cool air still surrounded them. While her eyes were focused on the hall, the female ghost hunter suddenly felt a hand move across her shoulder and down onto her breasts. Despite the fact that she should have been scared or bothered, as a professional in her field of expertise she was used to being touched. Certainly, fondling her breasts was different, but she remained calm, and told the others what was happening. "Something's touching me, especially on my breasts; it feels like a breeze, but it is definitely something real."

They all looked, and when the head investigator moved to feel the cold spot above her shoulder and measure it, something slapped his hand away. He reached again and was struck harder, but this time he heard a voice... It wasn't loud at all; most people wouldn't have even heard it, but it did seem aimed right at him.

"We have got to go," he said. He didn't give a reason, but he insisted that they leave and leave at that very moment. He quickly grabbed one of the voice recorders... the one closest to him, put it in his pocket, immediately left the hallway, and headed back into the room behind the screen and then into another hallway to find the rest of the group to discuss what had just happened. The other two took a few more minutes to gather their equipment, but they followed as quickly as possible.

As they entered the other hallway, a woman's voice warned, "Watch out for the carpet'"

They were not sure who said it, or even what direction it came from, but as they looked in front of them, they saw that a piece of the carpet was torn. It really wasn't anything, but it was just right for someone to catch their shoe or heel on and fall. Suddenly, as they watched, the tear got bigger and wider until it spread across the width of the hallway and was almost three feet from one edge to the other.

"What on earth is going on?" the lead investigator asked.

The floor beneath the carpet was red and amber colored granite. It was like nothing any of them had ever seen before. It was still beautifully polished for not having been touched for quite a few years. There was also a thick black vein, which ran through the granite like a crack. The texture was smooth and it had the appearance of glass. It was obsidian. True, it was rare in this area, but the head investigator had seen it before in museums, as the ancient natives of the area often used obsidian for weapons, so he knew exactly what it was.

"What are they trying to tell us?" he asked. Of course, several of the team had suggestions, each more ridiculous that the one before, but they were all considered.

The best one was that the granite and obsidian were part of some ancient temple that the natives used for animal sacrifices. The thing was, the Cuyahoga Indians lived in the area and they were never into any form of sacrifice, neither human nor animal.

"Besides that," the lead investigator stated, "the natives around here lived in that cave in The Gorge Metro Park. You know the one, the Mary Campbell Cave."

"Yeah, if I remember right, that cave is all sandstone," added another of the investigators, "and also that one prehistoric house some kids found years ago was made of sandstone boulders."

They all thought about it for a minute and then dismissed the idea of a native altar rather quickly. One of them lifted up another piece of carpeting and this time found that the floor was not made of the same material. It was made of wood. To be precise, the flooring was made of maple, that at one time had been highly polished, but it was now dull, worn, and basically looked its age.

"Let's all head back into the theater," the head investigator suggested. So they all gathered their equipment and started to head back into the theater itself.

"I wonder why that one piece of flooring was made out of stone?" the head investigator asked.

Just at that moment, he looked over and saw a figure walking across the stage. He hurriedly looked around and accounted for all of his people. They were all right next to him. The ones out in the van were contacted by walkie-talkie and they were both in their positions, so no one should have been anywhere near the stage. But, there it was… a full body apparition walking *across* the stage as if there was no one else in the building. At the same time, Tina walked into the theater and took her usual seat.

"Do you see that?" one of the investigators asked, pointing to where Tina was seated. They all said that they did.

They watched as Tina just sat there, drinking her drink, eating her popcorn and watching something on the screen. She too, seemed as if she didn't notice the intruders who had entered her special place. They just stood and watched as Tina enjoyed her movie time, and the full body apparition that had appeared, walking across the stage, just faded away. They checked the video cameras and digital cameras that they had with them. Every instrument had detected and recorded Tina's presence. Finally, one of them got the nerve up to walk over to Tina and try to record her voice.

She was just sitting there when one of the investigators, a young woman named Helen, went over to her. "Hello, can you hear me?" she asked. Tina just sat there staring straight ahead. "My name is Helen. I am not here to harm you. I just want to try and communicate with you."

Suddenly, Tina looked directly at her with a perturbed look. "I am trying to watch a movie," she said. "Could you please be quiet?"

Helen's face turned pure white, almost deathly white, but she did not lose her composure. "May I ask what your name is?"

"If I tell you, will you leave me alone?"

Helen promised that she would.

"My name is Tina," Tina stated softly. "I come here as much as possible to watch a movie without anyone bothering me, so please just leave me alone."

Helen looked over at her associates and they were all as shocked and excited as she was, so they signalled her to keep communicating, but when she turned back, Tina was gone, although the empty cup and popcorn bag were still there.

Just as suddenly, a voice, a huge booming voice said, "It is time for you to leave. Get out of here and don't come back."

Despite the fact that the majority of the investigators immediately began gathering up their equipment, the head investigator stood his ground. "Look, you may be able to bully the others, but I am not going anywhere."

Something unseen, yet extremely powerful approached him and once again ordered him to leave. Once again, the head investigator refused, but this time his refusal was a lot stronger.

According to one of the investigators, this disrespect must have done something to really piss off whatever it was that was facing down their leader, because the curtain leading to the stage area flew open and several bluish white "lightning bolts" came shooting from an empty room. Now, they didn't hit anyone, but the lightning did leave burn marks on the wall near the group, and stopped just a few inches from their leader.

"Christ, what the hell was that? Ben, did you get that on tape?" the lead investigator asked. Ben did not know for sure if there was a camcorder pointed in that general direction. If they were lucky, they may have actually recorded the "attack" on video.

No doubt, even for professional ghost investigators, this was the most bizarre, frightening experience they had ever encountered, so, directed by their leader, they quickly gathered up their equipment, and, after using the spare key Stephen had given them to lock up, they all headed back to the "office", which was actually the head investigator's apartment, to start going over everything they had gathered during the evening.

They sat all night listening to recordings and watching the videos. Yes, they did find a lot of very freaky evidence, such as voices screaming in pain, while others begged for mercy. There was one voice, though, that truly terrified everyone who heard it. They identified it as Jacques and it seemed to be the voice of the person in charge of the torture.

"Get out of my church," it kept repeating, over and over again. Each time it said those five words, it seemed to get angrier and angrier.

The videos were even better. Yes, they did get Tina on video, as well as the apparition that walked across the stage. It also captured countless orbs and a black mist that drifted between the box office and the hallway where they were standing. The last video showed a mist moving a large picture that had been hanging on the lobby wall. It wasn't moved far, just a couple of inches, but luckily they did catch it on video. This material they had gathered from their night at the Strand Theater they all knew was unbelievable, and would prove to the world what ghost hunters had known for years. They sat up for hours celebrating, knowing at long last all their efforts to prove ghosts really existed had come to fruition.

The next morning they met with Stephen and told him what they had found. They went to show him all the evidence on their recorders and tapes, but were more than dismayed to find there was nothing but blank tape. All of the audio recordings were filled with static, so nothing could be heard clearly, and it seemed that all the evidence they had collected had been destroyed. This had never, ever happened before; they had special equipment that protected against this type of thing, no matter how the spirits tried to cause havoc. Yet, this was apparently the exception, as the unseen forces here were too strong.

All they could do was confirm to Stephen all they had actually seen and heard. Their hopes of showing such evidence to the world were totally destroyed and there was nothing they could do about it. Of course, what they did tell Stephen only just confirmed everything he already knew.

The lead investigator drew in a deep breath and said, "Mr. Baker, with all the personal experiences we had and the evidence we did collect, I can safely say that this building is and has been haunted by at least two different beings. One, a girl named Tina identified herself and she actually showed herself to us. The other's name was Jacques. He is an extremely angry soul. We warn you, he is the one to watch out for."

"Did you find one named Edward?" Stephen asked.

"We didn't get that name," the investigator replied. "He may have been the one we saw walking across the stage. He didn't interact with us. He just walked across the stage and disappeared."

Stephen thanked them and escorted them from the building, after giving them a $2,000 donation to help pick up some new equipment. He also gave them all passes to every show that the theater was going to have for the next year.

As they all got to the door, Helen turned to Stephen and asked if there was any way that they could come back at another date and do another investigation, this time without the faulty equipment. Without a second's hesitation Stephen agreed.

After they all left, Stephen turned off the lights, checked the room out again, and locked the door… after all, he had to go to William's wake. However, he did leave one light on. He left the light on in the projection booth as a sign of respect for his lost projectionist.

CHAPTER 9

The next day, Stephen stopped by to collect the mail and make sure that everything was still alright. He got to the door, and as he went to put his key in the lock, he looked through the glass and saw Tina with two figures, standing near the concession stand. As soon as they heard the tumblers on the lock set, the two figures faded into nothingness, leaving Tina standing there all by herself.

She looked at Stephen as he opened the door and stepped through. Suddenly she appeared beside him with a bewildered frown on her face. "Who were those people I saw last night with their cameras and equipment?" she asked.

"They were here to learn more about you and your friends," Stephen replied, sensing that Tina was upset.

"Mr Baker, we did not like them here. They made us feel very uncomfortable," replied Tina.

Stephen was taken aback. He immediately realized how much all this must have upset her, just by the way she had addressed him so formally. All he could do was tell her he was sorry, that he did understand how much this had bothered her, and he promised her that they would not be back, despite what he had said to the investigators. The last thing he wanted to do was upset this beautiful, delicate young, seemingly very friendly soul.

"Tina, so how many of you are actually here?"

"As we are not allowed to go to heaven, the twelve of us are trying to get to Summerland," Tina said, with tears in her eyes. "But as well as heaven, we have been told that the gates to Summerland have been closed to people like us. They have kept us here for year after year after year, they said for all eternity."

"Who has kept you here?"

"Father has kept us here," she said. "He said that we were evil, we were bad people. I swear, Stephen, we did nothing wrong."

"I know. I read some things about it."

Tina then turned and faced the end of the hallway. She said something to somebody that Stephen couldn't hear. Suddenly, she turned back towards Stephen and she smiled as he looked past her and saw several other people walking up behind her.

"Stephen," she said, as she stretched out her arms, "these are some of the others who are trapped here with me. They have not yet found a way to make contact with those who are off the ethereal plane. It is only a couple of us who have gained such knowledge, and although we have tried to share it with the others, the Fathers will not allow it."

"How many of the "Fathers" are there?"

Tina turned and spoke to the others who had gathered around her. They nodded and then silently walked back down the hallway and faded away. Tina then looked around cautiously before she started to answer.

"There are two Fathers here," she said.

"Do you know their names?"

She lowered her head and told him that the names that she knew were Father Edward and Father Jacques DuMond.

"Father DuMond is the most vicious of the two," she said. "Father Edward at least has some, very little, but some compassion for those of us who are suffering. He wants to let us pass, but Father DuMond is too strong, even for him."

"What brought you to this place?" he asked.

"I came here in 1905. I was pregnant by a young man I loved who went to Europe as soon as he found out about the baby. I figured that any place named after the Sacred Mary of Magdalene would be a place of safety for a young unwedded pregnant woman. Oh, how wrong I was!" Then Tina started to cry, the tears streaming down her face, as she spoke about the cruelty she had suffered at the sadistic hands of Father DuMond. "The Father said that I was a sinner and that I was evil, as I attacked the beliefs of his church. Stephen, I was a good Catholic… I really, really was. I just fell in love with the wrong person, I made a mistake, and I have more than suffered for it. I am a good person, believe me, I am a good person, but Father DuMond says I must suffer for eternity to pay for my sins."

"Tina, I am so sorry. I do believe you," he said, trying to put his hand on her shoulder, but it passed right through her body.

"I was given shelter for as long as I was with child. The minute I gave birth, the baby was taken from me, they said for not following the teachings of God and Christ. It was then that they cursed me and abandoned my soul here, along with the others who were also murdered."

"What happened to your baby, Tina?"

"I heard them say…"

Just then someone knocked on the door. Tina immediately went through the curtain and disappeared into the theater. Stephen followed, but by the time he got to the curtain, no more than maybe ten seconds, she had already vanished. He didn't look for long, though. Rather, he headed for the door, where he had to tell some pimply-faced teen and his girlfriend that the theater was closed for three days because of a death in the family.

After that he locked the doors, turned the marquee off, and went down to his office. He sat in his office with the lights off, except for a very small amber night light, and he didn't even put his radio on. He didn't want anything distracting him. There was something that Tina had said that had grabbed onto Stephen Baker and wouldn't let go. Why would the priests only kill twelve? He thought that there must have been more than twelve sinners in Akron.

He opened all the books, he had taken from the library to try and find the answer, but every time he found a reference to the twelve, they all led him back to the twelve disciples of Christ.

"What were the twelve?" he asked out loud. Suddenly, his computer came on and Microsoft Word opened again.

"Christ's twelve were tortured and harassed for their beliefs," the message came across the screen, "just as were the twelve who died on this hallowed ground. They were tortured and harassed for their sins."

"Who is this?" Stephen asked. As soon as the last words left his mouth, the computer went black and the keyboard was thrown across the room. Stephen refused to let this intimidate him. "I want to know who is here with me and I want to know what you are trying to tell me, right now." There was no sound except for the echo of his own voice. After that faded, the room became perfectly silent and even the glow of the light seemed weaker than it did just a minute before.

Stephen immediately left his office and went down the hall and started walking around the theater. There were just a few safety lights around, but other than that, the building was completely dark. It was almost as if the sun had gone out. The building was totally black inside and Stephen had trouble seeing. His eyes strained to the point where it hurt him to look around or even move his head.

As he walked, he swore that once or twice he felt something take his hand as if it, or they, were trying to protect him, to keep him safe. "Tina," he whispered in a questioning voice, "is that you?"

Once again, there was no answer, and within seconds of his asking, even the guiding touches disappeared and he was left all alone. He was now in a room at the back of the screen and the safety lights were faint, to say the least, but there was just enough light to make out edges and corners.

In the distance he could hear the phone at the box office ringing and several people knocking on the door, but he was too far away and it was way too dark for him to bust his ass to get up there and see who it was. Occasionally he heard people talking in "normal" conversation, yet he knew that he was the only person in the building. Stephen figured that it was some of the spirits gathered together, but again, it was too dark for him to see anything, although he knew that they were there.

He found a stack of wood hidden in a corner of the room. Piece by piece he moved it. Occasionally he felt resistance, but for the most part it was easy to move since the pieces were not very big and they were pretty well stacked. He moved the last piece, and was surprised to see there was a door cut into the floor. He had certainly never noticed it before, but then of course the wood had been hiding it, and also he had been too occupied in the management of his haunted movie theater. The door was sealed and badly rusted, but it was a door cut into the floor nonetheless.

"I wonder where that goes?" he asked himself out loud. He turned to get something to help him pry it open, but as he reached for a piece of metal, the safety lights brightened and then died. Now he was in total darkness, in a part of the building he didn't know very well, and there was still a lot of debris lying all over the floor. He had some light a minute before, but now it wasn't there and all he had was his memory to find his way back.

It took him about 15 minutes to make it back to the main theater, as he kept getting lost. Eventually, he saw the sight he had been looking for... a room with some light. Stephen was bruised up a bit and had a few small cuts, mainly from tripping over things, but he was at least back in a room he knew. He quickly made his way up the aisle into the lobby and out of the front doors.

He looked back through the glass doors and saw the theater just as it was supposed to be... dark, quiet, and not a soul inside...

CHAPTER 10

It was a couple more days before Stephen, or any of the staff, went back into the theater. William's death had been such a shock to them all.

William's funeral came and went. Over two hundred people attended the service and it was surprising to Stephen how many had shown up to say their last goodbyes. Stephen did not know too much about William, but judging by the turnout, he was extremely popular in his own crowd. He even had a girlfriend that he had never talked about.

Laura and Meghyn both gave eulogies. Stephen wasn't sure how long the girls had known young William, but if their eulogies meant anything, they had all been friends for a very, very long time.

After the service, Stephen went up to William's parents, whom he had never met and offered his condolences. Since their son was murdered in his theater, he offered to pay a large amount of the funeral expenses. Stephen knew that he didn't have to do this, but he had always thought that William was a good kid, friendly, reliable, and smart, and to die like that was truly horrendous.

As soon as he had finished talking to William's parents, Stephen was about to head over to console his staff, but immediately he was approached by a young reporter from the Akron Beacon Journal.

"Mr Baker, if I may have a quick word. I am representing the Akron Beacon Journal to find out if there is any truth in the rumor that your theater where Mr. Jackson died is cursed and always has been," he stated. "Mr. Baker do you think that there is any truth to the rumor?"

"As far as I know, there is not now, nor was there ever a curse on the Strand Theater," Stephen replied. He was bothered and upset, not only by the funeral, but also by this young man's probing question. He knew that he couldn't tell the truth, but he also had trouble lying.

"But, Mr. Baker, I've talked to one of your employees, and they told me about some of the stuff that goes on in your theater. All I want is the truth."

"What is your name?" Stephen asked the young reporter, stalling for time. The reporter told him without hesitation. "Well, Mr...," Stephen was so upset he already forgot the name he just heard. "... of course, there are strange things... like some unexplained noises, but then, every old building has those. That does not mean that there are ghosts, demons or anything else supernatural hanging around in my theater, and you can quote me on that! Now, why don't you leave us to mourn in peace? Leave us the fuck alone, before I have to do something I really don't want to do at a funeral." Stephen then stepped toward the reporter, who made an immediate hasty retreat back to his car.

Stephen then turned and went over to Laura and Meghyn, who were standing at the edge of the grave, looking at the dark ebony lid of the casket. Meghyn was crying, while Laura was trying to be strong. Of course, it wasn't working. As soon as their boss walked up to them, they grabbed onto him. By now, both of them were crying, so Stephen just stood there with his arms around them both, holding them up. He looked into their eyes and the second he did... Stephen Baker felt himself tearing up. It was all too much!

The two women stood there crying and talking to Stephen for almost an hour before he took their hands and led them to his car. Over his shoulder, he heard the faint buzz of a camera motor, but he ignored it. He just didn't care. He and the two people who were the closest to him at that moment wanted to spend some time together and just mourn.

He wanted to drive them home, but they didn't want to be alone, so they all headed to a restaurant out on Arlington St, as far away from the cemetery as they could get. They spent the rest of the day and into the evening together just hanging out, being there for each other and supporting each other.

Stephen saw that reporter drive by a couple of times and he saw the flash of a camera more than once. He made a point to keep the girls from seeing it. They were still on the edge of crying, and "that asshole," as Stephen called the reporter, just wouldn't leave them alone to grieve.

Finally, they decided to go home. Meghyn decided to crash at Laura's house. They tried to get their boss to stay, but he thought better of it.

"You know what," he told the girls. "I am just going to go park my car at home and then grab a couple more drinks at my local bar and head on home. I just want to be alone tonight." He knew that he was lying, but he wasn't going to let them know it.

After he left the girls, he started walking down the street towards his car when he noticed that same reporter following him. He wasn't that close behind, but a few times Stephen heard some leaves rustle or the shuffle of feet behind him. Although he never actually saw the reporter, he knew someone was there and he knew exactly who it was.

He got to the corner where his car was parked, and it was then that the young man came out of the darkness and actually made himself known.

"You know, Mr. Baker, I am going to find out what happened to William Jackson," he said with a distinct voice that reflected his arrogance. "I am not one to give up when I think that there is a story out there and I definitely think that there is a story here, and you are certainly a part of it."

Stephen thought for a minute. A vision soon flashed through his head of what the headlines could be if he continued to ignore this ignorant gnat. Rumors, especially the ones endorsed by a local newspaper, had a way of growing and evolving. A curiosity, that was all the reporter had going for him, but no matter what the possible article would say, there wasn't one headline that Stephen could think of that wouldn't ruin the reputation that the Strand Theater had just started building.

"After all…" he said out loud to himself in a nearly inaudible whisper, "… no one is going to want to come to the scene of a murder… except maybe those fucking punks who used to break into the theater and twisted thrill seekers who might just get off on manic priests, torture and murder!"

"What was that, Mr. Baker?" the young reporter asked, as he leaned toward Stephen.

"Nothing," Stephen replied. Again he took a minute to think before he said the next sentence. "Okay, you want to know what happened."

"Yeah, I sure do."

"Well, then, come with me and make sure you bring your camera and I'll let you know exactly what happened."

The reporter and Stephen got into Stephen's car and they drove off down the street. The reporter did not say much during the trip, but Stephen kept a smile on his face the whole time. He knew what he had planned. He just hoped that if it worked, and that was a big if, even if the story did get printed, hopefully no one would ever believe it.

Stephen didn't talk for the entire trip to the theater. The reporter kept occasionally asking questions, but the only answer he ever got from Stephen was a slight smile or a cold stare. It took almost an hour to travel across town and Stephen knew that his silence was going to have one effect. He knew that it was going to piss this young man off on a grand scale, and that was just the way he wanted it.

When they arrived at the theater, Stephen noticed that the marquee lights were all on. They gave an eerie glow to the front of the ticket booth. Between the lights and the twinkling stars, it actually looked as if the box office, the lobby and the entire front of the theater were on fire.

"That's awesome," the reporter said, as he got out of the car. He took a small digital camera out of his pocket and asked Stephen if he could take a picture of the theater. Of course Stephen said yes. The picture was taken, they opened the door, and the two of them walked inside. The lobby and hallway were dark, except for the glow of some small nightlights that Stephen had installed for the nights he worked late... often well past midnight.

"If you take any pictures in here...," Stephen said, "... make sure that the camera is set to the high ISO setting. It is what I use and I always get the best shots."

The young reporter took his camera, and, after looking at the controls for a couple of minutes, he set the camera just as he was told.

"Another suggestion I have to tell you is set your flash on automatic."

The young reporter looked at the camera again and made the appropriate adjustment just as he was told.

Stephen looked up and observed the end of the hallway darken to the point where it was almost pure black. He just watched as the darkness spread up the hallway and disappeared mere feet away from them. As it did, the temperature dropped to where the area where they were standing became so chilly that the tips of their fingers began to burn as if they were out on a cold January day.

The reporter looked at Stephen and asked what was going on. Stephen replied with the truth this time. He explained that the theater was haunted and that there were at least five spirits that roamed the building. He then went on to say that there was one named Tina, who was very friendly and liked to communicate with people in the theater.

"Oh, come on," the reporter said. "How can you expect me to believe that?"

Stephen looked at him and replied, "Well, you just saw and felt that, didn't you?"

"That was just a cold breeze and condensation. That is all that was," said the young reporter.

"No," Stephen said with a slight hint of a smug attitude. "That was one of them. I don't know which one it was, but it was one of them."

Almost inaudibly a voice came from behind them. "Stephen..." "That was Edward. He does not like to be seen, but he wanted to let you know that he was here." Both Stephen and the reporter turned around and saw Tina standing by the concession stand. Stephen walked over to Tina, dragging the open-mouthed reporter with him.

"Tina, welcome back," Stephen said. He then turned and faced the young man. "Tina, this is... Sorry, you know, I never really did get your name."

"My name is Jefferson, Thomas Davis," said the young reporter. "And no, I am no relation to him."

"Okay," Stephen said, as he turned back to Tina. "Tina this is Jeff Davis. He is here to find out more about you and your friends."

"It is very nice to meet you, Jeff," she said, with a slight smile across her face. Stephen thought it reminded him of the smile on the Mona Lisa, but it looked a lot sweeter.

"It is nice to meet you too, Tina." Jeff replied.

Tina then smiled at Jeff. "Come visit us again, Jefferson Thomas Davis." Jeff turned round to ask Stephen, with a very confused look on his face, "And she... is she one of them?" Stephen nodded and calmly stated, "As a matter of fact, Tina has been here for over a hundred years. She is one of the lost souls that the urban myths are about." They both then looked around and Tina was gone.

"Oh, come on, Mr Baker. I do not believe for one moment that woman is a ghost." "She is a captive soul, Jeff, I can assure you of that," Stephen replied... Stephen then went into everything that Tina had told him about her time in L'église du Sacré Féminin.

When he had finished explaining about Tina, Stephen, then invited the reporter to follow him into the auditorium, and see exactly what it was that Tina did in the theater.

They opened the curtains and there she was, watching some movie, drinking pop, and eating some popcorn. Stephen explained that she did the same thing night after night. He also told Jeff that she loved watching the newer films as well, and that there were a couple of times when she even interacted with other members of the audience.

"Yet I still have no idea where she goes when she is done here," he said. "All I know is that she disappears behind the screen and we can't find her to follow her." He knew better, but he didn't want to give out too much information.

The young reporter just stood there and watched without saying a word… for at least five minutes. Then he asked if there was somewhere they could talk privately, and Stephen was more than happy to take him down to his office.

"I was in here when William died," Stephen stated. "I was doing some work on the computer and I suddenly heard a ruckus in the hallway. I ran out and there was William lying on the floor in the hall. I checked and found he wasn't breathing. We called 911, but unfortunately by then it was all too late."

"Did anyone see what happened?" Jeff Davis asked, while he wrote down everything Stephen was saying.

"I don't think so. I heard one of the girls scream and went running out. That is all I know."

"My source told me that it was Laura. Is that right?"

Stephen said that it was entirely possible that was who it was, but in all the confusion he wasn't sure and he didn't want to say anything that may be wrong.

"Just then the computer screen came on and words started to appear on the screen again. It said, "*Stephen, ne mentent pas. Dites-lui la vérité et tout sera bon pour vous.*" Both Stephen and Jeff Davis looked at the screen.

Stephen showed a little less confusion than Jeff, as he highlighted the text and opened Internet Explorer to get to a translation program.

"Why are you lying to me?" the young reporter asked, with a slightly angry voice.

Stephen looked confused for a second before he asked if Jeff spoke French. The reporter then said he had spent two years working in a bureau in Paris when he was an apprentice with the Times, and during that time he learned to speak French like a native. Jeff Davis got a kind of a cocky look across his face as he told this to Stephen.

"Now, this is just a loose translation, but it says, 'Stephen, do not lie. Tell this man the truth and everything will be good for you.'" When he had finished, Jeff Davis got a stern look on his face and asked Stephen why he was lying.

"To be honest, I didn't think you would believe the truth," Stephen confessed.

"All I want is the truth, Mr. Baker... just that... the truth. I want to know how and why William was killed."

Stephen then reluctantly admitted, "Jeff, I believe William was killed by the ghost of Father Jacques Marie DuMond. DuMond was a priest here back in the late 1800's and he severely punished those he deemed as not living the lives he thought they should be living."

"You mean this place was a church?" Jeff Davis asked.

"Yes, it was called L'église du Sacré Féminin... The Church of the Sacred Feminine," Stephen then informed Jeff. "It was burned down over a hundred years ago by the people of Akron, when they found out what was going on there." Stephen looked around cautiously. "This theater was built on the property where the church sat and it may have even been built of the original foundation."

Jeff Davis thought about all this for a minute. He had the feeling that what Stephen was saying wasn't quite right, so he asked, "So, why doesn't anyone know about this?"

"Think about it a minute," Stephen answered. "The stories that were fact at one time soon became urban legends and then eventually just weird stories that talk about the haunted theater over on 11th St.

"It isn't that people don't know about it; everyone has heard about it at one time or another. It is just that the stories and the facts have become so convoluted over the years that there isn't anything left to believe. It went from being history to just a story they tell around campfires to scare little kids."

Jeff Davis once again thought about what Stephen was saying and then recalled hearing something about the story years before, while he was sitting around a campfire exactly as Stephen had described.

Stephen then went on to tell the young man about the message he got right after William was killed. "It said that William was a thief, that he was to be punished, and the punishment was decided by Father DuMond. I guess he decided that a severe beating was a suitable punishment. That is what killed William. I saw it, and it was the most brutal thing I have ever seen, but…" Stephen paused for what seemed like forever, but it was actually only a couple seconds. "… How do you stop something you can't see and also when that something you can't see is holding you prisoner?"

"What did William steal to piss off these so-called spirits like that?" Jeff Davis inquired, thinking it was something big like money out of the concession stand or box office.

Stephen just stood there shaking his head in disgust. "We had an accident at the concession stand. The glass counter top got broken and glass went all over the candy inside. We were throwing it away for safety. William and Laura went out to the dumpster, where William took some of the candy out of the dumpster and put it in his pocket. Naturally, I would have given it to him if he had asked… I swear I would have… but I didn't have the chance. Whatever it was, it attacked him brutally in the hallway when he came back in. Then I got that goddamn message."

Remembering it all over again, Stephen tried to keep his composure, but it wasn't hard for the reporter to hear the pain in his voice and Stephen's eyes weren't hiding it any better either. It was obvious Stephen was very upset over all that had happened.

The reporter looked at Stephen and wasn't quite sure what to do. It was the first time in his five-year career that he had gotten such a reaction from someone he was interviewing. Finally, he decided that it would probably be the best thing to leave the office for a couple of minutes, and to give Stephen the chance to calm down and get himself back together again.

In the hallway, Jeff thought back to a couple of TV shows he had seen on the sci-fi channel about ghost hunting, so he thought that he might try a couple of the things he had seen them do. He paused for a minute to think and then started calling to the spirits.

"If there is anyone here I would like to meet you and talk with you to find out more about you. I do not want to harm you and I am not scared of you."

Stephen was still in his office when the black mist they had seen earlier appeared again in the hallway, right in front of Jeff Davis.

"What is your name?" Jeff asked. Then the hair on his neck bristled as the mist swirled around him and began to meld together. As he stood there, the temperature started to drop to a point where Jeff could actually see his own breath. It was suddenly very creepy and terrifying. "Who are you?" he asked again. Suddenly his voice changed as he noticed that he wasn't going to get any response. Rather, whatever it was, was definitely turning solid. He became quite perturbed, so he called out to Stephen, who came running out of his office to see what was going on.

"Stand there and don't move," Stephen commanded, with a sinking confidence in his voice. Although he had an idea of who it was, he wasn't one hundred percent sure and he didn't want to make matters worse.

"Believe me, I am not going anywhere," Jeff Davis answered, with a tremor in his voice. As he spoke, the mist closed in on him even tighter and became more and more solid. It almost looked as if part of the mist had formed into some sort of hand-like things which were holding Jeff's head and shoulders perfectly still. They weren't putting pressure on yet, at least not enough to cause pain, but it was making it impossible for Jeff to even look around.

"I'm going to try something," Stephen said. "Repeat exactly what I say but say it in French." Jeff agreed to do exactly what Stephen told him to and to say it exactly... nothing more... nothing less. "Father, I ask forgiveness for my behavior and my disrespect toward you and your church."

Jeff Davis thought for a moment and said, "Père, je demande pardon pour mon comportement et mon manque de respect envers vous et votre église."

"I swear by the sacred Mother, the Father, the Son and the Holy Spirit that I will live my life in accordance with the laws set forth by the Roman Catholic Church."

"Je jure par la Sainte Mère, le Père, le Fils et le Saint-Esprit que je vais vivre ma vie en conformité avec les lois établies par l'Eglise catholique romaine."

"Now Jeff, I want you to genuflect and show humility and respect," Stephen stated, as he observed the terror on the young man's face.

The "hands" that had held Jeff earlier faded away and joined back into the cloud swirling around him.

The young reporter did exactly as he was told, and as his knee hit the floor, the mist dissipated and he was able to stand up and walk around again. Stephen took him by the arms and escorted him back into his office. Jeff was shaking badly, but for the most part he was fine.

"What the hell was that?" Jeff Davis cried out hysterically.

Stephen took some tissues out of his desk and handed them to Jeff, while he made a sign for the young man to wipe his forehead, which was covered with thick beads of sweat.

"Jeff, I am not one hundred percent sure, but I think that you just met Father Jacques Marie DuMond, the former head priest here," he said. "He is one of those priests I was telling you about. You know… the ultra strict ones who used to run the church."

Jeff Davis' eyes opened wide as he listened. "From what I have been told and what I witnessed with William, you are lucky to be alive. I gather inquisitive reporters are not his favorite kind of people.

Jeff just slumped back into his chair and stared straight ahead, but it didn't take long for him to start to recover. As he did, he once again started asking questions, most of which Stephen could answer, but there were others that he couldn't and he wasn't going to find Tina to ask her.

Somehow a voice in the back of his head was telling Stephen that if he left, Jeff Davis was going to do something really stupid that would thoroughly piss Father DuMond off again, and maybe this time Stephen might not be able to save him.

The reporter then once again continued to ask for more details about how William had died. Stephen was very patient and took his time explaining in every minute detail what had happened that day. While he was explaining, he glanced across at the voice recorder Jeff was carrying and noticed that it wasn't turned on.

"Don't you want to record this?" he asked Jeff, with a small smile on his face.

Jeff Davis immediately looked down and saw that his recorder wasn't turned on, so he hit the button, but that didn't work. He checked again and found that the batteries were totally dead. Stephen knew that would happen. As soon as he walked in the building his cell phone had died on more than a few occasions, only to regain power the second he left. He wasn't the only one. He purposely didn't tell people to turn off their cells when the movie started, because the theater was kind of a black hole when it came to batteries.

Jeff reached down and started to replace the batteries, but Stephen told him not to bother and not to bother trying to get any of the pictures he had taken earlier since whatever it was also drained cameras as well as cell phones.

"You mean I don't have anything we talked about?" the suddenly frustrated reporter asked.

"I seriously doubt it," Stephen said. "You wanted to see the ghosts and they draw power from electronic devices to manifest, so the cells and cameras are the first to go."

"Why didn't you tell me about this before?" Jeff asked, as he became angry… very angry.

"First off, you wanted to see the place where William died, didn't you?"

Jeff answered, that, yes, he did.

"Second, you wanted to see if you could see the ghosts, once I told you about them. So, naturally, as they're here, I obviously had to bring you here."

Jeff agreed, and as he did, his tone started to calm down just a little. He was still pissed, but it wasn't quite as strong. He thought for a minute, before asking if he and Stephen could go somewhere else and do another interview.

Stephen thought for a minute. He knew that if they left the theater, the recorder would start working again and then this reporter would have the proof he needed for his article. Without it, no self-respecting editor would ever allow it to be written, much less printed.

"Look, I'm sorry," Stephen stated, as warmly as he could. "I have been with you all afternoon and I really don't have time to do another interview at present. After all, I do run a movie theater. Maybe we can do it some other time."

"But this story is very important," Jeff responded.

"It isn't that important," Stephen stated. "After all, we are just a small theater. Yeah, we have ghosts here, and for the most part they leave us alone, so between you and me, I like it like that."

"But, Mr. Baker… Stephen, couldn't we…" Jeff sounded now like he was begging. Well, almost begging, but whatever he did, he wasn't going to change Stephen's mind.

Instead, Stephen took the reporter by the arm and started walking him to the door. Tina was back at the concession stand. So Jeff quickly grabbed his camera and hit the shutter. He looked at the view screen as Stephen Baker gave him one last shove through the door. Jeff saw a picture with a strange shadow, but nothing he could use.

As he walked away, Jeff Davis also had a feeling that the theater owner, Stephen Baker, was a lot smarter than he had seemed. Jeff knew he now had no proof at all of everything he had seen and heard, and without that, he knew he had no story.

Stephen didn't notice as he was locking the door behind the reporter, but Edward Lloyd was standing there outside in the shadows, watching everything that was going on. Edward was not the jovial person he usually was, rather, he had an angry look on his face and his eyes weren't anything more than mere slits.

The young reporter walked down the street looking for a cab. Edward let him get about fifty yards away, before he started following him.

Edward Lloyd came back about an hour later. He stopped at the National News shop to get a couple of Coney dogs and a coke, before he settled down on the theater's steps to eat and observe the people passing bye.

Jeff Davis never did make it back to the paper, and was never heard from again.

CHAPTER 11

It was a couple more days before Stephen and the others were able to go back into the theater. Stephen was the first to arrive, followed a couple of minutes later by Laura and Meghyn. It was clear that there were still strong feelings about William's death, but at least they had come back and Stephen was grateful for that. They spent the first half hour or so just talking and wiping the last few tears away, but at least they were together working at the Strand Movie Theater. That in itself was a good start in getting their lives back to normal once again.

"Are we ready for this?" Stephen asked. He knew what the answer was going to be, but he felt that he had to ask anyway. Of course, just as he expected, the answer was a resounding "yes". So a couple of hugs later, everyone went and started getting ready for the audience they hoped would come.

An hour later, the concession stand was ready, as was the ticket booth. Each of the girls had taken the time to polish every inch of brass and bronze throughout the building. Meghyn went to the extra step of shining the marble pillars. Everything was as perfect as the day the theater opened only a couple of weeks before.

Stephen, as always, was fussing about every single thing, even dusting off every seat and placing on them a voucher for fifty percent off all ice creams and popcorn.

Laura eventually headed up to the box office and cleared away a couple of old tickets that were still lying on the shelf. She cleaned the glass again, but then after looking outside, she immediately called Stephen on the intercom, telling him that he had better come to the box office and see what was going on.

"Mr. Baker, you have to see this," she said in a voice that, through all of the static, sounded like she was either happy, or crying her eyes out. The intercom was one of the many things Stephen hadn't gotten around to fixing yet, so it would pick up so many signals from the police, cell phones, and static from the electronics store down the street. Again she called for him and when Stephen arrived his jaw dropped so hard that it nearly shattered the floor.

Outside, waiting in line to buy a ticket, he had been expecting to see eight, ten, or maybe even twenty people standing in line. Instead, there were literally hundreds of people lined up, all the way down the block, waiting to buy tickets. The thing he noticed was that each and every one was wearing either a black flower, or a black sash in memory of William.

"We're going to have to have two shows tonight," he said to Meghyn, who quickly agreed. "Sell to the first seven hundred and tell the rest to be back at 9:30pm." Then he thought for a minute and whispered to her. "Meghyn, all these people, they have come here to show respect to William. So no, don't bother selling tickets tonight. Instead, we are going to run movies all night and everyone gets in for free. Let's make this a wake… a wake that William would have loved."

She walked over and turned the lights off in the box office, and, as she did, she heard a rumbling in the waiting crowd. Both she and Stephen walked over and opened the doors, keeping them open with little ceramic wedges. They stepped outside and Stephen raised his hands to quieten the crowd.

"We thank you all for coming tonight to show your love for William Jackson, and we are not going to make a profit from your love and your grief," Stephen announced to the waiting crowd. "All showings tonight will be free. Just come in, sit down, and enjoy yourselves. I know that is how William would want to be remembered. Just one thing, though… I do not want to see any tears tonight. He was not that kind of young man and that is not how we are going to honor his memory."

The theater filled up in less than thirty minutes. More people came in and sat in the aisles or stood in the back.

Suddenly, Stephen heard a young woman's voice. "You are doing the right thing, Stephen. These people need to be together, so I will not be taking my seat tonight. Please save it for that young man. My seat will be his tonight, so he can say his goodbyes to everyone here."

"Tina, is that you?" Stephen asked.

"Yes," she whispered. "I want you to go be with all those people and say goodbye to your friend. I am not leaving, but I do not belong here tonight."

Tina never did physically appear that night, but Stephen knew that she was there watching it all, and for some strange reason that was a great comfort to him.

He went up to the projection booth and started the movie. The rest of the night he just sat there quietly and thought about everything that had happened in the last couple of weeks, all of the stories he had heard about the ghosts and the history of the building. It all made him wonder if he was doing the right thing, running the theater in the first place. Then, over the quiet, he could hear the people in the audience… more than seven hundred people… laughing and having a good time, and in that one moment he knew that he had to keep it open, no matter what.

A couple of times he thought he saw William walking around the projection booth, but when he looked back there was no one there. Stephen, out of all of those people, was the only one who cried that night, which gave him an inner feeling of pride that he kept with him, knowing that he had given all those people that loved William an evening of carefree happiness.

CHAPTER 12

Stephen got to the theater early the next morning. The clock said that it was almost 10:00am, but for Stephen, that was early. He opened the door and went in. He knew that he had forgotten something, but he couldn't at that moment remember what it was. The minute he opened the door, he remembered. He had stupidly forgotten to lock up the register at the concession stand.

Now, he knew that the night before wasn't for the money. If it had been, he would have charged every one of those people and made lots of money. But he did do quite well at the concession stand, in fact, nearly all the candy was sold and they had done well on other things as well, so he was wondering exactly how much they had taken in.

He got to the register and hit the total button. In the drawer was well over $2,500 and that didn't match with the total on the register receipt, which showed sales of only $1,700.

"What in the hell?" he asked. He was used to money suddenly going astray, or sometimes even missing candy, but he wasn't used to finding extra money left behind.

He gathered up the money and his paperwork and headed for his office to call Laura to see what had happened regarding this extra money in the till.

It took a couple of times calling before she finally answered the phone, and her voice was groggy when she did.

"Did you have a long night?" he asked in a good-natured voice.

"Yeah," she replied. "Some friends called and we went out until around 5:00am this morning. To tell the truth, towards the end of the evening I have no idea where we went or what we did, but I sure am paying for it this morning."

"I just have one question and then I'll let you get back to sleep." Laura was happy to oblige, as long as she could grab a couple extra hours rest to get her act together.

"Laura, I went into the register drawer at the concession stand this morning and found that the tally didn't add up to the money in the till."

Suddenly Laura became a lot more awake as she started thinking about what he was talking about. "Stephen," she assured him, "I would never steal from you. I think you know that. Every penny Meghyn and I made went into the drawer, and I double counted it before I left."

"I am sure you did," he said in a reassuring tone. "I know that you wouldn't steal from me, and, Laura, there is no money missing. As a matter of fact, it is quite the opposite."

Now fully awake, she asked exactly what he meant if there wasn't money missing.

"When I counted this morning there was about $800 extra in the drawer, and I just wanted to know where it came from."

She thought for a minute, and then another, and another, and he could tell by her breathing over the phone that she was getting flustered.

"Just calm down," he said. "You aren't in any trouble."

"Stephen, there was a guy who kept hanging around the concession stand. He was carrying an envelope, and I swear I looked away for just a second. When I looked back the drawer was open and he was gone. But no money was missing, I made sure of that. But as no money was missing, I didn't bother to say anything about it last night. I am sorry."

By now she was nearly crying, afraid that she was going to be fired. In all the time she had worked at the theater, she had come to love the place and thought of it as her home.

"What did he look like?" Stephen asked.

"He was around sixty to seventy or so, long grayish brown hair, and a beard that was almost all white. He had on an old duster," she said.

"Was there anything else?" he asked, his voice showing obvious excitement.

"You know, there was something else," she replied. "I think… I am not sure, but I think… he was wearing a priest's collar."

Stephen became silent as he thought for a couple of minutes, then he asked, "Did you happen to get his name?"

She again told Stephen that she had been serving several customers when he walked up to the counter, so she never got a chance to talk to him.

Once again Stephen reassured Laura that she wasn't in any trouble, and told her that he would see her when she got to the theater.

He took the money and slid it into his pocket. He counted the rest a second time and it matched exactly what the receipts said should be in the drawer. He put the start–up money, around $35, back into the drawer, and as soon as he did, he turned and started walking back to his office.

He opened the door, went and got out the box which he kept locked in a small safe under the floor, put the money in the box, and put the box back in the safe and locked it up again, making sure that the safe door was covered as usual by a red carpet. After that, Stephen settled down in his chair and started reading the book he kept in his lower drawer. It wasn't long before he became bored and decided to walk around the… well, at least to him, largely unexplored back areas of the theater.

It took him more than a few minutes, but eventually he made it back to the room behind the stage curtain where he had seen that old iron door cut into the floor. He looked around, found a light switch, and when he turned it on, this time he saw the same corroded iron door with huge black hinges, but now strangely there was a cross on the door running nearly from the top to the bottom. This he knew had certainly not been there when he first discovered the door. The cross itself was around four feet tall and was made of silver with a gold figure of Jesus nailed to it. The heads of the nails sparkled. Stephen thought it looked like they may have been tipped by rubies, but he wasn't sure.

"Where the hell did that come from?" he asked out loud. He didn't expect an answer and he wasn't disappointed. The room was totally silent. He did remember that he was sure the cross wasn't there a couple of days before when he was stumbling around in the dark, exploring the back rooms after William's death… Thinking about it even more, he was quite positive he hadn't seen the door looking like that before.

He also found that the room had suddenly become cooler. Usually the entire building was somewhere around seventy degrees, but now the temperature had dropped down to where his skin was actually cold to the touch. Stephen reached down to the door and it, in contrast, was warm to the touch, as if it was heated from below.

He slid his fingers around the edges of the door, and the air coming out of the thin crack was a lot warmer than even the door. He also noticed a strong smell coming out with the air. "What is that smell?" he asked himself. "I know I have smelled that before." He thought and thought, and suddenly remembered that it was the bittersweet smell of incense. He remembered it was kind of a spiced rose smell, which may not have been exact, but now at least Stephen recognized what the smell was.

He tried lifting the iron door open, but the door was heavy and the hinges were heavily crusted with decades of rust. Then he heard the cries of women, men and even children screaming for mercy. The screams stopped when another voice said to him,

"Stephen, you do not want that door to open. It is the gateway to a world from which you cannot return."

It wasn't any voice he had heard before. It was strong, even stronger than Tina's when she appeared in the theater.

"Who is this?" he asked.

His eyes were set for the dark now and he could see everything in the room. He looked all around, but there was no one else there. The voice did not answer or say anything else again. He looked at the door again. It was so tempting. He wanted to open and see what was on the other side, but he didn't have the strength to open it himself, so he decided to go back to work and get back to it later.

Before he left, he thought he heard a very young woman's voice saying over and over again, "No Father! Please don't kill my baby." He couldn't tell where it was coming from. He wasn't even sure he heard it, but he didn't want to stay there any longer. He had no idea what was going on or what he was getting himself into.

Meghyn and Laura arrived at the theater around 5:00pm. Though Stephen was still a little stressed by what he had heard, when they arrived, their apparent enthusiasm to be back at work again calmed him down and immediately he felt in a much better mood.

This time they brought a friend with them... a young man named Jason Kilpatrick, who had moved to Akron a few days before and was looking for a job. They told their boss how they had met Jason the night before at a pub, and how beyond all belief, he had been a perfect gentleman throughout the entire evening.

Stephen looked the young man over. Then on Meghyn and Laura's word, without even the slightest interview, he hired Jason to take William's place as projectionist. Now, Stephen knew that the young man didn't have experience as a projectionist, but he decided that it just might be worth training someone from scratch.

As they stood in the lobby, all of the lights in the theater turned off and the old stage light from back in the vaudeville days turned on.

"What was that?" Jason asked.

"Oh, it's nothing," Stephen replied with an unusual pleasantry in his voice. "It's just the ghosts that hang around here. They like to play jokes sometimes. The lights will fix themselves in a minute."

"Ghosts?" Jason asked, sounding really confused and a little doubting of tales of ghosts.

"Yeah, there are a few ghosts who like this place. For the most part they just like to play... you know, tease us... but please... PLEASE behave yourself and do not... I repeat... DO NOT touch anything that isn't yours. They don't much like it."

"Is that what happened to your last projectionist? Did he do something wrong?"

Stephen thought for a minute before he answered. He knew that there was no sense hiding anything. There were tons of rumors out there already and some were a lot worse and more believable than the truth could ever be.

He told Jason that what William had taken wasn't something he considered wrong, but the spirits thought differently and they took it on themselves to dole out a punishment, and that punishment went way too far.

Jason looked at Stephen. He never said a word, but in his head he was thinking that possibly his new boss was slightly deranged, but he needed the job, so if his new boss said there were ghosts, he was going to be the last one to argue, even though he did not believe any of it.

As they headed towards the projection booth, still talking about the ghosts, the theater, and a number of other things, Stephen saw Tina standing over at the concession stand. He saw her at the same moment she saw him.

"Hello, Stephen. How are you today?" she said with a smile on her face.

"I am doing quite well, actually," he answered. "How about you? How are you today?"

"I am fine," she replied, as her eyes drifted toward Jason. "Who is this young man? I haven't seen him around here before."

Stephen introduced Jason to Tina, and as soon as he did, Tina became very flirtatious. She walked over to Jason and stood very, very close and Stephen wasn't sure, but he thought he saw her try to touch his hand.

"I have got to go," she said, as she turned and walked away. "Jason, I hope to see you some other time." Jason looked at her and simply nodded his head without saying a word. Stephen just stood there and smiled. It was clear to see that he wasn't offended by Tina's attention to the young man, but rather he felt not quite as important, and he was surprised at his feeling this way. After all, Tina was a ghost, not some young woman he was attracted to, but the feeling was there and he did not understand it. Observing the expression on Jason face, he could tell the young man was immediately attracted to Tina, not realizing Tina was one of the ghosts Stephen had been talking to him about. Tina was heading to her usual seat in the theater, but she turned and then came back to where Stephen and Jason were standing. As she walked up to them, she paused and smiled again, but this time at Stephen and she said in a very, very soft whisper, "You know, Stephen, he is really cute".

Stephen just smiled back, but didn't say anything to Tina. He did, however, turn his attention to Jason, who wasn't sure what was going on and wasn't exactly sure he wanted to know.

"You should be honored," Stephen said. "Tina has been coming around for quite a while and she has only interacted with a couple of us, but never like that. She has always been friendly, but sweet and innocent."

"You mean she's a…" Jason said, having a very hard time getting the word out.

"Yeah, she's one of the spirits who live here. She has never been anything but friendly to anyone she's met, but she also is the one who likes to play little tricks. The first few days I was here… I hadn't met her yet… she liked to turn the lights on and off and we had a bell up at the box office. We had to take it out after a couple days because of her. She rang it every hour on the hour. It got really annoying. But we like her and she has become almost like our little sister."

"Does she know she's a spirit?" Jason asked, playing along, pretending this was a ghost and not a very old-fashioned attractive young female arriving early to see the movie.

Stephen then told Jason about the day that he and Tina sat down and had their first talk. He said that they talked for a couple of hours and that Tina told him about her pregnancy and how she was killed by the priests for not conforming to their level of belief. He wasn't sure how much, if any, Jason believed, but Stephen knew one thing... he had seen Tina's reaction to Jason and he had no idea what was going to happen.

He spent the next fifteen or so minutes showing Jason around the theater, before finally leading him up to the projection booth. There he showed him all he needed to know about running the movie projector. Jason was a quick learner and needed very little instruction, so eventually Stephen said to him,

"Jason, I've got to go. Get used to the place, get everything set up for tonight, and I'll stop back later to make sure that everything is okay."

Jason started looking around, touching things and seeing where everything was. "Mr. Baker..." he started.

"Please, Jason, call me Steve," his new boss stated with a smile. "Everyone else does."

"Okay, Steve. What do I do if Tina comes up here?"

"Don't worry, she won't. She goes from the lobby to her seat in the theater and then back behind the curtain. I have never seen her go anywhere else in the building. But if she changes that, then just be polite to her... Yes, for God's sake be polite to her."

That answer seemed to have relaxed Jason a little, but it also brought out a curiosity... the same that Stephen had.

Jason instantly wanted to know what was backstage and where Tina went when she left for the night. Judging by the time he had spent with Stephen, his new boss did not seem nuts at all, so maybe there was some truth to all he was saying after all. The thing was, Stephen didn't know the answer, so he honestly didn't have anything to tell Jason about where Tina went or what she did.

The show went well that night. Actually, nothing out of the ordinary happened, so, after cleaning up and the boss's usual obsessive compulsive re-cleaning, they all went home.

CHAPTER 13

The next morning was darker than normal. The weatherman had predicted rain for the late afternoon, but when Stephen looked at the sky, he had an idea that the weatherman was wrong, and that he would be lucky to make it to the theater before the clouds opened up. Well, he was partially right. He managed to take his shower, despite the sound of thunder a few miles away, get to his car and make it to the theater before the rain started, and when it did start… it was sheets upon sheets of rain.

The theater was dark when he got there; even the security lights and the lights at the edge of every step in the building were off and it was quiet… too quiet. There was nothing, not the air conditioner, not the beeping of the answering machine at the concession stand… no noise at all, just total silence.

He looked at his watch and it was still four hours before the matinee was scheduled. Looking around, he found an old, really old-fashioned pocket transistor radio in a drawer near the concession stand. It was already tuned to WAKR radio in Akron. From the way it looked, it was like the last person who listened to it heard The Partridge Family and Donna Summer on the old AM station. He looked in the drawer and also surprisingly found some new batteries, which he inserted, and also the earpiece that went with the radio. The cord was worn and pieces of the insulation cracked off the moment he touched it, but after trying it, it still worked but the reception was terrible, so he turned it off.

Walking to the door to get better reception, he looked through the glass. The wind outside was blowing the rain sideways, so the glass was flowing with thick streams of water, but he could still make out some images through it. There was not one light on anywhere in the neighborhood. The traffic lights were out. So were the street lights, yet it was dark enough outside for the street lights to be on. Even the emergency lights in the other stores were out. He hadn't thought about it, but now he realized the new emergency lights he had installed in the theater were also dead.

Turning on the radio again, after a few awkward ballet moves, he held the radio high above his head and was finally able to pick up a signal.

"Lightening struck the electric generating plant on the Cuyahoga Falls Boulevard at 1:25am this morning," the newscaster said. "Repair crews have been working on returning power to over twenty thousand customers in the Akron and Cuyahoga Falls area. However, Howard Lester, chief of staff at the station, said that the repairs would most likely not be completed until sometime tomorrow. He suggests that people stay at home and do not travel unless absolutely necessary." Another story came on right after, talking about the four inches of rain they had had since midnight and how a number of intersections were impossible because of flooding.

"Shit!" Stephen muttered to himself, wishing he had not been so eager to get to the theater.

He got his cell phone from his pocket and managed to find some shelter outside a couple of shops down from the theater so he could call all of his staff to tell them to take the day off. Most of them were happy until Stephen informed them about all of the flooding and then their mood changed as they realized this would cause a long power outage, and they were stuck indoors doing nothing. After he hung up from the last call, he was totally drenched, and at that moment Stephen cursed his haunted theater where mobile phones were utterly useless.

As he hurried back to the theater he really got soaked, as now the sidewalk as well as the street had a strong river (for lack of a better word) flowing down it. He then realized that, like his employees, he wasn't going to be going anywhere soon either.

Luckily he had a spare pair of pants and a T- shirt in his office, as well as a really old pair of sneakers. After he had changed, he made his way back to the entrance and looked outside again. Maybe he was hoping that things had changed and the rain had stopped, or maybe he was thinking about taking a chance and running out to his car and trying to drive home. As he looked, he decided that the first thought had just been wishful thinking, and the second was just fucking stupid! So Stephen resigned himself to settling in and making the best of it. After all, he had all the pop, popcorn, and candy he wanted, and it was all free... after all... he owned it.

Just as he poured himself a coke with no ice and opened a box of Junior Mints and a bag of chips, he looked back toward the door in a feeble hope that maybe... but what he didn't expect to see was Edward standing at the door, looking in and shivering so badly he looked like he was having a convulsion. He was wearing a raincoat and had an umbrella protecting him from the worst of the rain, but was standing there barefooted, as he was carrying his shoes. Even though he was not thoroughly soaked, he looked really miserable.

Stephen ran to the door, still carrying his pop and candy. He unlocked it and let Edward in.

"What the fuck are you doing out in this?" he asked, as he took Edward's raincoat and umbrella with his free hand. "You want to die of pneumonia?"

"I had nowhere to go," Edward said. "They blocked off all the streets and all of the restaurants are closed, so I came here just in the hope that someone would be here. Thank God I was right."

"I am stuck here too," Stephen said, as he finally set down his food. "Can I get you something?"

"No, thanks, I am fine," said Edward, as he started putting on his still fairly dry shoes.

"You know, Edward, I am actually glad that you are here. I found something in the back of the theater, behind the screen, and I could use some help checking it out," Stephen said cheerfully, as he once again picked up his bag of chips, gobbled down the last of the candy, and started walking into the theater.

Now, Stephen had been in his theater more than a few times when the lights were out, but this was different. There was not one light, even a small one, burning anywhere. It was pitch black darkness. Darker than anything he had ever seen. He thought for a minute. Yes, he thought, it was a blacker dark than he had ever read about. It was a shock to his system; it caused a sense of confusion and a sort of dementia that he wasn't used to. Edward followed him, but not too closely.

"Where are we going?" he asked.

Regaining his senses, Stephen fought to try to find the words to tell him about what he had seen and heard. It took a minute, but he finally said, "I was in this room behind the curtain and I found an iron door back there. I mean, it was big and it had a gold and silver cross on top of it. I moved it just a fraction of an inch and I heard voices… women… children and men screaming… crying for mercy from some kind of torture. I have to find out what it is."

"Stephen, from what I have heard, it isn't a good idea exploring this place," Edward said.

The farther he walked into the theater itself, the darker and mustier the air was becoming. Stephen stopped for a moment. It was almost as if he was considering what Edward had just said, but after searching around for a minute, he found what he was looking for… a lighter, so he continued down the aisle.

"Stephen, I am warning you, this isn't a good idea," Edward said, as he tried to step between Stephen and the edge of a seat, blocking his way.

Stephen, who by this time was getting more than a little pissed at Edward's behavior, shoved Edward out of the way and continued down the aisle, around the end of the stage, and through the curtain. Edward was left standing in the aisle, shaking his head and mumbling.

"Stephen!" he yelled, but there was no response. Again he called out to Stephen and again he was greeted with nothing but silence. He looked around and muttered to himself, "Père, s'il vous plaît être miséricordieux sur cet homme. Il est bon, mais sa curiosité est plus que son esprit ne peut manipuler." Then he turned without saying another word, walked out of the theater, and back out into the raging storm.

Stephen made it back to the door without realizing that he was alone. It was warm in that section of the building, much warmer than it was the last time he was in the room. There was a little light coming from a small crack in the brick that made up the external wall. It was muted, but compared to the rest of the building, it was enough for him to be able to make out shapes and some shadows.

Finally noticing that he was alone, he called out for Edward a few times before he realized that the old man wasn't there. He had no doubt left in a huff, as his warning words had not been heeded... which now left Stephen having to try to open the door all by himself.

He sat down on the floor near the door for a moment. Maybe it was in an effort to adjust his eyes better. Maybe he was trying to find the nerve to open that damn door and see the unknown, or maybe he was trying to build up enough strength to try and lift it. Anyway, it filled his mind with thoughts and doubts, and although he would never admit it, maybe even a little bit of fear.

Finally, he reached over and touched the edge of the door. It was cold... colder than the air in the rest of the building. Stephen placed one finger beneath the edge and gently lifted it. The door, although extremely heavy, lifted a hair's width. *At least it isn't welded shut*, he thought. He tried again with both hands and it lifted just a little bit further. *Damn*, he thought, *this isn't going to be easy.*

As the door moved he could smell something coming from the hole. This time the smell was something he had never smelt before and it was putrid. There was almost a sweetness to it, but not quite, and the smell, even though slight, started to make his stomach turn. It wasn't long before the smell got stronger and the urges in his stomach turned from queasiness to down right sickness. The door didn't close when he let go of it like he thought it would, it stayed open just enough to let fresh air down into the basement.

Suddenly he lost all of the feeling he had in his arms and legs, and he turned and vomited what seemed to be food from his last three meals all over the floor and walls. As he tried to rise, Stephen felt a tightening around his chest. It was as if someone had tied a strap around him and was pulling it tighter and tighter.

He couldn't get his balance to stand up, so somehow he managed to crawl back into the theater itself and immediately his body convulsed as he tried to grab a seat and pull himself up. Once again he collapsed onto the floor. Breathing heavily, he yelled out for help. He was sure that there was no one else in the building, but maybe there would be a miracle and Tina, or someone outside the building might hear him.

"Stephen, what is wrong?" a voice said.

"I am sick. I need some help," he said, thinking that help was at hand. Then he convulsed and passed out. When he opened his eyes, he called out for help again, but now there was only dead silence. He lay there, moaning and partially crying because of the pain in his gut, which was growing worse by the moment. "Please help me," he cried out again. He lay there for what seemed to be hours, praying for either someone to help him or for a God, if He was a merciful God, to end the pain even if it meant taking his life.

Then, as he lay there, he heard a voice he had heard a couple of times before. As the words started, he felt someone lift his head as if trying to comfort him. "Je vous ai dit de ne pas demander ce que vous ne connaissez pas. L'autre monde est dangereux et pas de place pour vous," it said, as it lowered his head back to the floor. "Vous serez bien cette fois, mais méfiez-vous de la prochaine."

"I don't understand," he said. "I don't speak French." He looked hard, trying to see who was there holding him, but saw nothing. He was also looking for an answer that never came. He just lay back, the pain now, thank the Lord, had slightly eased, but it was still agonizing, as he waited and hoped that someone else would come to help him.

"Mr. Baker?" a voice called from the back of the theater. "Mr. Baker, where are you?" The voice had the sound of urgency to it. "Mr. Baker?" it called again. Out of the corner of his eye, he could see flashlights moving down the steps, scanning back and forth, looking up and down the aisles.

"I am here," Stephen replied, in a very weak, strained voice. The pain again had increased so severely that he wasn't sure of what was real and what wasn't. "I am here," he said again. Finally, he looked up and saw two men dressed in yellow coats standing above him. As he watched them starting to care for him, he slipped off into unconsciousness, asking a question as he faded. He asked, "Do you speak English?" but he never heard the answer. His vision, mind, and thoughts all went black.

The paramedics said that Stephen went in and out of consciousness during the ride to the hospital, but he never developed a fever or any other symptoms. Once they got him to the emergency room, he was taken directly in, and, surprisingly, the diagnosis was quick in coming. The doctors said that it was, they thought, some kind of version of the Spanish Flu, the one that nearly wiped out the population of Europe back at the beginning of the 20th century. After a couple of bags of saline solution and some heavy antivirals, the condition was gone almost as quickly as it had set in.

They kept Stephen confined to his hospital room, no matter how well he was feeling, for an entire week. They never did really find out what exactly the virus was, but for that week everyone wore masks and gloves, and on the first few days, even science fiction type body suits.

Shut up in that hospital room, Stephen eventually was about to climb the walls. At the theater, his staff had been running the movie sessions as usual and had reported business was good, but he knew he needed to get back to supervise. Already Laura was sounding a little perturbed with paperwork missing, and Tina, it seemed, was having a little too much fun with the lighting system. He also wanted to get back to open that old iron door with the engraved cross, and find out exactly was down below there. He even had a strong feeling his virus had something to do with it, and despite all the dire warnings, he was determined to open that door again.

After an entire week, happily, Stephen was allowed to check himself out of the hospital. One of his doctors stopped him on the way out and explained that they weren't sure exactly what disease he had, what effects it had on his body, or even if the treatment they had given him was the right one. "Mr. Baker, we had hoped you might stay another couple of days. Of course, you are free to go, but I have some more tests I would love to do." Stephen didn't even look back except to say again that he felt fine and that he was, thank God, getting the hell out of there and going home.

He had called for Jason to pick him up, as his car was still back at the theater. Jason was outside waiting for him, but instead of taking his boss home straight away, they went to Krispy Kreme for a donut and a cup of coffee. No better way, thought Stephen, to celebrate still being alive. After several cups of coffee and a dozen Krispy Kremes, they headed straight over to the Strand Theater, supposedly to pick up Stephen's car, but now, the pre-warned and extremely curious Stephen Baker had other things in mind.

CHAPTER 14

Stephen and Jason had really bonded over coffee and Krispy Kremes. Stephen liked the young man. He seemed very straight, intelligent, and, from what he could gather, had an extremely likeable personality with a strong moral code. So when they were about five minutes away from the theater, Stephen said to Jason.

"It's really early and the theater does not open for hours yet. Luckily, the electricity is now back on, so what a good opportunity to finally get that door open, but of course I can't do it by myself."

"What door?" Jason asked.

For fifteen minutes, Stephen sat with him in the parking lot assigned to theater patrons and staff, and told Jason in great detail about the door, the screams for help, and the smell that made him so sick. "I have a feeling that there is something down there and someone or something is trying to keep me from finding out what it is." When he had finished, Jason smiled, got out of the car, and politely opened the passenger door for Stephen. He took his boss's arm as they headed to the theater and said, "Well, Steve, if it is that important to you, let's throw caution to the wind and go see what is down there."

Their entire conversation as they walked across the parking lot was about what they might possibly find once they were in that basement. The ideas ranged from a torture area to a hidden chapel in the church, or even a creature guarding an entranceway to the underworld... maybe even to Hell itself. The ideas kept flowing, and became stranger and stranger as the caffeine from untold numbers of coffees kicked in. By the time they reached the theater, the ideas they were coming up with would have made a blockbuster of a horror film.

The door was open when they arrived and Laura and Meghyn were standing there at the doorway into the theater, as if they were on guard duty keeping people out.

Immediately both of them rushed over to their boss and hugged him tighter than he had ever been hugged before.

"It is good to see you guys," said Stephen gratefully. "And let me tell you, it is such a relief to be out of that damn hospital, I cannot begin to tell you."

"I bet it is," said Laura, smiling at Stephen from ear to ear. "As you know, we all wanted to visit, but all that matters now is you are back."

"So how come you're both here so early?" Stephen asked.

Meghyn kind of started jumping up and down to get his attention.

"Steve, we both knew Jason was picking you up, and, knowing you, we knew you would come straight here, and we wanted to see that you were okay."

"I am fine," Stephen assured her, "Just fine."

"Well, boss," she said, while giving him another hug. "It has been an hour or so, so we were starting to worry all over again."

Stephen hugged the girls again and told them that he loved both of them dearly. "I do not think of you as employees," he said. "You are my family, and I know that no matter what, we will be there for each other." With that they all, even Jason, joined in a group hug.

"Now, I have to go see someone," Stephen said, as they all let the hug break apart. Stephen left the three of them standing at the door as he walked into the lobby and down to the concession stand. "Tina?" he called out. "Are you here?" The room was deathly silent; there was not even a breeze to move the curtains. Suddenly, he felt a soft breeze on his shoulder, and when he turned, Tina was standing directly in front of him. "Tina, are you the one who called to get help for me?"

"Stephen, I saw you fall and I felt that you were dying," she said. "I could not let that happen. You have a special place in my heart and I do not want anything to happen to you."

"How did you know who to call and their numbers?"

"You had passed out and I found that talking machine you always have against your ear," she said. "I pressed a button and someone came on and she got me the help you needed, and then I found a list of names and pressed a button near the person I thought you trusted the most. I could not let you die, Stephen... I truly could not."

"But, Tina," said Stephen, looking puzzled. "My mobile has never worked in this theater."

"Oh, well, it did for me, Steve," she assured him. "Mind you, I found it very confusing to use, but you needed help, so I did what needed to be done." As soon as Tina finished explaining what she had done, Laura, Meghyn, and Jason came over and joined them, and when they did, Tina asked them to come closer. This was the first time the girls had actually interacted with Tina, so understandably, they were quite nervous.

"Meghyn, please, can you move even closer to me?" Tina requested excitedly. Meghyn was reluctant, but she took one step and then another and finally she was facing Tina with less than a foot of space between them.

Tina leaned forward and whispered to Meghyn. No one else could hear, but Meghyn suddenly got a strange look on her face, and then nodded and agreed to whatever Tina had asked her. Tina then reached over and seemed to touch Meghyn on the forehead. As she did, a powerful wind blew in from both ends of the hallway, pushing them closer together. Suddenly Tina was gone, the wind had died, and Meghyn was standing there all alone.

"Stephen," she said, as she walked over to him. "You are mine to keep safe in this place."

Stephen looked at Meghyn, as did Laura and Jason. Stephen wasn't sure what was going on and it confused him.

Meghyn then walked over and put her arms around Stephen's neck and actually kissed him. It wasn't the kind of kiss friends gave to each other; rather, it was very passionate, deep, and very, very long. "I will be here if you ever need someone," she said.

"Tina?" Stephen asked.

"Yes, Stephen it is me," she said as she backed away. "I just wanted to show you how much I care, since I was so close to losing you."

As soon as she finished the last word, Meghyn collapsed onto the floor. The breeze kicked up again, and as Meghyn rose and got up to her knees, she looked very shaken but her eyes had a look of understanding, and inner peace.

Laura and Jason ran over and helped Meghyn up off her knees, and gently led her over to one of the chairs by the concession stand. "What happened?" they asked in unison. Stephen knew, but he sure wasn't going to say anything.

"She entered me," Meghyn said, in the midst of her own confusion. "I was still there, but it wasn't me. I was just there. She told me it was the first time in almost a hundred years that she had a body. It was the first time in a hundred years that she could feel. As she entered me, I could feel what she was feeling. I even saw her memories. I now know what she went through. Unfortunately I now even know how horribly she died."

Meghyn then spent the next few minutes describing the hell that Tina and the others had gone through, and answering as many questions as she could. Meghyn went into such detail that she revealed a lot of facts that Stephen hadn't heard before. Jason and Laura just stood there, silently, as Meghyn kept talking.

By the time she finished, Meghyn's eyes were flowing with tears and her body was shaking so badly that Stephen decided to take her into his office, to sit and relax for a while.

"Laura, will you please stay with Meghyn?" her boss instructed. "Jason, you come with me. We're going to get that door open backstage and find out what the hell is down those stairs, no matter what."

They all went with Stephen into his office. Once there, Laura placed her arms around Meghyn's shoulders and tried to convince her that she had nothing to do with what had happened to Tina. It took a while, but Meghyn finally calmed down. Once they knew the Meghyn was all right, Stephen and Jason left the girls in his office and walked down the hallway and into the theater. As they did, the main theater lights that had suddenly gone out when Meghyn collapsed on the floor, suddenly came back on.

Thank God, Stephen thought. *Now we can at least see what is going on back there.* He told Jason a little more about what he had experienced and the more he said… the more Jason wanted to go back and get that door open. When they reached the curtain, Stephen opened it slightly and asked Jason if he smelt anything.

"It just smells musty, kinda like it hasn't been cleaned back here for a while," Jason said. "Maybe you ought to consider putting an exhaust fan back there, to get that bad air out of here."

"Yeah, maybe you're right" Stephen wryly commented. Sure, it might prevent another trip to the hospital. Jason smiled at the comment, as Stephen said he would purchase it as soon as he could… that is, if they made it out of there in one piece.

Realizing that the overpowering sweet smell was gone, Stephen and Jason went through the curtain and walked through the back area of the stage into the room behind the curtain and over to the door on the floor. Stephen had been expecting the worst smell and mess ever as he had vomited all over the floor and walls. Surprisingly, it was as if nothing had ever happened there. The door was still open a crack, just as Stephen had left it. There was a hot, not warm air rising from the crack and that air did smell rancid, worse than either of them could have imagined, but at least it was bearable. The door itself was as cold, if not colder, than it was earlier.

I have got to do this, Stephen Baker thought to himself. *I'm not going to let this fucking door beat me.*

Suddenly, a voice started screaming at the two of them. Neither Jason nor Stephen could tell where it was coming from. It was almost as if it was coming from all around them. "Par la puissance de Christ ne pas ouvrir cette porte," it said.

Jason looked around, not confused, but he definitely had a look of concern across his face. "What was that?" he asked.

"That was Father Jacques Marie DuMond, I suspect" said Stephen. "He was the one priest who some say killed all those people."

"He told us not to go down there," Jason stated, much to Stephen's surprise.

"You speak French, Jason?" Stephen asked. Now, it wasn't a real question… more rhetorical than anything, but Jason said that he studied French in high school and minored in it in college.

"Par la puissance de Christ, ne pas ouvrir cette porte," the voice said again, but in a voice that was more commanding than anything.

"Père DuMond, je sais qui vous êtes et ce que vous avez fait. Pourquoi ne devrions-nous pas ouvrir la porte? Y a-t-il quelque chose que vous ne voulez pas que nous voir? " Jason asked the voice.

The voice said, "C'est ma parole, la parole de l'Église et de la parole du Seigneur notre Dieu. Entrée, à l'exception des condamnés est autorisé."

"What did he say?" Stephen asked.

"He said that according to him, his church, and God, only the condemned may go through the door." Jason looked around before addressing Father DuMond again. There was not a sound anywhere, except their breathing. Suddenly, he turned toward the door and shouted, "Votre église a disparu, vous sont décédés depuis longtemps, et Dieu ne vit pas ici plus longtemps. Vous bâtiment a été soulevée il y a des années.

Vous n'avez pas de place ici, ni les âmes que vous coincés ici. Nous y allons pour voir ce qui s'est passé ici. "

"What the fuck did you say?" Stephen asked.

"I told him that his church was gone, he was dead and that God was no longer here," Jason said. "We want to find out what happened here and we ARE going to go through that door." He took a step toward the door to see what would happen. Again, there was nothing, even the door felt warmer. It was nearly room temperature. He waved and brought Stephen over, and together they lifted the door.

It moved very easily, considering all of the corrosion on the hinges. Sure, it had some creaks, but then again so did every door in the place. Even the revolving doors at the entrance made a slight whining sound whenever anyone walked through them. But the door opened quickly and slammed to the floor as they let go of it.

As they stood and looked down in the chamber beneath them, both Jason and Stephen were struck with a combination of fear and awe. Jason looked at Stephen and stated strongly, "Steve, I have to say something to Father DuMond before we even think about going down there."

"Okay," Stephen said.

Jason glanced around again and said, "Merci Père, nous allons montrer du respect pour votre église."

"I think I understood that. Was it 'Thank you, father, we will show respect for your church'?" Stephen asked.

"Yes, it was," replied Jason

"That was a good thing to say," Stephen stated approvingly, as they stood staring down the stairwell, feeling apprehension, excitement and also fear.

CHAPTER 15

Stephen and Jason just stood there for a couple of minutes, looking down into the entrance now the door was open. It was dimly lit, but they could still see that there were stone steps down to the basement. Stephen thought there were at least twenty, maybe twenty-five stairs. As they became accustomed to the light, both men could see that the steps were made of red and black granite, not like the usual gray marble Stephen had found in other parts of the building. He had assumed that parts of the original church were used in the construction of the theater, but there was only one other place in the building where he remembered seeing this particular red and black granite, and that was the square he had seen in the back hallway floor. The stones were damp, moss covered, and suffered from heavy cracking from decades of neglect, as were the walls of the stairway.

Stephen looked up and saw Tina standing behind him against the wall. She looked calm. It was as if something that she was trying to share, something that was tearing her apart inside, was finally going to be revealed, and because of that she was feeling an inner peace. She mouthed something, but Stephen could not make it out. He mouthed, "What?" but Tina just faded away without saying another word.

"Well, we might as well get going. They aren't going to wait for us," Stephen stated, in a very pathetic effort to relieve the tension and be funny.

"I don't think they have any plans," Jason replied, also trying to join in the fun, which both men did not really feel at all.

They then turned on their flashlights and started down the steps. Stephen's obsessive compulsive disorder definitely kicked in as soon as he took the first step. He counted each one as he descended. There were thirteen steps, followed by a platform and then thirteen more steps. As they reached the bottom, they saw another hallway extending under the theater. The dim light of the stairway had changed. The hallway was well lit, too well lit, actually. Stephen and Jason covered their eyes to give them a chance to adjust. As they looked around, neither Stephen nor Jason could see where the light was coming from, since there were no lights or windows anywhere to be seen.

As they entered the hallway, the two of them noticed that although the air and the walls were still moisture laden, the moss no longer covered the walls. There were still spots of it in the cracks between the stones that made up the floor, but that was all. Instead, there were plants of other types hanging from the ceiling.

"I have seen those before," Jason said, as he took one of the vines into his hand and lifted it up. "My mom used to have them in her kitchen. I think they are called..." He paused a minute trying to think back to visualize the house he grew up in. "I think they are called philodendrons. She always had a lot of them, but I remember she used to have one that was so big that it had started to wrap around the ceiling. That thing grew like crazy."

"Are you sure?" Stephen asked.

"Yeah, I'd know it anywhere," Jason said, with a slight sense of pride in his voice.

Stephen smiled slightly as he reached over and moved a couple of the vines. As he looked, his eyes focused with the bright light and again and he saw something that he never expected... a picture. It wasn't religious or anything like that. Rather, it looked like a country meadow with trees, flowers, and clouds. In the distance was a picturesque village. There were people in the village: men, women, and children, who looked happy. Animals, like deer and panthers, wandered through the village and they too looked peaceful. In a few of the cottages, he could see that a family was cooking, because he could see the smoke from the cook fires rising from old-fashioned stone chimneys.

What in the hell? he thought. *Why didn't they want us to see this?*

"Steve, look at this," Jason said, breaking the semi-trance that his boss had locked himself into.

"What?" Stephen inquired.

Jason was now looking at the other wall. He had torn some of the vines down and could clearly see the picture before him. It wasn't the bright and sunny picture that was on the other wall. It was dark, very dark, with stone pillars, black smoke, and flames that burned a deep red, intermingled with some color that was nearly black but not quite. The people in the picture were tormented. Their skin was bloody and torn; when there was enough skin to see, and their faces showed so much pain it was well beyond Jason's and Stephen's understanding.

Stephen stopped in his tracks when he saw what Jason had found.

"What the fuck is that?" he asked.

"Steve, I am not sure, but I think this is the Yin to the Yang of the afterlife," Jason said. "Look at it." Stephen and Jason both moved closer to the picture. Their eyes darted between the walls as they tried to take everything in. "You have the image of heaven over there, and I think that this has got to be someone's idea about what hell looks like."

"No, that is not heaven. It's called Summerland. I read all about it while researching all about "L'église du Sacré Féminin," Stephen informed Jason, as he looked at the painting again, but he wasn't able to look for long before his eyes went back to the other wall. "Look at that," he said, pointing at the one of the figures in the picture.

"At what?" Jason asked.

"That group over there," Stephen said, putting his finger on the wall right below a group of tortured souls. "There are twelve of them. That is the number Tina told me were killed here."

"Oh, my God!" Jason yelled, in total shock. "Look at the one in the black dress with the white flowers." Stephen took an even closer look. "Steve, I think that's Tina." Stephen looked again and nearly passed out. The girl, chained to a large rock, was, in fact, Tina.

Suddenly, a woman's voice started calling Stephen's name from up in the theater, but it wasn't Tina. He was sure about that. "Who is this?" he yelled, as Jason started walking back toward the stairwell entrance.

"Steve, it's me, Laura. We've got people out front who want to come in for a movie. I heard a couple of them talking and they're tired of being stuck outside. What do you want me to do? We also really do need Jason here to start the movie."

Stephen looked at his watch and was shocked at the time. He thought for a minute and yelled back up for Laura to start getting everything ready. He then turned to Jason and said, "I'm afraid work calls, so we'll just have to come back down here tomorrow." He then did his best to smile reassuringly at his new projectionist. "Actually, Jason, I think this may be a good thing. It will give us a chance to think about all this." Jason agreed, and Stephen then suggested, "Jason, how about after we have shown the movie, let's go over to the donut shop and try and figure this all out." Once again Jason agreed, so they both went upstairs and ran the movie for the matinee session, which happened to be "Twilight," a movie about the undead.

Before they went out into the theater, Stephen and Jason took a fan from backstage and set it to blow air down the stairs, firstly, to make sure that the air was fresh when they when back in, and secondly, to maybe dry things out a little to make it feel a little less damp and eerie.

CHAPTER 16

The next morning Jason didn't even give Stephen the chance to wake up on his own. The minute, hell, the very second the sun came up, he was at the door pounding on it, just as if he were being chased by something deadly. Stephen barely had time to get a pair of jeans on and open the door before Jason came in and started talking about what had happened the night before.

"Jason, I told you last night, we can't say anything to anyone about what is below the theater," Stephen stated, as once again he and Jason shared yet another coffee and donuts, which Jason had presented to Stephen as he walked into his apartment.

"Jason, I am positive, if we tell anyone, they are sure to tell their friends, and then before we know it, suddenly there'll be throngs of people wanting to see backstage and they'll tear the place apart, if we even give the slightest hint of what is going on here."

Stephen certainly was not talking about the ghosts who lived there. He was more concerned about the media, archaeologists and ghost hunters… not to mention the world of loonies out there who may consider his theater a shrine to the devil or some deity that they might believe in. "In fact, Jason, there was a nosey reporter asking all kinds of questions, but this place must have scared the life out of him because I never heard from him again."

"That was lucky," stated Jason.

"Yeah, it sure was. Besides, Jason, think about it, what the hell would happen to Tina and the other innocents if suddenly the place was overrun by hoards of curious people and their world was suddenly torn apart?"

"Yeah, I agree, Steve, but don't you think we should get some kind of help?" Jason asked.

Stephen shook his head, insisting that at least they wait to find out more before they set about involving anyone else.

"Maybe if we find out a little more, we could let Laura and Meghyn help some. I know they can be trusted, but not right now." It wasn't what Stephen said, but it was the way he said it that made the point because Jason didn't suggest it anymore.

They stopped for breakfast at Mickey D's, picked up a two-liter bottle of Royal Crown Cola, and then headed to the theater. Being that it was only 6:30 in the morning, there was no traffic and the trip went smoothly, so it didn't take long for them to get to Stephen's parking spot. They sat in the car for a little longer chatting, which gave Stephen a couple of extra minutes to think… to try to figure out what he was going to do once he got back into that hallway below the stairs. By the time they got to the lobby door, his mind had thought through and figured out different scenarios, but in the end he had more questions than he did any answers.

The lock in the main door worked extra easily that morning. It usually stuck just a little, but this morning it was different. The theater lobby was spotless and the night had cooled off the air a little bit, so it was comfortable. They set their two liters of cola on the concession stand, walked through the theater, and hurried to the area behind the curtain. There was no sign of Tina anywhere and no voices either, so it was all extremely quiet. The iron door was open just as they had left it, so they moved the fan they had set up to the side and immediately headed back down the stairs.

The vines that were torn down the day before had grown back and were now even covering a large part of the floor. *It must have been the fresh air we let in*, Stephen thought. *I can't imagine that the air down here was right for them. Maybe that fan was a good thing.* He and Jason started tearing the vines from the walls again, so they could get a better look at what they had discovered the night before.

It was still just as bright as it was before, but now their eyes were used to the light and were able to focus better. They were looking at the picture with the people chained to the rocks. Something they hadn't noticed the night before was the fact that these people's clothes and their skin may have been dirty and covered with soot and ash, but they looked to be in pretty good shape.

Jason walked a little further down the hall. The pictures ran almost all the way from the steps to the other end, but there was a slight arch-shaped indentation about thirty feet from where Stephen was standing. Jason thought that it didn't look like it was anything special, except for one thing... it had a part of the painting on it that wasn't quite the same as the rest. This had what looked like a cave painted into the rocks. Neither painting had any other type of doorway or exit painted anywhere on them.

"Steve, come here and look at this," Jason said.

"What is it?"

"I'm not sure, but it is something you have to see."

Stephen stopped examining the section of the painting he was most interested in and went down to where young Jason was standing. Suddenly his flashlight stopped working, but as Jason still had his, it was no problem.

What is this going to be? he thought. "This had better be good," he jokingly said to Jason, yet half seriously as well, as everything once they were down the stairs gave such a sinister feeling at times that both men had a sense of total impending doom.

What Jason was showing him was actually in an area of the wall recessed about two inches from the wall around it. The painting style was once again different and even the stones the painting was on in this part of the wall were different. They were grainier, looser than the rest of the wall. Stephen stood there for a minute, and the longer he did, the more his feelings told him that there was something else there. Reaching into his back pocket, he pulled out a handkerchief and started wiping the paint on this part of the wall away.

"What the hell?" Stephen exclaimed, as he actually started to clean away the paint.

Jason just stood there and watched, as the piece of cloth not only took away the paint, but with every touch the rock itself started to dissolve right in front of them. "Steve, maybe this might not be a good idea," Jason said in apprehension, as he backed away from the wall.

No fucking shit, Stephen thought, trying to figure out what in the world would have made him try this. *This has got to be the dumbest thing I have ever done.*

It didn't take long for the stone to crack and finally break apart into a pile on the floor. The air was stale, to say the least, and it was hot, really hot. Where the wall had been, now there was a door, a huge wooden door carved once again with a large cross.

Before they opened the door, Stephen asked Jason, "Can you please get me a another flashlight?" Instantly Jason took off back up the stairs, returning five minutes later with two flashlights, one for an emergency backup. He handed one to Stephen, who gingerly pushed the door open and immediately saw what he somewhat expected, but yet didn't expect.

Inside was a table with shackles on the corners, a rack against the far wall and a fireplace with what looked like several pokers or branding irons still in the ashes. Ropes hung from the ceiling and there were places on the floor where it looked as if it were made of red stone, but it was easy to see that the stones were stained by years of being soaked with blood, over and over again. The smell in the room was beyond comprehension and the screams of people being tortured reverberated off the walls.

Jason immediately moved away from the doorway, went over to a corner of the hallway and threw up. It seemed to take him forever to regain his composure and he wasn't sure he felt better after throwing up, but it was something that, with what they found, was not unexpected. The room was simply beyond human understanding.

Stephen, in the meantime, had entered the room. The moment he did, he thought back to the time he was in New Orleans and had toured the cemeteries there. The smell he smelled in that room brought back memories of that trip. It was the smell of death and decay. As Stephen stood there, Jason threw up one more time, and then once he was able to compose himself, he entered the room behind his boss.

"Oh, my fucking God! What in the hell is this now?" Stephen shouted out, as he looked across the room at a stained glass, heavy wooden door at the side of the room. Some of the stained glass on the door was missing; it lay in broken pieces on the floor. The smell got even worse as Stephen began to walk towards the door, covering his mouth and nose as he did, but the odor got through anyway and nothing would keep it out. Stephen tried pushing it, but the door wouldn't open. Through the stained glass section he was able to shine his flashlight into one of the broken pieces and look through another. The air that came through that opening was, unlike the rest of the area, very dry. It was as if the moisture stopped at the door and never entered. Maybe it was part of the design, maybe just a fluke; either way it happened.

"Steve, what is it?" Jason asked as he tried wiping his mouth clean.

"I'm not sure, but I have an idea of what it may be," Stephen replied to the scared young man, who had by this time backed a little further out of the room.

Stephen looked through the glass opening deeper into the room, back to where the light just barely reflected off anything and he really had to strain to see anything at all. In the shadows he saw what he was hoping he wasn't going to find. Bodies, some almost fully decayed, others somehow mummified and in near pristine condition. They were dressed in clothes of the late 1800's and early 1900's. Some were dressed in their finery while others were in rags and tatters. There were men and women, but no children. He assumed that Tina's body was in there, but in the dim light he couldn't tell.

Once again Jason called out to find out what Stephen was looking at. Stephen didn't want to say anything… he really didn't, as Jason's reaction to just the torture chamber had been bad enough. He couldn't imagine how the young man would react to what he was looking at now. "Do you really want to know?" Stephen called back.

"Yes, I really do," Jason loudly replied, as he stood by the door of the chamber. Against his better judgment, Stephen told him that he may have found the place where the people who had been killed by the priests were stored after their deaths. "How many are there?" Jason asked.

"It's too dark to tell, but I think there are more than twelve," Stephen stated, as he waited for Jason to lose it. "We're going to have to get in there somehow. There is a huge lock on the door and I don't know what it is made of, but I don't think we are going to be breaking this down anytime soon." He looked again and guessed that the door was made of oak and was at least three inches thick. He could see metal banding holding the parts of the door together.

"Steve, look at this," Jason said, as he pulled some vines down from the ceiling. Behind the vines was a wooden plaque engraved so deeply that a lot of the wood was cracked and splintered.

"What is it?" Stephen asked, as his attention shifted from the door. Jason held his torch up to the plaque and they were both able to see what was written there. At the top of the plaque was a cross with a sphere of thorns where the cross bar and the main piece met. Below that was some writing. Stephen looked closer and saw that it said, "Mai ces condamnés subissent les incendies de l'enfer et du désespoir de purgatoire."

"What does that say?" Stephen asked.

Jason stepped in front of Stephen, actually pushing him backward and onto one of the racks. He looked again and said, "It says, 'May these condemned suffer the fires of hell and the hopelessness of purgatory.' I take it, Steve, this is what we were dreading to find." Stephen didn't want to think about it; he just sort of grunted and let it go at that. Jason rubbed his hand across the plaque and the dust fell like some of the snows they got in late January. "Steve, there's more here." Stephen asked what Jason was looking at and got an answer he didn't expect. "Steve," Jason started with a voice that was on the edge of quivering, but not quite, "it's a list of names and dates… I think it's a list of the people you found."

"How many names are there?"

Jason wasn't going to guess, so he went down the list, touching each name as he counted it. "Ten… eleven… twelve," Jason said, "thirteen… fourteen… fifteen… sixteen," he continued, finally reaching a count of nineteen. "Steve, there are nineteen bodies in there."

Stephen looked over at Jason and asked him again to make sure. Jason confirmed that there would, or should be nineteen bodies somewhere in that basement, since he assumed that none of them got a "Christian" burial.

"Is…?" Stephen started to ask.

Jason looked at the list, and along with looking for her name, he wanted to know where she was on it, how many died before, and how many died after her. "Here she is," he said with a mislaid sense of pride in his voice. "She was the seventeenth one… person… to be brought down here."

"When?"

"It says March 15th, 1905," Jason said, as he looked at the rest of the dates. "They must have been busy boys."

"Why?"

"There are two other names with the same date next to them." He cleaned off a little more and saw the names clearly. "Yeah, I see two… James T. Lewis and Deborah Standesh.

Tina was the first of the three. That is, if this list shows the order and not just the day."

"What in the fuck went on down here?" Stephen asked, in a voice that was filled with anger and nothing else. "What could these people have done, that made those fucking lunatics treat them like this?" He was more determined than ever. He was going to get into that room to look into the faces of those nineteen people. He wanted to know what their last hours, their last minutes, were like.

Jason looked around the room. "You know, Steve, in a place like this, if you went by every horror film ever made, there would have to be a metal bar or rod somewhere around here." And sure enough, Jason then saw, at the top of some shelves, an iron bar about an inch square and three feet long. "Steve, I'm sure it would definitely be more than enough to break a hundred-plus-year-old lock." He was right. With very little effort, the metal of the locking device inside the case turned to powder and the lock fell to the floor.

Stephen opened the door slowly. It creaked loudly as it opened and the sound amplified as it bounced and echoed off the stone walls. It stuck a couple of times, but for the most part, it opened just like it did back in the 1900's when the door, sadly, had been in regular use. He and Jason walked in and saw body upon body. Some were stacked and others were tied to the walls, hung like slabs of meat in a smoke shop.

"How could they have done this?" Jason cried out, choking on his words.

It is just part of the way of civilized man. The more educated he was, the more barbaric he became, Stephen thought. "Jason, just look back at our history. We've been doing this kind of thing ever since we first moved out of the cave. Actually, I would be surprised if places like this did not occur, and did not occur more often. What bothers me more is the fact that this was a church, meant to reach out to people with love and compassion, not retribution and mass murder," he angrily responded.

They carefully made sure not to touch anything in that room. After all, it was a grave... well, sort of a grave. Stephen looked at each body. The bodies were pretty much intact, but the skin and tissue had dried and contracted around the muscle fibers and bones so it was fairly easy to see some of what had happened.

Both Stephen and Jason could see one thing... before they had died, most, if not all, were beaten and tortured beyond anything they could imagine. They all had multiple injuries such as broken arms or legs, snapped necks, or joints pulled apart and then forced back together again. A few, Stephen guessed that they were the most defiant, had sections of their skulls caved in as if they were hit, very hard, with a blunt object. From what they could see... not one person there had died a quick death.

Jason moved a chair that was facing one of the bodies and suddenly, nearly shocking himself, he let out a scream. It wasn't a man's yell. It was more like the scream a little girl would let out after seeing a big spider. "STEVE!... MR. BAKER!... GET OVER HERE!" he yelled at the top of his lungs. Before him was a young woman, dehydrated but still with the look of sweetness and innocence across her face.

She had reddish auburn hair with beautiful blonde tints, which he saw even through the dim light of the room. It was down to her shoulders, but it was matted and dirty, but even with that it must have been something she was proud of. It still bore the ivory and pearl hair clip she must have always worn while she was alive. Her dress was long and black, with flowers decorating the sleeves, and she had just the slightest touch of makeup, but the red lipstick she was wearing had dried and chipped off, leaving only the slightest hint as to what she must have looked like. The last thing he saw were her eyes, which were wide open and full of pain. They were dried out, but it was easy to see the blue fire that must have shone from them at one time.

"STEVE, COME HERE, PLEASE!" Jason yelled again. Stephen was only about twenty-five feet away, but was deeply concentrating on one of the bodies, a young man who was, for some reason, smiling at the time of his death. Stephen was fully absorbed in what he was looking at, realizing this man was not going to let his tormentors win. Then he heard Jason screaming for the second time and so he immediately rushed over, and was shocked at what he saw when he got there.

"Tina!" Stephen cried, as he looked into her eyes. He just stood there looking at her pure innocence. It wasn't that he didn't know what to say; he just lost the ability to think, much less speak, so the words just languished and eventually died.

Finally, he looked down and saw blood stains everywhere. He could see that her body still carried the baby weight she had when she was alive. *Those rotten bastards*, he thought. *Why did they kill her right after she gave birth - or did they kill her during the birth?... Oh, my God, did she even see the baby... what happened to the baby?*

"I did see the baby, Stephen," Tina said from behind him. "It was a beautiful baby girl." Tina knelt down beside her own body and began crying. "I wanted so badly to be her mother. I know that I could have been a good mother... don't you think so, Stephen?"

Stephen looked at her and realized that he too was crying, so he went over to her and knelt down next to Tina, feeling even more pain at that moment. He could not touch her, as he knew she would feel nothing, but he made the gesture anyway, trying to take her hand. "Tina, I am sure that you would have been a good mother and that your daughter... what were you going to name her?"

"Eleanor... I was going to name her Eleanor," Tina said, as she also reached out, tears in her eyes, not able to grasp his outstretched hand.

"I am sure that Eleanor would have been a beautiful, smart young woman... just like her mother," Stephen said, with a soft encouraging smile, as he saw the last of Tina's tears slow to one single tear, which, in his mind, he wiped away with his finger. "Do you know what happened to her?"

"I never got to see her again," Tina said. "They cut her out of me, then as soon as she gave her first cry of life, she was taken away. I begged for God's mercy and was told that for someone like me, God had no mercy. I was evil, I had broken God's commandments and my soul would never walk up to the gates of heaven or even Summerland. I would remain here, an evil sinner for all eternity... That evil priest said the words, but I never believed anything he said. He was a cruel monster, not a man of God. After all, how could a God who would forgive us in heaven, allow us to be punished so severely here in his church? They never even gave me the last rites. I was just allowed to die without any salvation." Stephen tried to comfort Tina as best as he could, but the memories he had now brought back to her were too overwhelming. She dropped to her knees and started crying and shaking uncontrollably.

How could anyone do this? Stephen thought. *There was no need for this. I wonder if the other's stories are the same, or was Tina treated differently because of the baby?* As he had these thoughts, voices came from every direction. It was hard, but he made out a few sentences and from what he heard, they all told of the same torture and death, with stories that were just like Tina's, but in some cases, even worse.

Jason was just standing back watching and listening to what was going on. Suddenly, he was so upset with all he had heard, he had to do something So he moved away from the wall... stood straight and yelled,

"By the power of Christ, if there is anyone here I command you to show yourself!"

The air in the chamber, which had been still, despite their movements, started to blow around the walls, lifting a century's worth of grime and dust, making it nearly impossible for Stephen and Jason to breathe, much less see anything. The two of them ran back through the open doors with Tina right behind them. The air was clearer out in the hallway and they were, after a minute, able to clear their lungs and eyes and look back into the torture chamber and the tomb. The wind was still blowing in the tomb, but it contained itself to that one room. Then, just as quickly as it started, the air stopped moving and the dust settled. Tina walked in first and just stood at the door of the tomb.

"Stephen," she said. "Here are the ones Jason just summoned. They are the ones who have been imprisoned here with me for all these years." They followed her in and standing before them were the souls of twenty-four people. Jason counted eleven women, eight men, and five children.

"Who are the children?" Jason asked. "I didn't..." Stephen shook his head almost to the extent of dislocating the neck muscles, interrupting him before he had a chance to finish his sentence.

One of them, a little boy about nine years old with blonde hair and freckles, walked over to Jason and reached out as if to take his hand.

"Sir," he said, in as polite a voice as Jason had ever heard, "they found out I stole some dried meat and bread for my family. My father died a couple of months before and we didn't have any money. I am sorry I did it and I always have been, but my mom and sisters had to have something to eat. Sir, do you know... are they all right?"

Jason had no idea how to answer. This boy... this child was murdered more than a hundred and ten years ago. "I... I don't think..." Jason said, as he tried to avoid answering.

"What's your name?" Stephen interrupted.

"Tommy. My name is Tommy Harrison," he said, with the saddest eyes possible. "The other children are Susan Schneider, Bobby Lewis, Edith Harrison; she's my baby sister, and Linda Lane. They were all hungry and went with me when I stole the bread and meat, so Father blamed them as well as me. I was the last one to be punished." Tommy started to cry, as did Stephen and Tina. "I was forced to watch them cry and scream. They begged to see their moms and dads, have them come and save us, but we were never allowed to see them."

Jason walked over to Stephen and bent over to whisper in his ear. "Steve, I didn't see any children's bodies in that room."

"I know," Stephen answered. "I wonder where they are?"

Tina walked over and took Tommy by the hand and walked him back to the others. "Tommy, it is time for you to go back now. Everything will be all right," Tina said to the boy gently. Tommy took her hand and started walking with her, when Stephen interrupted them.

"Tommy, when were you brought here?" he asked. Tommy looked at Tina, as if he was asking for permission to answer.

"Go ahead, Tommy. He isn't here to hurt us, so go ahead and answer him," said Tina softly again.

Tommy looked up at Tina. She nodded and Tommy told Stephen that he and the rest of the children were brought to the priest on December 22nd, 1879.

"How old were you then?" Stephen asked, inside feeling so horrified to think that this had all been going on even longer than he had thought.

"I was just getting ready to turn nine at Christmas," Tommy said. "Edith was seven. Her birthday was three months before mine.

Stephen looked over at the little girl just standing there, not saying a word. To him she almost looked somehow incomplete. There was something missing. With her eyes so full of pain she looked like someone who needed someone to love her, or better yet, someone for her to love.

Suddenly, Stephen realized that all of the girls, hell, all of the children had the same dead look on their faces. Then he knew what it was, what would help them at least have a slim version of a smile. Not one of the girls had a doll… not one of them, and the boys didn't have whatever it was that made the boys happy back then, either.

"Tommy, where are your toys?"

Again he looked at Tina, who gave him a nod. "Our families never had any money. Our dads were either dead or out of work. We had trouble eating and having a place to live. We could never afford toys. We do have some toys here in that bad place where we died, a nurse gave them to us and we do play with them sometimes, but also when playing they do remind us of that terrible place and how we died. " Stephen listened, but the words he heard didn't sound like a nine-year-old's words. This was a young boy who was forced to grow up too soon. He wasn't able to play ball, or hide and seek, or tag and he probably never made it past the first grade in school… if he ever went at all. Odds are he had to work as a child laborer, to make a couple of cents a day to feed his mom and sister.

Tina took Tommy back to the rest of the people, and as soon as she let go of his hand, all of them turned and went back to wherever it was that they came from. Tina turned and looked directly at Stephen. She tried to smile, but it just wouldn't, or maybe couldn't come.

"Tina…," Stephen inquired, "where are the children?"

"I don't know," she said. "We knew they were here. There were only a couple of people who were brought here before they were. When I came, they told me about another room… somewhere… we don't know where, but it is supposed to hold the bodies of the children."

We're going to have to find that room before we bring anyone else in here, Stephen thought. "Tina, thank you so much for showing us all that happened," said Stephen very gently. "Jason and I are going to leave for now… but I do promise you that we will be back."

"I know," she said, as she started to fade away. "I know."

Stephen and Jason walked back into the torture chamber and back out into the hallway. It was then that Stephen noticed that the picture on the wall had changed. Instead of just the twelve souls that they had seen in the painting earlier, there were now nineteen. Also, the five children were now in the painting, secured to a pillar some distance away from the adults.

Stephen and Jason went back up the stairs, leaving the iron door open once again and the fan blowing fresh air down the shaft. They walked through the theater and as they started up the aisle, there she was. Tina was sitting in her regular seat watching something that Stephen thought had upset her, because she was crying like he had never seen a woman cry before. He sent Jason on into the lobby to get things ready for the evening, while he walked over to try to calm Tina.

"Tina, everything is going to be okay… I promise," he said, to no avail. Her eyes were staring straight ahead. Stephen thought back to the first time he ever saw Tina. She behaved just that way. "Okay, Tina… I'll leave you alone, but remember if you want to talk… I'll be here," he whispered to her, and then left the theater, walked into the lobby and joined Jason, who was at the front door letting in Meghyn, Laura, and Kelly so they could start work.

They had apparently been waiting there patiently for quite some time. Stephen glanced up at a clock in the foyer… and it read 6:30pm… they had about an hour before the doors opened for the evening show. *We were down there for eleven hours*, Stephen thought to himself. *It sure didn't feel that long.*

At 7:30pm the doors opened and Stephen, Jason, and the rest of the staff spent a normal evening with seventy-eight of their closest friends… their customers.

CHAPTER 17

The following morning, Stephen was up sometime around 10:00am. After stopping at Krispy Kreme for breakfast, he decided to head down to the library, as now he actually had some dates he could work with.

Luckily, every newspaper ever printed in Akron was stored on microfiche. He went up to the research floor that he had been to on his last visit and handed the clerk a piece of paper with two dates... December 22nd 1879, and March 15th 1905. It took her about half an hour to find the correct ones, but eventually he found himself sitting before a screen looking at stories written before his great-grandparents were born.

I think it would be best if I start with the 1879 stories, he thought. *There would no doubt be more coverage for five missing kids than there would be for a missing pregnant young woman.* Turning the crank, he finally got to the right date and there was nothing... absolutely nothing... not a single word about the kids. Now, although Stephen was fairly intelligent, he didn't at that moment realize that when looking for a news story that occurred on a specific date, you always had to look at least at the next day's paper to see if there was a story... possibly even the day after that, except on television, radio, and the ever-present internet, which, of course, always provides instant news just with the mere press of a button.

"Excuse me," he said, as he called one of the staff over and did his best to explain what he was looking for.

The young woman was most likely a volunteer from one of the local high schools since she didn't look a day past sixteen. She looked at him and gave the sweetest smile. "Sir, to find a story about something that happened... especially way back then... you know... before TV, you must look at papers after that date to find the story," she said, with what sounded like the beginning of an attitude. Feeling very stupid, Stephen defensively thought *What a little bitch,* as he graciously thanked her for her help. He even gave her a couple of passes to the theater. It wasn't clear why he suddenly did that, maybe by being extra nice to her, she'd realize that she was a little bitch and change. He doubted it, but there was a chance. But he did take her advice and check out the paper from December 23rd and there it was, a front page story about five missing children.

As Stephen read the report, he realized that the story was basically the same story Tommy had told him. It said, "The children: Tommy Harrison, his sister, Edith, Susan Schneider, Bobby Lewis, and Linda Lane were last seen walking home after a sandlot baseball game. Store owner Francis King said that he chased the children from his store when he caught them stealing bread from his counter. None of the five made it home. Police said that they are searching the area and every clue will be followed to its conclusion." Stephen kept looking through the entire next few day's headlines, but there was no further information about the kids or any further follow-up.

Stephen took that reel back to the librarian and asked for the one from March of 1905. He scanned quickly through. It was a lot easier, now that he knew what he was doing. The headlines from the March 16th paper were about a Liverpool shipwreck and the loss of twenty-three lives, as well as some speech President Wilson made encouraging young men to enlist in the newly created Army Air Corps. Page by page he looked and looked again, but there were no articles about a missing young woman.

I bet they thought she left town with the baby, he thought.

Then, on the third page, he saw a story about a baby that was found. It wasn't about the missing girl, so he had ignored it at first, but the third time he saw the headline it caught his attention. It read, "Abandoned Baby Found at the Church of the Sacred Feminine".

He started reading the story and it was about a baby who was born on March 15th. It said that the mother gave birth, and then after dropping the baby at the church, she returned to West Virginia to be with her family. It added that the baby was to be adopted by members of the church, Mr. and Mrs. Paul Olivier of Spicer Street in Akron.

Oh, my God, Stephen thought. *That's got to be her… that's got to be Eleanor.* He kept reading and getting as much information as he could about the story, especially the Oliviers. He was there for pretty much most of the morning and afternoon.

Across the hall from the room with the newspaper information was the room that handled documents related to genealogy. It contained things filed away like school records, births and death information, and, most importantly to Stephen, census records. He went in and asked to see a copy of the Akron census for 1910. The book the librarian brought out was thick. Stephen looked at it and said, "Oh, my God!" The librarian never said a word; she just grinned and went straight back to a book she was reading on vampires. It took Stephen a couple of hours to go though it all, but eventually he found the information he was looking for. "I thank the gods that we have computers," he said out loud. An older librarian heard what he said as she passed by and commented, "It sure makes things a lot easier".

Stephen smiled at her, so she walked over to him and said, "Honey, you couldn't be more right about that". Then she sat down at the table and asked if she could help him in any way, and what was he looking for? Stephen knew that she was just trying to be helpful and possibly also a little curious, so he said he was doing research about the turn of the century working class. It was obvious that she believed him, because she went and found him a few more books from 1905, tapping him gently on the shoulder as she handed him the books. Stephen thanked her and glanced through the pages, pretended to take some notes, and soon after went back to the census.

It read, "Name: Paul David Olivier - Age 32, Wife: Elizabeth Ann Olivier – Age 29, Children: Marie Elizabeth Olivier – Age 5, Joseph Robert Olivier – Age 1." It went on to say that Paul worked in one of the rubber factories as a tire maker while Elizabeth worked as a seamstress. It also listed Marie as a student.

She must have been in kindergarten, he thought. *I wonder what school she went to.* He knew the Spicer Street area, and the kids there either went to Mason Elementary or Spicer Elementary. He looked at the census book again and saw that their address was 678 Spicer St, so he knew that she went to the Mason School. It was a long walk, but that was where she went.

Just about then, someone else came and tapped him on the shoulder. This time it wasn't the soft touch of the librarian; it was firmer and definitely male. He looked up and saw Edward standing behind him. This time his face wasn't the warm, friendly face he had been greeted with every time they met. It was instead cold and hard like a piece of granite.

"Why are you looking into something you do not, could not understand?" Edward asked, with a voice that was as cold as his look. Stephen didn't answer the question, but he did ask a question of his own.

"Why aren't you trapped in the theater like the rest of them?" he asked.

"So you know? How did you figure it out?"

Stephen looked at him and smiled. "You just told me," he said as he stood up and stood face-to-face with Edward. "So, I repeat, Edward, why aren't you trapped in the theater like the others?"

They were both now in an aggressive stance and people around them were starting to notice, so, slowly, Stephen sat back down, and, surprisingly, Edward sat down next to him. They were both still on guard, but they tried not to let anyone else know it.

"I wasn't in the church when the people came in with torches and destroyed the place," he said. "They found me a few days after they were done with the Father and all his supporters. I was just walking down the street in front of the ruins of the church. Someone recognized me and they took me out into the woods and started beating me. They must have killed me, because I have been wandering around town since then. I can only go into that building for a short time... maybe a couple of minutes, before the pain gets too bad."

"Why would you have been part of such horrendous things?" Stephen asked him.

"It was the will of God," Edward said. "It was the will of God. The church sent down a doctrine that said that parish priests must become more active in making the parish free of all sin. Father DuMond took it to heart and acted the way he thought the church wanted him to act. He stopped sinning."

"But what did those poor people ever do to receive such punishment?" Stephen asked.

"It could have been anything," Edward explained. "If the Lord's ten commandments forbade it, then of course Father DuMond was there to set it right."

"But stealing a loaf of bread, and..."

Edward did not even allow Stephen to finish his sentence, as he banged the table violently. "Remember Exodus 20:15... 'Thou shalt not steal'... that was a commandment from God. It was one of the ten commandments, so there was no alternative; it had to be enforced."

"But why didn't you try to stop the torturous punishments?"

"I wanted to, but, believe me, it was the word of the church. Sadly, I was even excommunicated from the church by Father DuMond when I objected. Father DuMond said he didn't want any dissidents around him, so that is why I wasn't there when they came." Stephen thought for a minute and asked Edward if he, or anyone else, had ever seen the doctrine from Rome."

"No, of course not. Believe me, Stephen... he... Father DuMond... was well aware of its importance, so he always kept it locked safely in the church office and would not allow anyone to see it. He said it was for the head priest's eyes only."

"So you don't really have any idea if... it was real or not?" Stephen inquired, without realizing his tone was sounding more like the cops on television... than a man talking to a dead deacon.

"I wasn't allowed to see it, but, of course, I believed Father DuMond... so did everyone else. The Father was chosen by God, to rid us of all sinners."

At that moment, Stephen was seething inside. He had quite liked Edward, but that he could condone all that had been done in God's name was beyond understanding. He did not want to be anywhere near Edward, so he made an excuse he had to get back to the theater, as he had been at the library far too long. He quickly gathered up the papers he had been writing on, headed over to the main counter with the books, and handed them to the librarian. Edward had followed him over there, so he turned to Edward and told him that he had to go; he was needed at the theater. As Stephen walked out of the library, he looked back, and Edward was gone.

Stephen really did want to get back to the Strand, so he didn't stop to eat, drink or anything else. He just drove straight to the theater, where Laura, Meghyn, and Jason were standing at the door, eager to get started. Their boss apologized for keeping them all waiting, and, as he did, he looked at his watch. It was once again 6:30pm and the show was set to start at 7:30pm, so once again they all rushed in to get things ready for the evening.

The doors opened and the movie started right on time, and, of course, Tina was right there in her seat, drinking her pop, eating her popcorn, and watching a movie she loved, "Casablanca".

CHAPTER 18

After the movie finished and the people left, the staff did their usual re-cleaning, and when all was to Stephen's satisfaction, also left to go home. Once they were all gone, Stephen locked the doors for the night. Jason had wanted to stick around and go back into the basement, but Stephen insisted that he go home for the night, because before they did anything further, he had some more research to do. He was in his office thinking about everything, when Tina came to the door. At first he thought it was just to say good night, as she had not acknowledged him since they were in the basement the night before, but then he realized that she did now want to talk.

"Stephen, how are you tonight?" she asked.

He replied that he was doing okay… he then gestured to her and said, "Come on in and have a seat". Deep in thought as she entered his office for the first time, Stephen was thinking… *How am I going to tell her about her daughter?* Stephen was worried about how Tina would react.

As she sat down, Tina had her sweet look down to a T, then she looked at him, sensing he had something to say to her. "What is it, Stephen? Do you have something to tell me?" she asked. After all, Stephen now knew all about the lost souls trapped in his theater, so she really did not want to hear if what he had to tell her was something bad, but, being Tina, she tried to act as if she did want to hear, just in case it was something good.

"I went to the library," he stated. "I was down there doing some research about what happened downstairs." Stephen's voice suddenly became strained, as he tried to think while he spoke. "I looked for a newspaper story about you disappearing, but they never wrote anything about it."

"Stephen, did you really think they would let anything out about the people who came here for help and ended up murdered?"

"Not really," he replied. "But… I did find a story about a two-day-old baby girl back in 1905. The article said her mom, they thought, went off to be with family when she abandoned the baby at 'The Church of the Sacred Feminine,' and was never heard from again. The baby was then adopted by a couple who were members of the church."

The computer, which was turned on in Stephen's office, suddenly opened a word processing program and starting typing, letter by letter. It continued until the message, "Ne pas le dire. Ce n'est pas à elle de le savoir," appeared on the screen. As it did, Tina faded from view.

"Stop that French shit!" Stephen screamed out, upset that this had frightened Tina and caused her to just disappear. "I figured you'd be listening, you son-of-a-bitch, so show yourself to me. I want to talk to you face-to-face."

He heard a rustling in the hallway outside his office, and, since Tina wasn't there any longer, he opened the door and went out. There, in full white robe and silver vestments, stood a priest. Stephen just stood and looked at him for a moment. He wasn't as tall as Stephen thought he would be… maybe five foot eight or five foot ten at the most, and he looked like he only weighed about a hundred and eighty pounds. He had a beard of deep blue-black, with eyes that matched and they were cold penetrating eyes that could, and most likely would, look right through you. Other than that… he was nothing special at all.

"Vous avez appelé pour moi… Je suis ici aujourd'hui ce que voulez-vous," he said in a voice that was, to say the least, impressive, if not overly scary.

"Look, you bastard, I know you spent enough time running this place to learn to speak English… probably better than I do, so if you won't… I don't want any further dealings with you," Stephen said, trying to sound as powerful as he could. He then turned his back to the priest and mumbled something that could barely be heard over the pounding of his heart, which had swelled so much because of the stress it felt, like it was going to choke him. "Yes, I do speak English, but I am more comfortable speaking French," the priest said, making Stephen turn back around and face him. "I take it you are Father Jacques DuMond?" "I am."

"And this was your church?" Once again the answer was yes. "Well, I hate to tell you this, your church is long gone," said Stephen, with as much authority in his voice as he could muster. "I own this building now and a number of people you murdered are still here. I want to free them… allow them to cross over to the reward they deserve," Stephen stated, hoping to get this all over with as quickly as possible.

"They are sinners and their punishments were handed down by God through the laws of the Catholic Church, not by me," DuMond coldly stated back, puffing his chest out like a primed out peacock. "These evil sinners ARE NOT going anywhere; they will remain captured here for eternity."

"Bullshit," Stephen responded. "If Pope Pius, yeah, Pope Pius, you ignorant prick. See… I grew up a good Catholic boy… If Pope Pius gave you instructions… then tell me why no one else ever saw them?"

"They were not for anyone else to see; it was an order sent to me and me alone," DuMond stated coldly.

"Why not? Wouldn't it have made you more believable?"

"I do not have to explain myself to you or anyone else. Beware, if you persist in this I may condemn you for heresy and sentence you to eternity in damnation just like the others."

"What if I won't go?" Stephen stated, in an even harder, colder voice, with a defiant indignant look on his face, which obviously confused and greatly angered DuMond.

Father DuMond obviously wasn't used to being spoken to this way, especially having someone he considered beneath him stand up to him with such impudence. Inside, Stephen was literally so scared he just wanted to run, and if he had been like so many others, he would no doubt have been begging for forgiveness for his immortal soul. But Stephen Baker was different… he had strength and he knew this fiend did not, under any circumstance, represent God, the Pope, or the Catholic Church.

"Sinner, take heed," DuMond warned in an icy voice, "Do not disrespect the church, its laws or me. Be warned, it would not be good for you."

"Yeah, right," Stephen said, as he turned his back on Father DuMond and started walking back into his office. Then he turned again to face DuMond and said in a loud powerful voice, "Well, Father, mark my words, the people who followed you believed in that religious claptrap you spewed out. I don't… so you have no power over me." As Stephen turned and stepped into his office, Father Jacques DuMond faded from view. Then, suddenly, every window in the building shattered, including the ones in the box office, which were not attached to the building. "What the fuck!" Stephen yelled, as he ran from the office and looked up into the lobby. The streetlights were shining through the empty spaces in the doors, making the broken glass look like stars on the deeply colored carpet.

Stephen stepped outside and called Jason on his mobile to let him know what had just happened. Jason was asleep when the call came, but the first words out of his mouth were, "I'll be there in a few minutes". It took Stephen more than ten minutes to talk his young projectionist into staying home, but eventually he was successful and Jason went back to a less than restful sleep.

The next call was to the emergency glass company to get someone out to fix all of the windows. It took about an hour for the workmen to get there and another six hours to get all of the glass in. Stephen spent the time sweeping up shards of glass, then he noticed that the concession stand was also shattered. It was a couple more hours until all the glass could be cut and shaped. In all that time, other than the workmen,

Stephen was alone. Neither Tina nor Edward showed up, and Father DuMond was suddenly very quiet.

The sun was coming up when all the work was done and it was just six hours before the doors opened again, so Stephen just curled up on his couch and fell into a very, very light yet troubled sleep.

During his sleep, his dreams kept going back to the Church of the Sacred Feminine. He watched the five children being beaten and tortured, being told that they were going to hell to be punished for all eternity.

He saw Tina, lying naked, strapped to a table spread-eagled, having her baby ripped from her body. He saw the blood, heard her cries. He watched as in another area of the church the baby was handed to that couple, before Tina had the chance to even know if her baby was still alive or had been taken and murdered by Father DuMond. He saw the others tortured and killed for little reason. And in every dream, he saw Father Jacques DuMond watching, almost enjoying, every act that was being performed.

After a couple of hours Stephen gave up. It was like he was awake more than asleep, so he just got up, locked the front door, and went home… to do what, he wasn't sure. He just didn't want to be in the theater anymore right then.

On the way home he swung by Meghyn's house to see if she was awake. He knocked a couple times softly, and a minute later, she came to the door dressed in a white sweat suit and a pink hoodie, which she forgot to tie shut.

"I'm sorry to bother you," he said, as he tried not to look at her, since she was disheveled, and Meghyn always made it a point to look her best. He thought that maybe him seeing her like this was going to embarrass her.

"It's no bother," she said, with a big smile on her face. Stephen tried, but couldn't figure out how she could be so freaking cheerful so early in the morning. "I've been up a couple of hours now. I always get up early and go for a run, or if the weather's nice enough, I go for a swim." He looked and her hair was still damp, so he figured she had chosen the swim. *Why the hell would anyone get up this early on purpose?* he thought. *I try to stay in bed as long as possible.*

She invited him in for some breakfast, but he graciously said no, that he wasn't hungry. "I just wanted to drop these off," he said, as he handed her the keys to the theater. "I am going to take the night off. You are in charge, so do a good job for me." She said that she'd do her best, as she put the keys in her purse.

That afternoon, the theater had a decent crowd and Meghyn proved that she could run the place. Tina did show up. She was later than usual, but this time she just sat in her seat watching the movie and did not talk to anyone. The one time Meghyn observed her at the concession stand, she thought that Tina looked tired and her eyes were all red and drawn as if she had been crying... a lot. She did try talking to Tina, but Tina ignored her and just returned to her seat without even a glance back. The exact same thing happened during the evening shows... *She may not be acting like herself, but at least she is here,* Meghyn thought to herself. Then her mind really began working overtime and she started wondering what had happened in the last couple of days... It had to be something interesting, as no one, including Jason, would tell her anything.

CHAPTER 19

Jason was up in the projection booth all evening, looking through a small window that faced into the theater. It was there so he could make sure that the movie was lined up and in focus that night, though he didn't care much about the movie. As a matter of fact, there were a couple of times that it went out of focus and he didn't realize until Meghyn came up and told him that a customer had complained. He was more interested in the door behind the screen and all that he had seen with Stephen.

"What in the hell is wrong with you?" she finally asked him, the last time she came up about the movie. "Your mind is like it's a million miles away."

"Actually, it's about one hundred and sixty feet and one hundred and four years away," he said.

"What do you mean?" Meghyn asked. Jason replied that he wasn't supposed to say anything about what he had learned that day, but he could not help hinting to Meghyn that it did have something to do with Tina and all the weird stuff that had been happening in the theater. Naturally, this piqued Meghyn's interest. "You mean you guys found out why these spirits are here?" she asked.

"Yeah, we sure have," responded Jason, trying not to say more than that, but of course that answer was far too brief to satisfy Meghyn's inquisitiveness.

Meghyn's curiosity had been totally aroused. "Oh, Jason, please! You know you can trust me. I promise not to tell anybody. Just tell me all about what you and Steve found out about this place," she begged, as she moved closer to Jason smelling of jasmine and snuggling up to him with a, "Pleeeeeaaaaassssssseee?"

Unable to resist Meghyn, Jason weakened immediately and said, "Okay, I'll show you what we have found, but you HAVE to promise that you will NOT tell Steve that I took you down there. I'll get fired if you do," he stated. Elated that her pleading had worked, as it always did, Meghyn agreed not to say a word to their boss. Once again she agreed. Jason then said he would meet her in the lobby when everyone had gone home.

Eventually the last show ended. Laura and the others all went home. Laura hoped her boss was not sick again. It was so unlike him not to attend every show. What she didn't know was that her boss had stayed at home to try and get a good night's sleep before he once again had to confront Father DuMond.

So by the time Jason met Meghyn, the theater was totally empty, and even Tina was nowhere to be seen.

As agreed, Meghyn met Jason in the lobby. She greeted him with a soft kiss on the cheek, and, seeing how perturbed Jason looked, once again promised that she wouldn't say anything to anyone, especially Stephen.

Once they were inside the theater, Jason turned the house lights back on and then he led Meghyn down the aisle, towards the backstage curtain. Meghyn was actually feeling slightly apprehensive, but there was no way she was going to show it to Jason.

"Now, Meghyn, please stay calm," Jason warned, "because I assure you, you are going to be shocked… really shocked about what you are going to see. So please try not to show it," Jason warned.

"What am I going to see?" she asked.

"Just wait."

"Wait for what?" she asked. It wasn't hard to see that her curiosity was getting the better of her. "What am I going to see?" Once again Jason told her to wait, and, of course, this made Meghyn even more curious.

Once they got to the door, they immediately felt the cool air blowing down the shaft from the fan, which had been left running. The light from the bottom of the stairs was just as bright as it was the night Stephen and Jason went down the stairs for the first time.

Jason moved the fan and then instructed Meghyn, "I'll go down first and you follow when I call for you". Jason touched Meghyn's arm reassuringly, then started down the stairs. It took Jason a couple of minutes… maybe five at the most… before he called up to her, "Okay, Meghyn, you can come down, but promise you will not touch anything," he asked her.

Meghyn carefully climbed down the stairs, feeling a little nervous. Once she reached the bottom of the stairs, she looked around, not at all expecting to see what was there. "Oh, my God," she said, sounding shocked, scared, and surprised. "What the hell is all this?"

Jason couldn't answer her question. Or maybe, even though he could, he just didn't want to. In fact, suddenly he started to regret having listened to her pleas and being so stupid as to bring her there. There was nothing he could do about it now, except take her by the hand protectively and lead her down the long hallway.

Meghyn's eyes glanced back and forth between the two walls. "Oh shit!" she stated in horror. "I have heard about places like this in several books I've read. I never believed it really existed. It's apparently a place where heaven and hell meet. The hallway must be the divider. Some say that there is a thin veil between the two realms. It is supposed to be nearly impossible to cross between them."

Jason stopped and turned around to look at her. Meghyn was saying stuff he couldn't believe she was saying and even shouldn't be saying. He then explained to her that Stephen had said that the good side was called Summerland, not heaven, although the way he talked it sure sounded like it was the same thing. He then asked Meghyn how she knew so much about this type of thing.

"My mother was a clairvoyant," Meghyn said. "Before she died, she taught me a lot about her abilities and how I could develop them for myself. I dabbled in it a little when I was a teen. I actually got people thinking I was a witch for a while… that is, until I realized that boys didn't want to date witches. Then I just let it go. My God, it has been years, but I guess you never forget."

"I guess not," Jason said, laughing a little. "Here, come this way." He took her by the hand and led her down to the hallway. After clearing some fresh growth, he moved a couple of rocks that he and Stephen had just stepped over. "Close your eyes, and try not to get too upset with what you see," he said, as they started through the arch. Meghyn did exactly as she was told. She was feeling very strange and was relieved that Jason was there with her.

Once they got inside the room, he told her to go ahead and open her eyes… which she did. The moment she did, her eyes opened as wide as they could and she stood there for a minute in total shock. She hadn't seen anything like this in anything other than history books and that was the stuff used by Catholic priests in the Inquisition. She put her hands up over her ears and she started to cry.

Immediately, Jason once again became very concerned that he had exposed Meghyn to this horror, and wished he had not been so totally stupid as to agree to take her down to the basement.

"My God… I can hear them. They are crying, begging for mercy, but no one will listen!" she cried out. "I hear the cries of children and women. They didn't want to die. They came here for help and were murdered. Jason, their cries are so loud, it is unbearable!" She was on her knees, resting on stones still stained with blood after all those years. "Oh, my God, no!" she yelled. "Right over there, that is where Tina was killed. I can feel them cutting her open. She was still alive and she felt everything. God, it hurts so bad! They took the baby and left her cut open."

Jason just stood there feeling numb and not saying a thing. He knew Meghyn was actually seeing all that had happened.

"I see her lying there suffering, begging for them to give her the last rites before she died, but they ignored her pleas. She eventually just passed out with the pain and then stopped breathing. Oh no, Jason it is unbelievable but I can see so much of what they did to Tina, and also everyone that was here. They were all tortured horribly, and just left to die in the most agonizing pain imaginable. I can also see what they did to the children. Oh, please let this stop. I just can't take any more... those poor children, oh, those poor, poor children..." Meghyn suddenly went very quiet, the tears pouring down her face.

"What about the children?" Jason asked. "Why on earth were they brought here?"

"They were guilty of stealing food," Meghyn cried out, shaking all over. "Jason, they tied them to the walls... over there." She was crying as she pointed to a corner of the room that neither Jason nor Stephen had checked out before. "They were forced to watch everyone else die."

"So, how did the children die?" he asked, not wanting to hear the answer.

"They were starved. Then, as a punishment for their so-called sins, they would tease them with food. Let them smell it and then take it away. The children were allowed water and they got a lot of it to fill their bellies but very little food. They lasted a long time before they were allowed to die."

"Oh, my God, do you know what happened to their bodies?" the horrified Jason asked.

Again she pointed at that corner. "They are there," she cried out. Suddenly, Meghyn didn't look like herself anymore. Jason stood back watching her; it looked like she was in a trance or something. "They are behind that wall!" she screamed.

"There's an alley on the other side of that wall," he replied, completely forgetting that they were, at that moment, thirty feet below the surface of the ground.

Meghyn immediately walked over and placed her hand on a large stone. It was solid black. Not like the gray stones that made up the rest of the room. She placed her other hand on the wall and started to sob violently. "They are behind here," she stated.

Fearing for her mental safety, Jason immediately walked over and grabbed her, dragging her out of the room and back into the hallway. "Oh, Meghyn, I am so, so sorry I showed any of this to you. What just happened to you, Meghyn?" he asked, as she eventually snapped back into her senses.

"I felt everything," she stated in a broken voice. "Jason, I literally felt their pain. I saw what they saw." Jason looked at her again. Tears were flowing down her face in streams. "I can't go back in there ever, ever again, it was far too horrifying."

Jason took her hands in his and promised her that she wouldn't ever have to go back in there again.

They went back up the stairs. Meghyn cried all the way out and Jason nearly had to carry her, but they made it. As soon as they got to the lobby, Jason laid her down on one of the couches, gave her some water to drink, and as soon as she had calmed down a little, went off to call his boss and let him know what had happened.

It took two calls and an additional five rings for Stephen to get up and answer his phone. He was groggy and still had a little bit of a buzz from a couple Jack and cokes. "Hello?" he mumbled.

"Steve, this is Jason. I am still at the theater with Meghyn," he said.

Suddenly Stephen's mind cleared and he realized what the young man had said to him. "What are you doing there?"

"Meghyn and I are just hanging; we were going on out."

This statement from Jason got Stephen kind of suspicious. "What are the two of you doing and what happened? Why are you calling me so urgently?"

"I'm very, very sorry, Steve, I broke my promise to you. Meghyn suddenly suspected something was going on, so I weakened to her pleas and took her downstairs to show her what was down there…" Jason stated hurriedly, with genuine remorse.

"And…" Stephen asked, as his senses cleared even more.

"She knows where the kids are actually buried," Jason said quietly. "She's some kind of psychic or something and she learned a lot while we were down there."

"You two stay right there and don't do anything else," Stephen stated, finally realizing what was going on and getting angrier with Jason by the second. "I'll be there as soon as I get dressed."

In fear for Meghyn and Jason, Stephen quickly got out of bed, got dressed, and, after, grabbing a quick cup of coffee to wake himself fully, got in his car and started for the theater. *What in the hell was that stupid son-of-a-bitch thinking,* he thought, as the street lights passed him by in nothing less than a blur. *I told him not to say anything to anybody. What the hell did they do down there? Did I speak English? I thought I did, but maybe not…* It didn't take him long to get there, mainly because the traffic was light and he didn't bother stopping for red lights… he just slowed down a little to make sure there were no cars coming and then drove straight through them.

Finally, he got to the theater, and, as he looked through the lobby doors, he could see Jason sitting on the lobby couch trying to comfort a very traumatized Meghyn.

Opening the door, he let himself in and quietly but quickly made it through the lobby and stood next to the two of them. Meghyn looked up and in her eyes he could see an almost unbearable pain. Calming down, or at least acting as if he was calm, Stephen inquired of Jason exactly what had happened.

The moment he spoke, Meghyn started to cry again, so Jason and Stephen walked further down the lobby outside of her hearing. Jason explained how he and Meghyn were alone and talking in the projection room, when he foolishly let her know strange things had been happening, and then, after a little prodding from Meghyn, the truth about what was going on just came out. "I didn't mean to say anything, Steve. I really don't even remember the conversation or how it started," Jason said. "All of a sudden I was telling her about the basement and I found myself taking her down there."

"Okay," Stephen responded.

"Steve, when we got down there, we eventually went into the torture area. Shit, Steve, it was unbelievable. She knew everything! She told me how Tina died and what they did to those kids. Nobody should ever have to go through something like that." Jason looked over and saw that Meghyn was sitting there watching them... still crying... but watching them nonetheless. "She knew that we never found the children. She knew that they are behind a big black rock in the corner of the room. Somehow she knows where their grave is."

"Okay," Stephen said again. "What did she say about Tina?"

"I can tell you," a voice replied, coming, it seemed, out of nowhere. Stephen looked in the direction it came from... thinking it may have been Meghyn. It wasn't. The air behind Meghyn shimmered a little and then Tina materialized behind her. She looked calm and she rested her hand on Meghyn's shoulder. It looked as if she was massaging it in an effort to try to relax her. Of course, Meghyn only felt a soft, soothing breeze. "Stephen, I will tell you what they did to me, but only if you promise to finish telling me what you were going to tell me about my daughter... what you found out about her."

"Tina," Stephen sighed. "Please, come over here. I have a feeling that you are going to need to be near a friend who sincerely cares about you, after you hear what I have to say."

Tina did as he asked, sitting so close she was nearly passing through his body as she looked into his face.

"What is it?" she asked, with a tear already forming. Stephen gazed into her eyes. They were beautiful, full of life and hope, although that life and any hope that she had in her heart was tempered by all of the pain she had endured throughout her life, and for many years after her death.

He smiled a bit of a smile, as he told her that he did have some good news. "I found out about Eleanor, your baby daughter. She made it and she was happy."

"What happened to her?" Tina asked, between sobbing and smiling.

"She was adopted by a family named Olivier. They named her Marie Elizabeth, and she had a brother named Joseph Robert. I am not sure, but I think maybe the Oliviers adopted him too. I also found out that Marie Elizabeth went to Spicer Elementary School." He stopped talking and just as he had predicted, Tina started shaking so badly it almost knocked Stephen to the floor, as the furniture started moving erratically.

"What else did you find?" she cried, as she tried to grip his arm and her hand passed through his body. "Please, tell me."

"That's all I know right now," he said, as he reassured her. "Believe me, Tina, I promise I will find out as much about Marie Elizabeth as I can. Now that we have a name, it should be very easy to find out more about your daughter."

Tina stopped crying, and smiled at Stephen in gratitude once again, and then moved over to Meghyn, who looked like she was in a trance or something. Tina touched Meghyn's hand, but, of course, Meghyn felt nothing but once again only a gentle soothing breeze as Tina sat down next to her. Stephen was slightly concerned, but he had learned not to comment. Tina knew what she wanted to do and there was no point arguing.

Stephen sat down on a chair across from the girls and gently reminded Tina that she had said she would tell them all about what had been done to her before her death.

"It is not nice to hear, but just talking about it may help ease the memory, especially now you tell me my baby daughter was adopted and they did not kill her because of my one transgression," she said.

"I came here for help when I was nine months pregnant, when I had a few labor pains. They took me before the priest, but he condemned me. He said I needed absolution and must be punished for my sins... I have no idea who it was, but someone tied my arms and legs and took me down into the basement. When I went into labor, I wasn't given anything for the pain, but there was a nurse. I remember her... she was an older woman... she kept telling me I was going to be okay. The priest came down and untied my arms and legs. At that moment I also thought I was going to be okay."

"Was there anyone else there?" Stephen gently asked.

"No, I just saw the priest and the nurse, but my head was restrained by the priest so I couldn't look around. So maybe there were others there; I do not know. The priest stared at my body and removed all my clothes. He looked at me like I was something disgusting, but that didn't stop him from "blessing" my sexual organ.

"Did he...?" Stephen asked.

"Oh no... no..." Tina replied, he just made the sign of the cross and stroked the outside of it. Anyway, when he was done, the nurse took me over and laid me on a wooden table. The splinters hurt my back. I could feel drops of blood falling from the small cuts. Then the priest came over and tied me spread-eagled on the table. He pulled so hard my legs and arms were pulled out of their sockets. I remember asking for something for the pain, but he looked at me with pure hatred and said I didn't deserve it. The nurse also begged him to give me something, but he utterly refused.

"This might sound strange..." Tina said, "... but strangely, I did like her."

"What happened then?" asked Stephen, observing both Jason and Meghyn were also listening intently, Stephen himself felt sick to the stomach and dreading what he was to hear next..

"The priest went over and took a knife off of the wall. It wasn't a scalpel. It was more like a butcher's knife... the ones you cut meat with. I could see that it had a LOT of dried blood on it, so I knew it had been used before. He came over, said something in Latin, and stabbed into my belly just below my ribs. By then I was screaming, but my body was numb. I didn't feel anything other than my skin being sliced. He cut down and took the baby out of me. I only heard the baby cry once, so at least I knew she was alive, but I never heard her again as they got her out of the room so quickly. But I did see her beautiful little body and face. I will never ever forget it, she was so beautiful. The priest said something else in Latin and then just left me tied to the table, bleeding to death. I felt myself go weak. I knew I was dying... I begged for the priest to return to give me the last rites but he never did... then everything went black. There was a white light as my vision faded, I reached out for it, as the priest suddenly appeared, but he pulled me away from the light, screaming I was not allowed near it for all eternity.

"The next thing I knew I was walking around the church building. Then later on it was destroyed by very angry people, but fortunately for us, all the areas in the basement remained, so we all did have shelter and a place to go that we knew. Then they eventually built this theater and called it The Strand Movie Theater and they then started showing movies in this building where the church had once been. Everyone I had ever known before was gone, and along with the others, I was captured here for eternity. Then the movies suddenly stopped being shown, so we just wandered around the building trying to comfort each other, and then, happily, you came along, Stephen, and I was able to watch the movies once again."

"Did you know the priest who murdered you?" Stephen asked softly.

She thought a minute, scared that by saying his name she might cause Father DuMond to cause Stephen harm.

"Yes," she finally answered. "It was Father DuMond. I met him when I first came in and he didn't bother to wear a mask when he took my baby, so I saw his face the whole time."

"That is exactly what I saw in my vision," Meghyn said. "I felt everything you felt." She looked at Stephen and told him that he had to take her back to the basement. "There is something else these murdered souls want to tell me."

"But, Meghyn, you told Jason, it was all so real and horrific to you, you did not want to ever go down there again!" stated Stephen, not understanding why Meghyn now wanted to go back down there.

"I know I said that, Steve, but I know I must go down there to help those poor captive souls."

Stephen shook his head "No, Meghyn, I cannot put you through that mental torture again. If something happened to you, I would never forgive myself." Meghyn became more demanding and insisted on going down again. At that moment, Tina suddenly faded away, as Meghyn still kept on insisting she must go back to that room, so finally Stephen gave up and the three of them went through the curtains into the room behind the stage and down the stairwell.

Once they got down into the basement, they went straight to the torture chamber. The minute Meghyn walked into the room, she could once again hear the screaming and cries for help. This time, though, she was expecting them, so it wasn't nearly as shocking and painful as it was the first time. She didn't yell and she remained calm, as she did her best to drown them out. "There… over there," she said, pointing to the corner of the room where she had seen the children.

"This stone?" Stephen asked. She nodded her head as she stepped toward Jason and took him by the hand.

Stephen estimated that the stone was about four foot by six foot. It was black, just like Meghyn described, but he also noticed it had the same red veins that he had seen in the stone tile up in the main room. He and Jason walked over and put their hands on the stone. He thought it looked like granite, but when he touched it there was something very strange about it… it felt light, not heavy at all. *This thing should weigh a ton*, he thought to himself, but when he and Jason put the smallest amount of pressure on the side of it… the stone moved easily… too easily.

"Steve, just look at this," Meghyn called out to him. She was standing beside where they had pushed the stone too. Pointing at the stone she called to him once again. The tone of her voice was excited and upset, yet curious at the same time.

Stephen went over to Meghyn and once he did, he could understand why the stone was so light. It was barely an inch thick and a crack in the side showed that inside the granite-like shell, the stone was porous… a sort of sponge like material.

This immediately turned their attention from the stone and back to where it originally sat in the wall. The stone had been concealing a brick doorway and another set of steps going even deeper down. The doorway this time was just a basic door, no arch or cross or anything like that… just a big, rectangular, entrance door in a brick frame. There was not a bit of light coming from the entrance, so Stephen and Jason lit the torches they had brought with them again and started down, closely followed by Meghyn.

These walls were made of rough-hewn stone. The walls in the basement hallway and even the torture chamber were at least smooth… these walls were not. Some places were so rough that even a soft brush against them could open a very bad gash in your arm or leg. Stephen hit a couple of sharp rocks, as did Meghyn, but eventually they made it down the twenty-five steps into another small room.

Meghyn, Jason, and Stephen looked around and what they saw really surprised them. This room was different from the ones upstairs. The wall at the left side was smooth and painted with scenes of children playing. It even had shredded curtains hanging from wooden rods.

"It seems obvious someone actually cared about these kids," Stephen stated, as he pointed to a corner of the room which revealed a pile of antique boys' and girls' toys. "Look, he said, as he pointed toward the toys. There were dolls, toy tools, carriages, and hand-carved wooden horses. The pile itself wasn't messy, though, the way a kid would just throw the toys in a corner. It was neat, like the way a parent would put the toys away.

"Too bad they weren't around to play with them," stated Jason angrily, "and no doubt when they could do so, the memories were far too hideous."

Their torches were running low, so they used the light from the small flames of their lighters which reflected off of the walls in a beautiful kind of dance. In that light, they saw five shelves on the far wall and on all but one shelf was a child's body. On one of the lower shelves were two little bodies lying side by side... holding hands.

These bodies were not as well preserved as the ones in the upper chamber. Stephen assumed that it was because of the high humidity, with this room being so deep down under the building. Along the right side of the room there were more shelves... four in all. *They were no doubt expecting to kill more kids*, Jason thought, as kids are so often doing naughty things.

"What kind of kids are they?" Stephen asked.

"What do you mean, Steve?" Meghyn asked.

"How many boys... how many girls?" Stephen asked, as he continued to look around.

"Going by the clothes, I would guess two boys and three girls," Meghyn said. "Steve, that brother and sister you saw... who was eldest?"

Jason answered that when they saw the kids earlier, the brother Tommy seemed to be the older of the two.

"If you remember, Jason, Tommy told us that he was nine and Edith was seven when they came here."

Jason immediately replied that he remembered most of the conversation, but not that part. It had all been far too traumatic for him to hear everything that he had been told.

"Come over here and just look at this lower shelf, with the two young bodies holding hands," Meghyn said. "The little girl seems slightly younger. I bet this is Tommy and his sister." Stephen and Jason looked closely at the young bodies and they agreed with Meghyn that, most likely, the two skeletons were indeed Tommy and Edith Harrison.

Suddenly, very faintly, they heard a kind of clicking sound from the corner where the toys were piled up. Meghyn was the first to look over and she saw a little red rubber ball bouncing up and down. *I used to do that when I was playing Jacks as a kid*, she thought.

"What's going on?" Stephen asked.

"I'm not sure, but I think that maybe one of the girls is over there playing Jacks," Meghyn replied. She turned back towards the bouncing ball, walked over, and sat down next to it.

The ball continued to bounce as she moved closer. "Hello, my name is Meghyn. What is yours?" There was no reply, but suddenly the ball stopped bouncing. "Can you do something for me?" Meghyn inquired. Intuitively with her abilities, she suddenly knew the names of all the children there. "If this is Edith... can you bounce the ball once for me?" The ball sat perfectly still. "Okay, so it is not Edith. Is it Susan, and can you move the ball for me?" Again the ball didn't move. "Then you must be Linda... Linda, can you move the ball for me?" It took a couple of seconds and then the ball started bouncing again. "Hello, Linda," she said. "It is very nice to meet you."

"Keep talking to her," Stephen said. "Maybe she will actually answer you."

"How many children are here playing with you?" Meghyn asked. The ball stopped and then bounced five times, which Meghyn realized meant that all five of the children's spirits were in this room with them. "You know… I know it might make you really tired, Linda, but is it possible for me to see you for a minute or so?" The ball stopped for a minute and bounced once. Meghyn realized that this most likely meant a yes, but there was no way to be sure.

"Linda, was that a yes?" she asked.

"Yes, Meghyn… that was a yes," a sweet young voice answered, as a hand formed around the ball, and the next thing Meghyn, Jason, and Stephen knew was that they were face-to-face with a young girl who looked to be about nine years old. She was extremely pretty, but she also looked very worn and tired. Meghyn guessed that was because it took her so much energy to cross over. She looked past Meghyn and saw Jason and Stephen standing there watching. "I remember you," she stated softly, pointing to Stephen. "You were talking to Tina?"

"Yes," Stephen gently replied. "Tina is my good friend."

"She is a friend of mine too," Linda said. "She takes great care of us."

"How does she do that?" asked Stephen.

"When we cry or feel sad because we miss our moms and dads and our brothers and sisters, she helps us feel better. She holds us and talks to us and makes us laugh," said Linda in sad but pleasing voice.

Stephen smiled and somehow even managed to reach out and give little Linda a make-believe hug, at least as much of a hug as he could, as he could not really touch her, and told her that Tina seemed like she was that kind of person. "I like her a lot," he said, even loudly enough for Meghyn and Jason to hear. He had a feeling that they already knew that, but he just wanted to actually say it. Maybe it was to let him feel that Tina was a real live person and not just a ghost, or that he was just able to connect with someone, whether they were alive or not.

After Stephen spoke to her, Linda went back to playing with the ball and eventually started to fade from view. Before she was completely gone, she looked at Stephen, Jason, and lastly Meghyn. She smiled that sweet little smile that all little girls have… the kind that shows pure sugar and spice and everything nice. "Meghyn, Stephen, and you…," she said pointing at Jason. "It was very nice meeting you and I hope that you will come and visit me again." Meghyn didn't say a word. Neither could Jason or Stephen. As the ball rolled away and settled back into the pile of toys, suddenly all three of them broke down and cried.

At that moment, for some reason, Jason looked at his watch. It was if they had been in a time warp or something, but he remembered going down into the basement at 12:30 in the morning. His watch amazingly now said that it was 6:47. "Steve…" he said, "… do you know that the sun is already up?"

"What?" Stephen asked.

"Boss, it's daylight outside. I think we all need to unwind, and, believe it or not, it is 6:47am, and time to get some breakfast. Meghyn is looking extremely drained and I must admit I am also feeling extremely worn out, as if I had been through the gates of hell."

Stephen agreed it was time to get back upstairs. "There is nothing else we can do here right now," he said. "Jason is right; let's go get some rest and something to eat. We can come back later."

As they eventually climbed the last set of steps and went through the curtain into the theater and headed to the foyer, they could see the bright glow of the sun coming through the lobby windows. It wasn't the orange sunlight you'd expect from a sunrise, rather, it was pure white.

"What time did you say it was?" Stephen asked.

Jason looked at his watch again. Meghyn checked her cell phone, which miraculously hadn't rung all night. Both the phone and the watch said the same time… 9:28am.

"When you told us the time before, how long ago was that?" Stephen inquired with a perplexed look on his face.

"Ten… maybe fifteen minutes ago," Jason said.

"Where did the other two hours and forty-five minutes go, or come from, or whatever?" Stephen asked, but none of them could answer; they were all extremely confused. Stephen tried thinking for a bit and even tried figuring it out by talking to the others, but they all had no idea where the lost time had gone. Finally, he suggested that they all go home and get some sleep. No matter what time it really was… the sun was up and they were all tired and upset.

Stephen emptied the cash register, turned off the lights, and locked the front door. He loved his theater, and, looking back into the lobby as Jason and Meghyn walked ahead of him, he knew that something was going to have to be done to get the bad karma out of the building. He had to find some way to send the captive souls of Tina and all who had suffered there, to their rest. He thought to himself, *They shouldn't be stuck here because some sick son of a bitch mad priest believed all sinners had no right to go to heaven and had to be punished.* Stephen, still deep in thought, turned away from the door and started walking under the marquee, thinking to himself… *I have got to help them. I just have to figure out how I am going to save them all from Father DuMond and reverse his damnation of these captured, innocent souls.*

CHAPTER 20

Later that same day, Meghyn and Jason arrived back at work around half an hour after Stephen. Not one of them had really been able to sleep, and Laura and the rest of the staff noticed that in their faces and wondered what the hell had been going on. They figured that most likely the three of them had gone out on a bender, and that did get some jealous reactions going, since the rest of the staff had not been invited to join in the fun.

When Stephen had entered the theater, he noticed that Tina was there, as usual. That, at least, was a good thing. She had her popcorn and Coke, but for the first time she wasn't watching the movie. Instead, she was just walking across the lobby, down the aisle and back again. Over and over again, he observed her doing this, never changing from her course. Even when people walked in to go to the actual movie, she just walked, staring straight ahead. Concerned, Stephen waited patiently until he had the chance to catch her.

"Tina, what's wrong?" he asked.

She stopped for just a moment and told him that there wasn't anything really wrong. She just felt suddenly so strange, knowing that no longer was she or the others alone. For the first time they had people who were alive, caring about all they had suffered, and that meant so much. "Stephen, Linda told me how kindly the three of you treated her," Tina said. "Oh, Stephen, it is all so terrible. That little girl, she never did anything wrong. She doesn't deserve to be here. But then, neither do any of us!"

"I know," Steve gently replied, but that was all he had the chance to say. Tina started walking again and continued through both showings before she faded away. After the last customer left, Stephen called Jason and Meghyn into his office.

Laura and the new staff member, Kelly, were supposed to have left, but instead they hung around, and eventually became so curious about what was going on, they did what they would never dream of doing normally and gained enough courage to try to listen to what was going on, outside their boss's office door.

"Guys, I forgot to mention it last night, but I suddenly remembered something else I need to tell you," Stephen stated to both Meghyn and Jason. "That stone we found last night… I know where there is another piece of it in the theatre itself."

The two women listening outside the door started to get a very confused look on their faces, as they listened intently.

"There is the same tile under the carpet on the left end of aisle two, row four. I found it some months ago when the carpet was being cleaned. Naturally I thought nothing about it, but now I think it could be very significant and I want to pull it up tonight to see what is under there."

By now Kelly had heard enough. Something else was going on in the theatre besides Tina, and she immediately wanted to know what it was. Kelly had been a mystery fan ever since she was a little girl. She just loved the intrigue, and was constantly watching old Charlie Chan and Sherlock Holmes movies, and she had got to figure it all out so easily that she could solve the crimes half way through the movies… much to the dismay of anyone watching the movies with her.

"I am going in there to find out what they are talking about," she said. "Laura, we have a right to know, as we already know there are ghosts haunting this theatre, therefore for our own safety, we have a right to know exactly what is going on!" she stated firmly to Laura, but it seemed Laura was not so keen to barge in uninvited!

"Don't do it, Kelly," Laura warned, but Kelly certainly didn't listen, as she opened the office door, grabbed Laura by the arms and actually dragged the resisting Laura into the office with her.

"Steve," she stated boldly, "we want to help out with whatever is going on here. And I also think, as your loyal staff, who have accepted the fact there are ghosts haunting this theatre, we certainly do have a right to know what is going on," Kelly declared brazenly, as she barged into her boss's office. The surprised Stephen, Jason and Meghyn jumped, as if they had just seen yet another ghost… which was surely a possibility in Stephen's haunted theatre.

"What are you both doing here, barging into my office uninvited?" Stephen asked angrily.

"I saw the way you three came in earlier and we wanted in on the fun you guys seemed to have been having," Kelly stated.

Laura suddenly felt very embarrassed at Kelly's boldness, so she tried to apologize for the intrusion. "I am so sorry, Steve, if we have annoyed you. We were both just really curious about what was going on," Laura stated, trying to her best to support Kelly, but also trying to appease Steve.

Steve looked at Meghyn and Jason, and realized that maybe these two would never cease bugging him unless he allowed them to know at least part of what had been going on, and possibly Kelly was right; maybe they did have a right to know anyway. So regaining his cool, he then had them both sit down, and began to tell them part of what he, Jason and Meghyn had found in the basement, and some of the stories they had learned over the past couple of days. Then, after continual pleading from Kelly, once she had heard what was going on, he asked Meghyn if she felt up to it, to take Laura and Kelly down the stairs on a short tour of the torture chamber and the two crypts.

Meghyn hesitated for a minute and then agreed.

Once the three women had left, Stephen looked at Jason and smiled. "Jason, come with me. Best we investigate this without any female hysterics," Stephen stated jokingly, as he started for the door. Jason immediately got up and followed his boss. Steve headed into the theatre and straight to aisle four, where he had found the tile under the carpet some months ago. As they removed the loose carpet and found the stone tile, they suddenly heard a scream, actually, two screams, coming from behind the screen area.

"Guess who that is screaming?" Jason said, with a laugh in his voice.

"Yeah, I think we should have gone into more detail about what was down there," Steve said, both men trying to find some relief from all they had seen the night before.

They stood there, just looking at the stone for at least five minutes. It wasn't like they were figuring out what to do. They knew all they had to do was simply pry the stone up and see what was underneath. Steve for some reason felt a little apprehensive, but after what they had already seen, how could it be any worse? Finally, he got tired of thinking about all they might find and he just decided to do it.

"Jason, let's get this done," he said, and he knelt down beside the stone. Both of them forced their fingers down into an extremely small crack between the stone and the wood floor. Surprisingly, it moved easily. Like the door that covered the entryway to the children's tomb, it was way too light for its size.

"Look at that," Jason said, as he reached down into the hole in the floor. He grabbed at something. Bringing it out… he held in his hands an ebony box with bronze and gold trim and the symbol of the Catholic Church inlaid into the lid in ivory. There was a small lock, simple looking, but still fancy, with the appearance of being made of gold. Jason handed the box to Steve and placed the stone back into place.

"Let's go up to the office and get this thing open," Stephen stated. His curiosity was piqued and it was hard for him to wait and not open the box right then and there, but he wanted to be in a place where he felt more organized. The two men didn't even speak; they just walked up to Stephen's office, went in and closed the door behind them and set the box on the desk, as Stephen went to his filing cabinet and took out a screwdriver to pop the lock.

"I don't want to damage the lock too much," Steve stated, as he put the screwdriver into the lock and pried it forward. The clasp broke quickly and the lock fell to the floor.

"After all we have seen, even the contents of this box have me feeling very apprehensive," Jason said with a forced laugh.

"Me too," agreed Stephen. "But, Jason, I know we must see what's inside," said Stephen, as he stared at the box.

Slowly, he reached over and opened the lid. The first thing he noticed was a red velvet bag with a black rope holding it closed. That was the first thing Stephen opened and he dumped its contents onto the table. What poured out shocked both Stephen and Jason. They were gold coins... about 50 of them, from what they could estimate. Both men took a coin each and examined them closely. They all looked alike, a five-pointed star with the words "One Stella, 400 Cents" engraved on the back and the image of a woman on the front.

"You know what is actually amazing, Steve!" Jason stated happily. "I actually know about these coins. My dad was an avid coin collector. We attended many coin auctions together. One we attended a couple years ago actually auctioned off some coins just like this. A few of these were found on a shipwreck and they went for... if I remember right... about $130,000 a piece."

Stephen Baker paused for a moment and counted the coins. Their original estimate was slightly off. There were only forty-two coins on the table. Steve thought for another second... doing some quick calculating and stated..."My god, Jason! If these coins are as valuable as you believe them to be, then we have just found way over five million dollars worth of coins!"

Jason looked at his boss, and it was almost as if he couldn't quite grasp that idea, because he immediately asked Steve what else was in the box. Jason then didn't even wait for Stephen to answer. Instead, he reached over and dumped the rest of the box onto the desk. There wasn't any more money, but there was a lot of old, yellowed papers and a black leather-bound book, which was tied shut with a deep blood-red ribbon. It was tattered and worn but it was still tied tightly.

Stephen placed the coins back in the pile and grabbed the book and cut the ribbon. The book was hand written. That was easy to see because of the level of calligraphy. It looked high quality, like the way the monks have done, and still do, when they hand copy religious documents. He leafed through it a little and saw that most of the pages were empty. It was only the first twenty-four that had any writing on them.

"Holy shit," Stephen stated in shock. Jason turned quickly and looked at Stephen, whose eyes were just staring at the book in amazement.

"What is it?" Jason asked.

"Jason, these are the actual records of everyone we found," Stephen stated. "It gives names, dates, what they were accused of and how they were all killed." He looked through the pages. There were the five kids, but he found out that there was someone else killed before them. It was a forty-four-year-old woman who left her husband to live with another man. "Listen to this…" he said, "… it says 'Jennifer Lynne Foster, aged 44, 12/15/1869, adultery, abandonment of minor children and speaking falsehoods to a member of the clergy, stoned to death.'"

"I wonder which one she was," Jason asked. Stephen could not answer, as he was not sure of all the other bodies. The only one he recognized was Tina, because her body was in the same dress she was wearing when he first saw her.

Stephen didn't look anymore at the book. He just set it down, gently, and started looking through the rest of the papers. There was the deed to the property and the original charter for the church, as well as some letters from parishioners. Then he saw an envelope with the seal of the Vatican in the corner. It was obviously opened, resealed and opened again, since the glue was wrecked by something more than just age. Gently he opened it. The paper was dry and brittle, but he managed to slide the letter out of the envelope and set it on the desk.

"What's that?" Jason asked.

"A letter from the Vatican," Stephen said. "I wonder if it is the one that DuMond told me about."

"There's only one way to find out," Jason said, as he looked at the folded, brown paper lying in front of him. Steve hesitated. He really didn't want to touch the paper in case it fell apart and they ended up with a pile of dust instead of the answers they wanted.

"I know what to do," Stephen stated, as he opened his desk drawer and took out a letter opener. Slowly and very gently he slid the blade into the fold and lifted the top edge of the paper and then the bottom section. A couple of cracks appeared along the fold, but, other than that, the letter opened in a very good condition. Stephen looked carefully at the letter and saw that, amazingly, it was written in English.

What does it say?" Jason asked, as he finished his third counting of all the gold coins.

"It's from Pope Leo XIII," Stephen replied, with an extremely surprised look on his face. "It says that under a papal decree the Church of the Sacred Feminine was to be dissolved, and that Father DuMond and all others connected with the trials and murders of innocents were to travel to Rome to face a tribunal to explain their actions."

"When was it dated?" Jason asked.

Stephen looked carefully, and just below the signature was the date the document was signed... June 12th, 1871... six months after the children were killed. Stephen informed Jason what the date was and then added, "Jason, do you realize, according to this document, that that motherfucker had already been expelled from the church, when he went ahead and in the name of the church killed all those poor people. He did it on his own."

Jason just looked at Stephen, and didn't say a word. He felt sick to his stomach, as Stephen shouted angrily. "Those people died for nothing but that prick's, sadistic, psychopathic ego," Stephen cried out in despair and frustration, as he slammed his fist onto the desk.

At that moment, the door to Stephen's office opened and Meghyn stood there. "What's going on?" Meghyn inquired, as she entered the room and saw all the papers scattered all over. Laura and Kelly followed her in, still talking about what they had seen down in the basement.

"I found the papers DuMond was talking about and he lied about everything," Stephen informed the girls." The church had nothing to do with what took place here. Pope Leo defrocked Father DuMond and disbanded the church in 1871."

Stephen then went on to tell the three women about the book and the coins. Then he very generously gave, Kelly and Laura a coin each, Meghyn four coins and Jason five. Then he with a smile informed the women about the possible value of the coins. At that moment Stephen's generosity did not sink in at all, they were too overcome with all that had taken place, so the three women just thanked him with a warm hug and then went on to talk about the evilness of Father DuMond and all the captive souls in their movie theater, and what could possibly be done to help them be freed from their imprisonment in the Strand Movie Theater. Then, without any real answer or suggestion from anyone, in frustration, Stephen gathered the rest of the coins and the papers together, and asked Kelly and Laura not to say anything about what they had seen, and he also once again reminded Jason and Meghyn to keep all to themselves. Then, after he had put everything in his briefcase, they accompanied him out of his office into the foyer. Stephen turned off all the lights, locked the main door, and they walked together in silence to the theater's staff parking lot, nodded at each other as Stephen told them all to drive carefully, as they all got into their respective cars and went home for the night.

CHAPTER 21

The next morning Steve awoke around 7:00am. This time it wasn't Jason who woke him up. He just woke up on his own. He had once again not slept well, maybe for a couple of hours toward morning, but even then he remembered he had heard the Amtrak go by and it always ran at 4:25am, when it was on schedule... which was about 75% of the time.

This morning he was going to be different. He didn't know why, but for some reason he changed his routine. Instead of going out for coffee and donuts he made himself a breakfast of three eggs with double the 'normal' servings of bacon, pancakes and hash browns and instead of coffee, he found an unopened can of grapefruit juice in the back of his cupboard, so he poured a glass, and, after making a funny face, he decided that he liked it.

He thought about the juice and remembered that his ex-wife loved the stuff, but she had left him more than five years ago. *Could it have been in that cupboard that long?* He thought. *No, it couldn't be that old. I must have picked it up somewhere or maybe someone else left it here* " Then, as he finished the glass, he started wondering about his ex. *I wonder how that old bitch is going.* He then thought to himself, *No matter how bad it was with her, arguing all of the time over the smallest shit, I still miss her.* That train of thought for the moment made him forget, just for a few seconds, all the terrible things he had seen, heard and learned over the previous few days.

He took his time eating. That was strange in itself, as he usually started and finished in less than five minutes, but he really needed to relax and get his thoughts together. It was something like 8:15am before he stopped eating and got the dishes in the sink for the evening's wash. Still in his underwear and robe, he went back to his bedroom and decided what to wear for the day. This, like the eating, took longer than it usually did.

At a 9:15am he was out the door, with the envelope under his arm that he and Jason had found the night before, along with all the papers found in the box.

As soon as the door to his house closed, Stephen's mind went back to the events at the theatre. He quickly got into his car, set the envelope gently on the passenger seat and started driving.

He knew he wasn't going to get any help from any of the churches in Akron. It wasn't that they wouldn't help; he just didn't think they could. In his mind this was not something a parish priest could deal with. It had to be taken to the diocese in Cleveland, since they would not be as concerned about each individual church the way a local priest would be, also they would have the knowledge of the history of all of the churches in the area, and that was something he needed.

Stephen Baker pulled out of his driveway and started down Hall St, turning onto Maple and heading into downtown to get to the expressway. On the way he turned on an AM radio station he listened to as a kid. He wasn't even sure it was still on the air, since he listened almost exclusively to FM, but there it was, WAKR 1590 AM and it was playing the same music it played so many years ago.

"This is so cool," he said to himself, as he turned onto the freeway. He listened to it all the way to Cleveland, at least, until he stopped for directions to the diocese's offices. He was not too far away when he stopped, so, instead of having to look for a parking space near the building, he paid the guy at the gas station ten bucks and walked the rest of the way.

When he entered the office there was a nun working at the reception desk. She immediately looked up from her paperwork and asked who he was there to see.

"I'm not sure, Sister," Stephen said. "I found some documents from a 19th century church down in Akron. They are really very disturbing, because they document the activities of a rogue priest." He felt a little uncomfortable addressing her, as he hadn't talked to a nun since Sister Florence, the nun who was his history teacher in middle school. *God, that woman was a bitch,* he thought. *My ass is still sore from the whippings she gave me.*

"I see," the nun said, as she started leafing through a Rolodex on her desk. "Here it is... you should see Brother George. He is the historian for the diocese and he'll know exactly what you are talking about. His office is in the basement... level 2."

Of course he's in the basement, Stephen thought. *Where else would he be?* He laughed at the thought, and the nun looked at him with the kind of contempt nuns are rumored to have when people are having fun. He looked at her, smiled and thanked her... of course this made her scowl even more intensely, which, in turn, made Stephen Baker even happier.

He turned and found the elevator. When the doors opened, he stepped in and pressed a button that said simply, "S2". It was a bit of a bumpy ride down, as it was an old building and an old elevator. Steve thought about some modern elevators he had ridden in and how you couldn't even feel the motion, or hear any sounds other than the standard digital music that played overhead.

The door opened and Steve found himself in a hallway lined with beautiful white birch paneling with dark cherry trim. The lights were more than ample for the space, and over each door was a lighted sign with the department name and room number painted on it. About halfway down the hall was the office he was looking for. It said, "S2-5, Historian". Steve walked down the hall, and, without knocking, walked in. The office was crammed with books, papers and computer discs and CDs. In the corner, an old man, bald with a bluish grey beard, sat looking at some painting on a computer screen.

"Hello, are you Brother George?" Stephen asked.

The brother turned and looked surprised and apologetic.

"Oh, I am sorry," Brother George said. "I didn't hear you come in, and, to tell the truth, I usually don't get many visitors down here." He took a second to think before he spoke again. "How may I help you?"

"My name is Stephen Baker and I own the Strand Theatre in Akron. We found a loose stone tile under the carpet in the theatre itself and when we lifted the stone tile last night, out of curiosity, we found a box of papers from the church that used to be there."

"What church was it?" Brother George asked.

"It was called the Church of the Sacred Feminine. It was run by a Father Jacques DuMond."

"Just give me a moment," Brother George stated with interest, as he went to his computer and pushed some buttons and opened some files until he found his database. He stared at the screen and suddenly turned to Stephen. "That church was disbanded by Pope Leo XIII in 1871. It was disbanded because of the death of six people at the hand of the priest you mentioned."

"Brother George, I am extremely sorry to inform you, but unfortunately that information is incorrect," Steve replied. "That priest and his people killed a lot more than just six people."

"What do you mean?" Brother George asked.

Stephen immediately took the book out of the envelope and set it on another table beside the priest.

"Here, look at this," he said. The brother took the book and started leafing through the pages, as Steven started to explain in the best way he could, all he had learned. "Brother George, it is sad to relate, but those six people you have a record of were just the beginning. There are records here for twenty-four people who were murdered in the name of the church. The last one was Tina Dameron in 1905. The church was destroyed, and Father DuMond was killed by locals in 1907."

Stephen then took the rest of the documents and laid them on the desk with the book. "This one is the actual papal order dissolving the church." He handed the paper to the brother, who nearly fainted when he saw it, and glanced at the other documents from Father DuMond .

"I will be right back," Brother George said, as he regained his senses and got up out of his chair. He then turned and rushed out the door, still holding the papal order and the other papers in his hand. Steve wasn't sure, but he thought he heard the man almost weeping as he went down the hallway. Five minutes later he returned. He found Steve reading a church magazine he had found on the desk.

This time Brother George had walked back down the corridor accompanied by the head of the diocese. As they had been walking, Brother George told his bishop all he knew about Stephen. "Bishop, Stephen Baker is the man who just brought us these papers and he is the owner of the Strand Theatre in Akron, where the Church of the Sacred Feminine once stood."

As they entered the room, Steve immediately stood up and was face to face with what he assumed was a bishop or maybe higher in the church rankings. Bishop Duncan didn't wait for Brother George to formally introduce the two of them; he stuck his hand out and welcomed Stephen to the building.

"I am Bishop Duncan, and, to tell the truth, I am more than horrified at what Brother George just showed me of what you have found," he said. "It changes a bad part of the history of our diocese, and unfortunately with these papers you have brought us, it makes what we knew about the past even worse."

"Bishop," Stephen said as gently as he could. "I am sorry to say, that isn't the worst part. The bodies of the people DuMond killed are still in the basement of the theatre and their souls are being held prisoner there by DuMond." Bishop Duncan said nothing; he just stood there listening and shaking his head.

"Bishop, a young woman, Tina Dameron, has wandered the halls of the theatre since it opened. She is a sweet, gentle soul who wouldn't hurt anyone, and she was tortured by Father DuMond. There are also five children who wait in a tomb in the basement. When I saw them there, one was a little girl named Susan Schneider. She was playing with a small rubber ball."

"And you actually saw all of this?" Bishop Duncan asked, with a look of sheer horror on his face.

"Yes, and so did two other people…" Stephen Baker replied, "… maybe two more after last night." This, and all the other information Steve now shared, had Bishop Duncan's total attention and he was quite overcome.

"Mr. Baker, if I went to your theatre, would you be so kind as to show me what you found?" he asked.

"I would be happy to," Steve replied. "I would, and so would my staff so appreciate it if you would. Maybe you could, with your knowledge, even help those wretched captive souls be released from their torment."

Bishop Duncan thought for a minute and then told Stephen that, if everything he said could be proved, then he would do the best he could to help free those lost souls. "So, Stephen, tell me, if they really do exist, and I am sure after what you are saying that they do, what was it that Father DuMond punished these poor captive souls for?" he asked.

"Pardon the language, Bishop, but they were MURDERED for small shit," Stephen stated angrily. "Those sweet kids were killed for stealing bread and dried meat for their families. Tina was killed for being pregnant and not married… Yes, I know society was once far less tolerant of women having children out of wedlock, but such retribution is incomprehensible, especially within the sanctity of the church. Did these people who came to the church for help deserve this kind of treatment?" stated Stephen angrily.

"No, not at all," Bishop Duncan replied. "No doubt they came to our church for help. They should never have been punished for anything like that, certainly not here in America and certainly within our own church."

"Why, is what I ask, why? How could this horror go on for so many years?" Stephen shouted out in his frustration. "In 1871 it was supposed to have all ended. What went wrong? How on earth this did Father DuMond continue if he had been defrocked? All those bloody hellish years, causing such unbelievable suffering!"

"I do not know quite what to say," Bishop Duncan replied. "Apparently something went wrong in our administration somewhere. A defrocked priest continuing on in the name of our church is quite incomprehensible, so I really do not know what to say. From what these papers say, he had been recalled to Rome, so quite truthfully, I do not know what to say except God forgive us for not knowing all this. Let me assure you, we will leave no stone unturned to find out what happened. Let me assure you, in all my years in the Lord's service, I have never felt so ashamed."

He looked Stephen straight in the eyes and asked him what time the last showing at the theatre was for that evening. Stephen said that the last show started at 7:30pm. "I will be there at 7:15pm. I want to watch the movie so I can observe this young woman, Tina, you talk about, and then when the audience and your staff have gone home, you can show me everything that I need to see… if that is okay with you?"

"That's fine," Stephen stated. "I'll even make arrangements for you to get a room at a nearby motels, so you don't have to drive back that late at night." Bishop Duncan thanked him and said that he had to go to make some phone calls, so he left Stephen and Brother George alone in the office.

"Mr. Baker," Brother George asked, "Would it be possible for me to borrow those papers so I can research them further?" Of course, Steve replied that it wouldn't be any problem, as long as he made sure that everything would be returned so they could be put back in their resting area. The brother had no trouble agreeing to that. So Stephen left the book and all the other papers and headed back to Akron. But before he left

Brother George's office, he also informed him that they had also found some coins which he would talk about later with Bishop Duncan.

Once Stephen got back in his car and the radio started blaring again, his thoughts went back to something a lot more enjoyable. He wasn't sure why he was thinking about what he was thinking about, but he knew he needed to relax… maybe he would take a vacation once all the bullshit was over, but he knew that for the first time in a long time, he was feeling good. At least this representative of the church, Bishop Duncan, was just as horrified as he was at what had happened.

Stephen made one stop on the way back to Akron. He stopped at a Dairy Queen in Independence and grabbed a coffee, and then headed right back to the library. He had to find out what had happened to Tina's daughter, Marie Olivier.

When he finally got to the library, he went straight back to the genealogy department and started digging through some of the city's school records. He was right. She attended Mason School for the first seven years and then went to Thornton Jr. High and then she must have moved, because she finished her school days at Central High School in downtown Akron. The records also showed that she was smart, really smart, since she graduated with honors. He couldn't find out if she attended a university or not, since those records were not public.

After going through all those papers, he found out that marriage records were now computerized and fairly easy to use. Typing in her name, it only took seconds to find out that she was married on August 12th, 1928 to a man named Fredrick Davidson.

Writing that information down, he headed over to the census records. First, he checked 1930 and found Marie and Fredrick listed, but no kids. Then on further research, the 1940 records showed that they had two kids… a set of twins in 1934 named Fredrick Jr., and Eleanor.

"Oh, my fucking God," Steve exclaimed out loud. "She actually named her daughter what Tina had wanted to name her."

He decided that he would look up the children's names and see what he could find out about them. Eleanor had apparently married and divorced, and then married a man named Geoff Wagner, who worked as an attorney for a firm in Cleveland. They had one daughter named Susan.

Fredrick Jr. had a career in the military, working his way from private up to gunnery sergeant. He married a girl named Marion Potter and she gave birth to a son in 1959. The boy was named Fredrick the 3rd.after his father and grandfather.

A little more tracing found information about Fredrick the 3rd. He, like his father, had a career in the military, but he, unlike his father, was an officer, after graduating from the University of Akron with a military science degree. He married in 1983 and had one daughter named Meghyn Davidson in 1984.

Oh, my God, it is impossible. It just couldn't be, he thought. *It just couldn't be.*

As soon as recovered from the shock, Stephen gathered his thoughts, took his cell and called Meghyn. "Meghyn…" he said, without any explanation, "… what is your dad's name?"

"Fredrick," she answered. "Why?"

There are a lot of men named Fredrick, Steve thought, *and Davidson can be a common name. Stay calm, stay calm, do not jump to conclusions.*

"Meghyn, when were you born?" he asked.

"February 29th," she answered.

"No, no, I am not asking what month, I am asking what year," he replied, with a slight touch of impatience in his voice.

"1984," she replied, with the same impatience in her voice. "Steve, what is going on? Why do you want to know when I was born?"

Steve's mind was racing with excitement. Then he tried to calm down and give it all a little more thought, so he paused for a minute to think and realized that he shouldn't at this moment tell Meghyn what he had found out... that maybe it would be far better to tell her in front of Tina. No doubt it would thrill both of them to know they were part of each other, and certainly Tina would be ecstatic, he was sure of that! *That explains a lot*, Stephen thought. *That must have been how Tina could blend with Meghyn so* easily.

"Steve, are you still there?" Meghyn asked impatiently.

"Yes, Meghyn, I am. Look, it was just that I ran into a man who thought he knew your family," he stated, lying through his teeth, but it was the best he could do on such short notice. "He knew you worked for me, so he asked how you were doing and if I knew your dad," Steve said, trying to cover himself.

"I do not understand. So why did you need to know the year I was born?" Meghyn asked. "Are you sure you are feeling okay, Steve?"

"Meghyn, please, just trust me. To tell the truth... I think, I may have some important information for you. Just meet me at the theatre at 5:00pm, if you can."

Meghyn wasn't sure what was going on, but she did agree to be there, as Steve asked. Then, as she didn't have anything to do all day, she suggested, with a distinct sound of flirting in her voice, that she was hungry and might be willing to get some lunch, if someone was kind enough to invite her out.

Stephen got the hint and immediately suggested, if she was free, why didn't they get something to eat. They met at a restaurant in Highland Square at 1:30pm, and, over a steak and fries, they talked about the bodies, the ghosts and the theatre. Meghyn also tried her best to find out what Stephen was so secretive about, but he would not budge. So instead, they took time to find out about each other, but every time she tried to get information out of him, Stephen was careful not to say anything about what he had found out. After that lunch, he then knew for certain that young Meghyn had ceased just being a staff member and that they had become real friends. That she was Tina's great-great-granddaughter made it even more special.

He walked her to her car, and, very unexpectedly, she gave him a kiss on the cheek and promised that she would be there at the theatre at 5:00pm, and although she was curious as the Cheshire Cat, she didn't ask any more questions.

It was only 2:30pm when he left Meghyn. He had achieved a lot in a short time. So, completely out of character, since he owned his own movie theatre; Steve decided to go to a rival movie theatre near Chapel Hill, and, after chatting with the manager, he was given a free ticket, and he sat down as a part of the public to watch the last half of the movie . The thing was, it wasn't a movie even he particularly wanted to see. He just wanted to be around other people and he wanted to take an hour or so just chilling, without thinking about anything, especially mad priests, tortured souls and especially Tina, a ghost that was now not only haunting his theatre, but far too constantly also his dreams.

The movie finished at 4:00pm, and while he was there, he stuffed himself on pop, popcorn and candy.

Stephen arrived at the Strand at 4:30 pm. He walked in and sat down at his desk. The door was left open for Meghyn, since his office was at the other end of the building and he couldn't hear if she knocked.

Tina showed up sometime around 4:45pm and started to do her normal thing, but Steve stopped her at the concession stand and told her that when Meghyn got there, they needed to have a talk. Tina said "Okay" and then went on into the theatre.

Meghyn showed up at exactly 5:00pm. She walked in and started looking around for her boss. She checked the ticket booth, the concession stand and the theatre itself, where she saw Tina sitting in her usual seat. She went over to Tina and sat behind her. "Hello, Tina," Meghyn said. "Have you seen Steve?"

Tina placed her pop and popcorn on the seat next to her and turned to look at Meghyn. "Meghyn, Steve said that he wants to talk to us. He wouldn't tell me what about, but he just said we needed to talk," she said. "I wonder what he wants to know."

"I don't have a clue," Meghyn replied. "He also told me that he had something to tell me, but he didn't say what."

Both women made their way out of their seats and up the aisle. "I bet he's in his office," stated Tina

The two of them went out of the theatre and walked toward the office. Between them there was extreme curiosity about what Steve wanted to discuss with them, but that was all it was… conjecture.

The door was shut when they finally got there, so, politely, Tina knocked with a very ladylike knock. Of course it made no sound, so Meghyn knocked for her. Before Stephen even opened the door, eager to know what he wanted, Tina entered his office straight through the door and stood impatiently by his desk as Stephen opened the door to let Meghyn in. He smiled warmly and seemed very excited. "I think maybe you both should take a seat," he said, as he smiled once again. They walked past him and sat on the couch. *This is good*, Steve thought. *They'll be able to support each other. No doubt this is going to be a shock.*

"What do you want to tell us?" Meghyn asked. Tina echoed the sentiment, then suddenly her mood changed and she had a look of distress across her face.

"It isn't what I want to tell you. I just want to introduce the two of you," he said.

"But we know each other," Tina said.

"No, you don't," Stephen said. "Not really." Both of them got really confused looks on their faces. "Meghyn, your father was Fredrick Davidson… right?"

"Yeah, I told you that earlier, Steve."

"His father's father was also a Fredrick Davidson… right?"

"Yeah. So what?"

"Do you know who he married… the first Fredrick Davidson, I mean?"

"Yeah, great grandma Marie. I met her once when I was very, very little, but she died when I was five."

Tina's eyes suddenly got a light to them as she realized what was coming next. "Steven…" she said, before Steve put his finger on her lips so she couldn't finish her sentence. He looked at her and nodded his head, which made her face light up as she moved a little closer to Meghyn.

Meghyn looked over towards Tina, who, surprisingly, suddenly reached over and tried to hold Meghyn's hand. Of course, Meghyn felt nothing except a very warm glow, as Tina tried to hold her hand tightly. Meghyn could not believe a ghost would try to hold her hand like that; it was all very strange. This sure was getting weirder and weirder.

Then Stephen turned to her with a solemn look on his face and stated, "Meghyn Davidson, I would like to introduce you to Tina Dameron…"

"Okay," Meghyn said. She was confused, since she had known Tina for a while now.

"Meghyn, I repeat, I would like to introduce you to Tina Dameron… your great-great-grandmother."

"My what?" Meghyn's eyes glanced between Tina and Steve, as if she was trying to understand something that was just out of reach.

"Your great-great-grandmother," Stephen said, smiling. "Marie was Tina's daughter, who was taken from her when Tina died here, so long ago."

Tina just sat there trying to hold Meghyn's hand tightly, and unfortunately unable to, as her hand just floated through Meghyn's. She was also crying and smiling all at the same time and was looking at Meghyn with such heartfelt love in her eyes.

"Oh, my god, are you sure?" Meghyn asked.

"I followed the records of Marie's adoption through all her descendents' marriages and it leads to you. So, yes, I am sure."

Meghyn looked at Tina and finally got a smile on her face. "Oh, my god, are you really my great-great-grandmother? I cannot believe it! Ghost or not, this is the most thrilling news ever!" Meghyn stated excitedly, as she reached over and tried to give Tina a hug. Of course, Tina's body just passed through her, but she still tried hugging anyway. Her voice still had a tint of shock to it, but it also had a large amount of pleasure shining through, and then she suddenly, like Tina, burst into tears of joy.

"You know what," Steve stated, smiling from ear to ear. "You two have a lot to talk about, so I am going to get across the street and get a drink. I'll be back later. Neither woman said anything, at least not to Steve; they just sat there, unable to really touch each other, but thankfully able to chat away to each other in sheer excitement, and Tina was able to learn all about her daughter Marie, and all the family history of which she had been robbed, and which she had so longed for.

As Steve had left the room, he doubted that they even noticed that he was gone… they were that into this bizarre and unique "family reunion".

He got back to the theatre about 7:00pm and, although he hated to do it, he had to interrupt Tina and Meghyn because the theatre was getting ready to open and Meghyn had to take her spot in the concession stand. At 7:30pm the doors opened for another night of movies, snacks, popcorn and soda, the movie patrons not at all realizing the unique events that were taking place behind the scenes in the Strand Movie Theatre.

CHAPTER 22

At 7:15 that night Bishop Duncan arrived for his appointment with Steve. He started to buy a ticket, but immediately Stephen saw him at the ticket booth and went out and humorously admonished him for even thinking about buying a ticket. Stephen then escorted Bishop Duncan into the lobby and down into the theater entrance. Standing with the priest at the door, Stephen pointed to Tina already seated, waiting for the matinee movie to begin.

"See that beautiful young woman in the middle of the theater," Stephen stated, "who seems to look just a little out of place?"

"Yes, Steve... I see her," Bishop Duncan replied.

"Well, Bishop, as I mentioned before, she comes here all of the time, sitting there watching a movie, pretending to talk to someone and eating snacks from the concession stand."

"I gather she is the young woman you spoke about," stated Bishop Duncan.

"Yes, that is Tina Dameron. Her name is on that list I left with the brother," Stephen replied. "She was the last one killed here in 1905. She's the one they killed, just for being pregnant and not married."

"Are you serious?" the bishop replied angrily.

"Yes, I am. She has been captive here for more than 100 years. There are others in the basement, but Tina was the only one really able to adapt and interact with me and even a few of the staff here. After the movie is over and everyone leaves, two of my staff, Meghyn and Jason, will join us, and we will take you down into the basement and show you all we have seen."

"That sounds excellent," stated the appreciative and curious Bishop Duncan.

Aware of what was going to happen later, to relax his guest, Stephen said with a smile, "Welcome to the haunted

Strand Movie Theater, Bishop, and before the movie starts let me go get you a Coke and some popcorn. I am sure you do not get to the movies often, so you might as well enjoy this part of the evening before we go down into the basement!"

"Thank you, Stephen, I'd appreciate that, but let me come with you," Bishop Duncan stated politely, as both men made their way back to the concession stand.

Meghyn was the one who waited on them. Immediately Stephen introduced them. "Meghyn, this is Bishop Duncan from the Cleveland Diocese. He's here to check out what's been going on here. He is not to pay for anything while he is here. Do you understand?" Meghyn said that she did, and she gave Bishop Duncan a large Coke and large popcorn with a lot of extra butter.

The movie lasted about 90 minutes, and, once the rest of the audience and the staff had left, Stephen, Bishop Duncan, Meghyn and Jason went back through to the backstage of the theater, and, after descending the stairs, they made their way along the hallway in the basement.

Bishop Duncan looked at the paintings and saw the tortured souls depicted on the one side. He took his cross in his hand and started praying. "Heavenly Father," he said, "please take these souls and protect them as your children." Then he made the sign of the cross and followed Stephen, Jason and Meghyn into the torture chamber. His eyes showed pure shock and disgust as he looked around the room. He closed his eyes and all Stephen heard him say was, "My Lord, how could this have happened?"

"Bishop, look at all these torture devices," Stephen stated, trying to direct the priest's attention to all of the devices in the room.

Bishop Duncan walked over to the door and just froze. He saw all of the bodies piled on top of each other, but he didn't panic the way Stephen thought he might. Instead, he remained very calm.

"How many bodies are in there?" he asked. He looked around and finally went in. He was shocked at the way the bodies were treated. It looked like some of the films he had seen of the concentration camps the Nazis ran during World War II. Before Stephen had a chance to answer, Bishop Duncan started going from body to body with a small bottle of holy water he always carried with him and drew a cross on each of their foreheads. Finally, he looked at Stephen and said, "And I Corinthians said, 'And now abideth, faith, hope, charity, these three; but the greatest of these is charity'. Mr Baker, let me assure you, with all I hold dear in the church, these tortured souls WILL feel the charity of our Lord."

"19," Stephen said, as he looked at the priest with a very appreciative look. "There are 19 people in this tomb."

Bishop Duncan soon got another shocked look on his face as he heard Meghyn call both him and Stephen to the other side of the chamber.

"Bishop... please look," she said. "We found this earlier when we were down here." The stone had, somehow, been replaced, but just like it was earlier, it was easily moved, and again the room was totally black.

"What is it?" the bishop asked.

"It's the rest of them," Jason answered.

"The rest of them?" Bishop Duncan seemed surprised to hear that there were more.

"Yes, Bishop... it is the bodies of the children who were murdered here," Meghyn said, as she walked in and lit her torch, closely followed by Stephen and Bishop Duncan. "We counted five of them... all ages and both boys and girls."

The light from the torches, for some reason, flickered and dimly lit the room. Bishop Duncan just looked for a minute. It was doubtful that he could have said anything, even if he knew what he wanted to say. Finally, he gripped his cross and said a prayer for the children.

"Steve, you better come out here," Jason said quietly. "We have a visitor out in the hallway and it isn't a good one."

"Bishop… " Stephen started, "… if it is who I think it is, please forgive me the language I will have to use." Bishop Duncan didn't know what Stephen was talking about, but he immediately gave Stephen absolution for all sins that he had committed and all the sins he was going to commit in the near future.

Jason was backed against the wall as Stephen walked into the hallway. There he was. The one Stephen Baker knew would be standing there, in his usual white frock with gold trim.

"Que faites-vous avec les enfants?" DuMond asked.

"Look, Father DuMond… I fucking told you that if you want to talk to me it has to be in English," Stephen yelled. "No one here understands that French shit."

Father DuMond got a very angry look on his face, before he replied. "I told you not to come down here," he said. "I want to know what you are doing here. You have no right to be here!"

"This is my building and I can go anyplace I damn well please," Stephen stated angrily. "What does it take to get that through your head?"

"It is my church and it always will be," Father DuMond screamed back.

"Actually, no it isn't!" stated Bishop Duncan, as he stepped out of the room. into the hallway "This church was closed in 1881."

"Who are you?" DuMond asked.

"Please allow me to introduce myself," Bishop Duncan said. "My name is Bishop Duncan; I am the Bishop of the Cleveland Diocese." Immediately on hearing this, Father Jacques DuMond backed off and assumed a passive stance.

"Father DuMond, you have no authority here. This church was closed and you were removed as its priest by the Pope in 1881."

"I…" Jacques DuMond started to say,

"I… nothing! You are a renegade priest and you have brought utter shame to the Catholic Church. I command you to release these captured souls and leave this building," Bishop Duncan stated firmly, as he brought out a document from the diocese. "The Church of the Sacred Feminine will be erased from the records of the Catholic Church and its name will never be spoken or used for another church for all time. It has been written and it will be done."

"Who says this?" Jacques DuMond asked, as he regained his maniacal attitude. "These sinners are to remain here. It is decreed by me and I will not tolerate any interference. Bishop or not, you have no right, to interfere in my church!"

"I do have the right," Bishop Duncan stated, as he stood firm, using all the powers he possessed to overpower this demonic priest. "Any deacon has the right, any priest, bishop, cardinal and certainly the Pope. You do not represent the church, the Pope or God… you are evil incarnate. I decree this church has never existed, and will never exist again… Jacques DuMond, you are no man of God, so heed my words as the representative of the Catholic Church. Release these souls you have so hideously tortured, and leave." Then Bishop Duncan became so angry, that for a man of God he had a very hard time controlling his anger as he looked at Jacques DuMond and shouted, "NOW GET OUT!"

Jacques DuMond backed up a little, smiled contemptuously and faded from view without another word.

Stephen looked around and immediately thought, *That was just a little too easy. Jacques DuMond will not tolerate this interference*, and, sure enough, he was right.

"Bishop, keep your eyes open," both Stephen and Jason warned.

"For what?" the suddenly bewildered Bishop Duncan asked.

'Over there… by the door," Meghyn yelled.

As they watched, cracks developed along the walls and ceiling of the hallway. They weren't near the paintings, but closer to the exit. Then, piece by piece, sections of wall and ceiling fell to the floor, ripping the vines out by the roots. It only lasted a couple of minutes and there wasn't enough debris to seal them in but it was enough to let them know that DuMond was not going quietly into his night.

As the last piece fell and smashed on the floor, Stephen, Bishop Duncan, Meghyn and Jason all quickly exited the hallway, climbed up the stairs and closed the door on the floor shut behind them, and placed a wooden plank across it.

"What was all that about? Suddenly I felt like I was once again involved in an exorcism," Bishop Duncan stated, as they left the back stage area, and headed into the theater.

"That was DuMond getting pissed," Stephen replied. "The last time he became mad at someone it was our former projectionist William Jackson. Father DuMond thought he was stealing candy, and he literally beat him to death, just because William took some unopened candy out of the trash after we threw it away. Jacques DuMond literally freaked out. He had me pinned down, unable to move like I was caged in an invisible prison. What he did to William was horrific to witness. When DuMond eventually released me, I went to help William but it wa too late, he died shortly after, way before the ambulance even arrived. Of course, the police did not believe a word we told them. They investigated and eventually put it down to a sinister intruder."

"Over trash candy?" Bishop Duncan asked in disbelief. Stephen just nodded his head.

By now Jason and Meghyn were over at the concession stand. Eating some leftover popcorn and sharing a candy bar, Stephen couldn't hear what they were talking about, but Jason was smiling at Meghyn, who was smiling back at him and tossing her hair in a very feminine gesture. It was easy to see that she was flirting with Jason, but he couldn't quite tell, if Jason was into it or not.

"You two stop eating all the profits and get out of here," Stephen called out. He then looked at Bishop Duncan and asked, "Bishop, it has been a very eventful night. You must be feeling very depleted; it is already very late …the Steak & Eggs over on Market Street is the only place that is still open and close enough to your motel. Would you like to have something to eat before you go to the motel?"

"No, I do not think so, Stephen. To tell the truth, I hate waking the motel owner as it is already so late, to stop to eat would make it even later.. Also, it has been an extremely emotional night for me and I need to think about my next plan of action regarding Jacques DuMond and the evil he has instigated here in the name of the church." As Bishop Duncan finished speaking, Meghyn and Jason waved both Stephen and Bishop Duncan a good night, and, hand in hand, headed towards the front door.

At the door, Meghyn turned and called out, "See you tomorrow, Steve. It was very nice to meet you, Bishop Duncan." Bishop Duncan smiled warmly at the young couple as Stephen excused himself for a few seconds and went over to Meghyn and Jason, reminding them that he was having the carpets cleaned in the early afternoon so that they should not arrive before 6:00pm. "Okay, boss," stated Meghyn, as she took Jason's hand and both of them exited the building. Stephen locked the door and then returned to Bishop Duncan.

"Bishop," Stephen asked, "you have seen so much tonight and you have met DuMond. Do you believe you can free all these poor captured souls and actually rid this place of Father Jacques DuMond?"

"I will have to go back and talk to the cardinal and the rest of our staff, but I am sure… together we can find out something that we can do," he replied. With that, Bishop Duncan shook Stephen's hand, and got up to walk out. But before he did, he told Stephen he had changed his mind. Yes, he was hungry, and he asked Stephen for directions to the restaurant.

Stephen thought for a minute, looked at his watch and stated it was 3:00am. The restaurant was possibly closed, so instead he invited the bishop to forget going back to the motel and to come to his house for something to eat, and then he could crash there for the night. Bishop Duncan tried to argue, but when Stephen told him that it was actually 3:00am, he accepted the invitation. He left his car in the staff parking lot and went with Stephen to his house for some food, a couple drinks and some sleep.

Stephen woke up some time around 9:00am. Bishop Duncan was gone. *Well, that sucks*, Stephen thought. *I finally get someone to spend the night and they split without even a note or a goodbye. I feel so cheap.* This thought got a smile going across his face. It was something that he couldn't have imagined happening with everything that happened in the past... a smile and just a touch of a laugh. He finished a cup of coffee, made a couple calls and left for the theater.

It was 1:30pm by the time he finally got there and the carpet cleaners were already there waiting for him. "We were just getting ready to leave," the boss said. Stephen apologized profusely and let them in.

"What the fuck?" he said. Inside, the floor was covered with dark black dirt. "Where the hell did that come from?"

"I don't know," the cleaning boss answered. "But we'll get it clean for you. It may take some time, but we'll do it." Stephen thanked them, paid them what they agreed upon and $200 extra because of the mess. He left the crew to do their work and went into his office.

"DuMond, you fucking prick," Stephen called out in a raised voice, but not loud enough for the workers to hear. "You get your fucking ass in here right now."

The room shimmered and suddenly DuMond was standing in front of him. "Sinner, do not talk that way to me,"

Father DuMond said in his typically arrogant voice. "You do know just how powerful I am?"

"Yeah," Stephen said. "I know just who you are. You're a defrocked priest who has illusions of being a god yourself, so you punish anyone who disagrees with your bible. Isn't that right?"

Jacques DuMond didn't answer.

"Is that what all the dirt is…a punishment?"

Again DuMond didn't answer. He just raised his hand and a wind blew in from the theater and blew all of the dirt out of the front door. "No," DuMond said. "That was not a punishment. It was a minor warning, a promise of what I can do if I choose."

The boss of the cleaning crew came to the office door and looked in. "Mr. Baker, I must be losing my mind," he stated. "All that bloody dirt has suddenly gone and we did nothing!"

Stephen thought as quickly as he could. "I know," he said. "I saw that too. Every once in a while we get a wind like that from the basement. Just clean up what is left and you can keep the extra I paid you. Just please do a good job."

"Okay," said the cleaner, as he stepped away from the door. "I am sure you'll be pleased."

Stephen then turned again to face Jacques DuMond. "Why would you do that/ Why have you always caused me such fucking problems?" he asked.

"Who was that man you brought in here?" DuMond asked. "Who was that Bishop Duncan? He does not understand all I have done. He spoke to me as if I was evil and not working in the best interest of the church."

"He was from the diocese," Stephen replied. "He at first was upset about your work, as it had continued for so long without the sanctity of the church. This did enrage him, but later he told me possibly he had misjudged all you have done here."

Of course Stephen was lying through his teeth, but he was very afraid for Bishop Duncan's safety. He knew Jacques DuMond did have demonic powers and he knew he had to appeal to his ego, not enrage him even further.

"Yes, I am sure once the church realizes all I have done, they will understand I had to do this to punish evil. I knew this so long ago when by mistake they sent me that letter. This is my chance to let them see all I have done to avenge the sins of these ungodly sinners."

Listening to Father Jacques DuMond, Stephen suddenly realized this evil bastard had a major weakness that could be actually used to destroy him. *Oh yes*, Stephen thought to himself, *I have found his weakness at long last… the easiest way to get to this defrocked priest is through his ego. How remarkable, I didn't think things like that followed after death.*

"You know how I feel about you, Father, you make me sick to the stomach," said Stephen, "but then I have never understood why sinners must burn in hellfire and never go to heaven. Maybe you are right, maybe you can let this bishop understand all you have done. Maybe at long last your work here can be acknowledged by the church after all."

Father Jacques DuMond actually smiled. His eyes lit up and he threw out his chest with pride. And then as quickly as he had appeared, he faded away.

Stephen also smiled to himself. Oh yes, now he knew exactly what he had to do and how to do it.

The cleaners finished at the same time that Meghyn and Jason got back to work. Stephen quickly observed they were both wearing the same clothes they were wearing the night before. He greeted them, gave them their paychecks and sent them to start getting ready for the shows that night.

The movies did okay that night. Not good, but okay. The people seemed to have fun despite some loud bangs and a few of the lights flickering on and off. Somehow, despite the fact that Stephen had tried to keep it quiet, people in Akron had heard that the theater was haunted and the people came, not only to see the movies but also to "enjoy" the ghosts and their antics.

CHAPTER 23

For the next couple of days Stephen Baker went about his normal day: getting up, having breakfast, showering and heading off to town. He was concerned that he hadn't heard anything from Bishop Duncan, but he didn't let it interfere with his day. True, he thought about calling him a couple of times, especially since he had figured out what DuMond's weakness was.

Finally, on the third day he got the call he had been waiting for, and as soon as he hung up he hopped in his car and took off to Cleveland. It was completely unlike him, but he didn't stop... not once during the trip. He passed a lot of the places, which was quite a few, that he usually stopped at whenever he went to Cleveland, but it was like they didn't exist.

Now, it is a 36-mile trip between Akron and Cleveland and Stephen took less than a half an hour to make the trip. Everything seemed to have gone right. He hit every light, there were no traffic jams and he even managed to find a parking space right outside the front door of the diocese.

He didn't stop at the reception desk.

"Can I help you, sir?" the nun at the reception called out to him.

"No, thanks," Stephen replied, without slowing his pace a beat. "Bishop Duncan told me to go straight up to his office when I arrived."

Stephen headed down the hall and to the elevator. Luckily, the elevator was right there, since a nun had just got off, so he stopped the door from closing, got in, hit the button for the fourth floor, and, as the door closed, he listened to some religious motivational song from years ago. It had been a hit, but he didn't know the words to the song, but he mouthed words that he made up, which were probably, he thought, even better than the real lyrics. He knew one thing... they weren't the type of words that a song played in a Catholic Church office building would be playing, but he was having fun making them up anyway and it sure helped relieve the tension he was feeling inside.

The door opened, and, just the way his luck was running that day, the office was directly in front of the elevator. *I know I shouldn't be wondering, but how the fuck is all this good shit happening to me?* he thought. Just as he stepped out of the elevator, across the hall Bishop Duncan opened his office door and stepped into the hallway. *What the hell?* Stephen thought.

"Hello, Steve. You got here quickly," Bishop Duncan said. "Come on into my office. I have some good news for you." Bishop Duncan smiled and put his hand out to shake hands and naturally Stephen was more than happy to reciprocate.

"Hello, Bishop. It is good to see you," Stephen warmly replied. "I also have some good news for you."

Bishop Duncan reopened the door to his office and told Stephen to go in and have a seat, and said that he would be back in a minute. "I have to go find a couple of people who have an interest in this, and want to be in on our meeting."

Stephen walked into this elaborate office, with an excellent view of Akron, and picked a seat at the left of the desk. He sat down, took out a piece of gum and started chewing it. That also was something he never did. He didn't even remember buying any gum, but he enjoyed the strong peppermint flavor it had. He sat there about five minutes. A pretty little nun walked in and set down some papers and walked out after saying a polite hello to the bishop's guest.

Finally, Bishop Duncan walked back into his office with two men. One was Brother George from the archive department, but the other priest was a stranger.

"Steven, you know Brother George," Bishop Duncan said. Stephen immediately smiled at Brother George and shook his hand. Bishop Duncan then introduced the other man as Father Lawrence Talbot, first assistant to the cardinal.

"A pleasure to meet you Father Talbot," Stephen said, as he shook the man's hand. "No doubt Bishop Duncan has told you all about what has been going on in my theater... We need help!"

"He told me that you have spirits haunting the theater... how many people?" Talbot asked.

"24," Stephen and Bishop Duncan said in unison.

"Unbelievable! I have never heard of so many... 24 people trapped in the basement of your theater and a rogue priest keeping their souls from moving on," Talbot said in a very questioning voice.

"That's right, but remember, which is very strange, Father Jacques DuMond is also a ghost," Stephen stated, as he went on to explain that the people were murdered by the priest for small sins like stealing bread and meat, to getting pregnant before marriage.

"That is nothing," Talbot stated. "No more than a couple of Hail Marys and an Our Father," and that is only if the priest is having a bad day. Other than that, it is just asking for absolution, which is granted without a penance... especially in the circumstances of that time."

"You know, I didn't think that anything any of those people did was a mortal sin," Stephen stated.

Father Talbot repeated again that it wasn't and should never have been allowed to get that far.

Stephen could tell hearing all this was very hard for these sincere and devout priests, so he quickly tried to change the subject "By the way, Bishop Duncan, I talked to DuMond after you left."

Bishop Duncan immediately asked what was said.

"I was afraid for your life, in fact, I am afraid for all of our lives. Jacques DuMond has extraordinary powers, so, as he was becoming so enraged he was reaching boiling point, I made up some ridiculous story, that though you were very angered that he had continued running the church after the

Pope had declared it was to be closed. I told him that maybe you would possibly see in a positive light all the work that he had been doing over all those years in the name of the church and God. Ghost or not, the man is an egotistical maniac. He immediately brushed aside all you had said to him and now is looking for praise from the Catholic Church for all the horrific deeds he has done. I tell you, he is truly insane. He truly believes that what he has done to all those poor people was in the church's name and God's. To appeal to his ego, I told him you would investigate further and then contact the cardinal and possibly even the Pope," Steven stated. "I made it sound very positive and he seemed to get a sense of pride about it all."

"That is amazing," Bishop Duncan said, "especially after all I said to him." As he spoke, Bishop Duncan looked at both Stephen and Father Talbot.

Stephen also glanced back and forth between the two priests, as brother George sat quietly listening and saying nothing. "Gentlemen, I think I may have a way to help those people and get rid of Father Jacques DuMond at the same time." They all looked at him intently, waiting for Stephen to explain more.

"We have to play on his pride and make him feel special and wanted by the church again, then, when his defenses are down, we can swiftly, with your help, send his soul to purgatory." They all discussed the idea some more and then agreed that they would all meet at the theater later that night.

CHAPTER 24

That night Stephen got to the theater about 6:00pm and waited for everyone else to get there. It wasn't a long wait. Meghyn and Jason showed up at 6:15pm and Laura showed up a couple of minutes later. As soon as they arrived, Stephen escorted them back out of the front doors and down the street. He did not want Jacques DuMond overhearing what he had to say.

"Tonight I want the three of you out of here as soon as the movie ends," he said. "Don't bother cleaning up. Just leave everything the way it is and get out of here."

"Why?" Meghyn asked.

"I have something planned tonight that may put an end to all the shit going on here." They asked some more questions, but he didn't answer them, and told them that sometime around 1:00am to meet him at the Steak & Eggs and, if it worked, he would explain everything then. They all agreed.

Three men from the diocese arrived at the theater about four hours later. Stephen had been expecting the two priests, but there were three, and the third priest was someone he had not met before. He let them in without asking about the third man. They went right into the theater, sat down and watched what was left of the movie.

As soon as the credits ran Stephen got the audience out. There were a couple of stragglers who hung around the lobby talking, but he told them that a repair crew was waiting out back to repair a weak spot in the screen and they needed everyone out of the building because of the fumes from the chemicals they had to use to make the repair. Then he offered them a couple of passes to a future movie and escorted them from the building. Meghyn, Jason and Laura followed them out and headed down the street. Stephen immediately locked the front door, checking it a couple of times, and then went back to the priests, who were still sitting in the theater.

The three of them stood up as he entered and then even before Bishop Duncan had a chance to introduce him, Stephen shook the hand of the third man. "It is a pleasure to have you here. I am Stephen Baker. And you are?"

"Steven," Father Talbot said, "this is the head of our church, Cardinal Thomas Morrisey."

"The honor is mine, Cardinal Morrisey. I am extremely honored to have you here and very thankful the church is taking this matter so very seriously," Stephen stated warmly, without the normal pomp that a man of Morrisey's title entitled him to.

"Nice to meet you too," Cardinal Morrisey said. "Father Talbot and Bishop Duncan told me about the situation and what you talked about and I am all for it." He looked around the theater and commented on the beauty of the building, and then asked if DuMond was around somewhere.

Stephen thought about the question for a couple of minutes and then said that he hadn't seen Father DuMond at all that evening. *You know what,* Stephen thought; *come to think of it, I haven't seen Tina anywhere either.*

Can you get him here?" the cardinal inquired.

"Well, let me try. Seeing that you all are here no doubt will have piqued his interest. All I can say is: I know you are all extremely experienced in these matters of exorcism, but do remember we are all in danger at any time, especially asking to speak to Father Jacques DuMond right now."

"Please try," the cardinal requested.

"Father Jacques DuMond, can you hear me? There are some people here to meet you," he called out loudly. "They are from the Cleveland Diocese and they want to talk to you."

It didn't take long. As soon as he said that these men were from the church, a wind blew down the theater, dropping the temperature by at least 20 degrees, and a darkness formed three rows down from where they were standing. Suddenly Father Jacques DuMond appeared and he was wearing the same formal vestments as Stephen had seen him in a few times.

Qui sont–ils?" DuMond asked, as soon as he became solid.

"Look, you rude renegade priest," Stephen stated, after glancing over at the three priests. "How many times do I have to tell you to speak English? Think about it? Did you ever give your sermons in French?... Oh, I doubt it."

"No, they were always in Latin" replied the angry priest, as he looked at Stephen with a look that could kill, if he wanted it to. "I know that priest," Jacques DuMond said, as he pointed to the bishop. He was the one who spoke to me with such contempt. If it wasn't for you saying I have a right to defend myself to show all I have done here for the good of the church and for all true Christianity by punishing all sinners, I would certainly not acknowledge any of you. So tell me, who are these other two men?"

"As I said, they are from Cleveland Diocese," Stephen stated once again. "This is Father Talbot..." Stephen pointed toward Father Talbot, who was just standing there, looking as if he were trying to figure out if this was real or some illusion created by his own mind. ... He had dealt with many things within the church, but never ever anything like this.

"And this is Cardinal Morrisey. He has taken precious time from his busy schedule to come here to meet you."

Cardinal Morrisey didn't show any reaction to Jacques DuMond's appearance. It was like he just happened to run into him on a street corner and they had just met. He, without thinking, reached his hand out to shake hands, but naturally this could never have happened, so he withdrew it immediately. Jacques DuMond immediately dropped to his knees and tried to kiss a ring that Morrisey had on. Naturally, this failed, as Jacques DuMond's face just slid through the cardinal's body, leaving no question in any of the priests' minds that Father Jacques DuMond was truly a ghost..

"Your Immanence," Jacques DuMond said, looking up at the man standing before him. "How may I serve you?"

'I have heard about your work here and want to know more," Cardinal Morrisey said. "From what I have heard you were misunderstood, by the church at that time, about your strong dealings with the parishioners of the Church of the Sacred Feminine, and I just wanted to let you know, that the diocese and Rome have, after all these years, now seriously taken notice of what you have done here."

Father Jacques DuMond's chest swelled with pride and his eyes lit up with pleasure. Actually the cardinal had really said nothing about what he felt about what had happened so many year ago, but naturally Jacques DuMond interpreted the words the way he wanted to interpret them, just like when he had totally ignored a papal order.

"We have discussed your work and we think that your job here may well be done," Cardinal Morrisey stated, as Father Talbot took a paper out of a cloth bag he was carrying, handing it to Cardinal Morrisey. "It is our opinion that you could better serve the church if you were assigned to a parish which is suffering the way this city was when you arrived."

"But there are still sinners here, Your Immanence," DuMond replied. "There was a thief not too long ago stealing food and just today I caught a vandal in one of the back rooms. He was punished the way Rome instructed me to."

All four of the men looked at each other with a mixture of confusion and a touch of fear.

"What did you do?" Talbot asked.

"He will sin no more. That is what I am supposed to do... stop sinners," Father DuMond said.

What the fuck is he talking about? Stephen thought. "Father DuMond, where is this vandal?"

Jacques DuMond still had that proud look on his face when he told Stephen that the sinner was in the room at the back of the building. He knew exactly which room DuMond was talking about. It was the one he used as a lounge/coffee house when he had private parties. Stephen didn't wait. He grabbed Bishop Duncan by the shoulder and both men ran down the short hall beside the screen.

"We will be right back, cardinal," Stephen called out to Father Talbot and Cardinal Morrisey."

They went into the coffee house. The lights were on. That was strange, since Stephen had sent everyone home and didn't have any parties planned for the evening.

The walls of the lounge were covered with murals by a local artist, and the few spots where there wasn't a mural, there was a painting hanging there by the same artist. Stephen liked art and always had, so he never thought of repainting the room or taking any of the painting down. On the wall by the coffee house counter there was a beautiful eagle painted all in red, black and gold. Stephen looked around and didn't see any damage, but he did see the body of a man lying by the counter, who looked to be about 45 years old.

The two of them went over and immediately started to examine the body. It was easy to see that the man had been badly beaten and had been dead for a couple of hours, so of course there was nothing they could do to help him. They needed to find what he had supposedly damaged to cause his death, and why he had been murdered by the insane Jacques DuMond..

"Do you see any damage?" Stephen asked, as he continued to look around.

"I don't see anything," Bishop Duncan replied.

They continued to search under the furniture, behind the paintings and even in the two bathrooms at the back of the room, without luck. Finally, they found it. It seemed the man had snuck back and was making a pot of coffee when he dropped the coffee pot and it broke.

"Look at this," Bishop Duncan said, as he picked the coffee pot up off the floor. "Do you believe this?"

"When it comes to Jacques DuMond, I believe anything," Stephen said, as he finally went over to the body to see who it was lying there. He did not recognize him at first, he was so badly beaten, so Stephen took the man's wallet out of his trousers and searched through it. The man's name was Scott McClelland. He was actually the former owner of the building… the man Stephen had bought the theater from.

Scott McClelland was well known in Akron as a gambler and a thug, who had been arrested a few times on vandalism charges. Actually, Stephen then suddenly remembered that right after he bought the building, there was some equipment missing from the original inventory, and he was sure that it was Scott who had taken it, but he couldn't prove it, and even if he could, it wouldn't have done any good. McClelland had been arrested a number of times over the years, but never convicted because he used the fact that his father was a summit county judge and because of it, the district attorney never followed through.

"You know what," Stephen said, "I didn't like McClelland, but he shouldn't have died that way… especially not over a broken coffee pot." Bishop Duncan either didn't know what to say, or he was in such shock from finding the body. "Believe it or not, you do get used to it," Stephen stated.

"You know that isn't nice," Bishop Duncan stated.

"I know, but I can't feel any other way about it. Remember Bishop, this evil bastard for so many years remained here, preaching the word of God and punishing sinners and your people knew absolutely nothing about it and your diocese was only 35 miles away." Seeing the look on Bishop Duncan's face, Stephen wished he hadn't just said what he did, but actually it was true; if the church had only opened their eyes to what was going on, none of this would have happened.

"Bishop Duncan, please forgive what I just said, but unfortunately it is the truth. But let us do something about it now. So let's get back up front and see what's going on. We'll take care of this later." Bishop Duncan made no reply, but the deep sadness in his eyes said it all.

They went back into the theater. It was empty, but out in the lobby they found Father Talbot, Cardinal Morrisey, and, incredibly, Father Jacques DuMond, sitting on the couches in the lobby. To Stephen they actually looked relaxed and almost friendly, and that scared him a lot. As soon as Cardinal Morrisey saw Stephen, he asked Father DuMond if he could see how things were handled where sinners were concerned.

Jacques DuMond stared at Stephen with a contemptuous, commanding look and nodded, then he instantly disappeared. Stephen took that as a sign that he was supposed to take Cardinal Morrisey down into the basement to see the crypts.

"Your Immanence, if you could please follow me." Cardinal Morrisey followed Stephen back through the curtains and to the door on the floor and then down the steep stairs. On the way down Stephen made a point to tell him about the recently murdered Scott McClelland, the former owner of The Strand, and the fact that he was killed over a broken coffee pot.

As soon as Cardinal Morrisey ascended the stairs and was in the hallway of the basement, his coolness immediately dissipated. Stephen looked into his eyes and saw what he thought was concern, bordering on fear.

"Where are the paintings you spoke of?" Cardinal Morrisey asked. Stephen took him down the hallway and pointed out the paintings of the people in the hallway. They had changed. The souls looked more tortured than they had been before. "What must these souls be going through?" Cardinal Morrisey said out loud, while feeling deep inside himself such total sadness and shame for his beloved religion and church.

"Well, Cardinal, I cannot really answer that. You would know that far better than I would," Stephen replied. "I just show movies… the immortal soul is your business."

Cardinal Morrisey smiled a little and agreed. "Where are the rest of the captive souls?" he asked. Stephen took him down to the archway and into the torture chamber.

"Would you believe all this stuff was used in the church's name?"

"In the middle ages, maybe, but it should have stopped back then," Cardinal Morrisey said. "We learned from those bad times and became more humane."

"Please, your Immanence, let me show you all we have found down here," Stephen said. Cardinal Morrisey followed him and saw all of the bodies stacked up in the small room.

"How many are here?" the cardinal asked. Stephen told him the count they had was 19 adults and children, and that total was certainly supported by the documents he had given to Brother George. Then he asked the cardinal to follow him again. They went back through the chamber and Stephen led him into the children's tomb. The minute Cardinal Morrisey saw the bodies all laid out nice and neatly, as well as the pile of toys in the corner, he actually could not control his emotions any longer and started to cry openly.

"What's wrong, mister?" a little girl asked.

Cardinal Morrisey looked down and the tears flowed even heavier. There was a little girl standing before him in a tattered dress and black buckle shoes with a hole where her big toe stuck out.

"Your Immanence, allow me to introduce you to Susan," Stephen said. "She was one of the children punished for stealing bread and dried meat. Susan, this is Cardinal Morrisey, a very important man from the Catholic Church in Akron. He has come here, especially, to visit you all."

Cardinal Morrisey knelt down so he was eye to eye with the little girl. "Hello, Susan," he said. "You look like a very pretty little girl."

She thanked him and asked him to please stop crying. She had never seen any priest from the church cry before.

"Would you like to play with me?" she asked. She took a doll from the pile and told Cardinal Morrisey that her doll's name was Sheila and she was her best friend.

"The thing was…" Stephen stated, in total frustration. "Susan wasn't even the one who stole the food. She was just with the boy who did."

"Is that true?" Cardinal Morrisey asked the little girl. She handed him the doll, which he happily took. "Very nice to meet you, Sheila," he said with a big smile, as he shook hands with the doll." Seeing this, little Susan's eyes lit up with pleasure.

"Yes, sir," Susan said. "I was always a good girl. My mommy and daddy always said so."

"I can see that and I think your mommy and daddy were right," Cardinal Morrisey said. "You are a very, very good girl."

"We should start to go back upstairs," Stephen stated, as he tapped the cardinal on the shoulder. "I have a feeling Reverend Jacques DuMond will be waiting for us to receive your report on all he has done here. It is incredible to believe, but that mad fiend literally believes he has the blessing of the church for all the evil he has committed."

"Susan, I am very sorry, but we have to go for a little while," Cardinal Morrisey stated gently, as he handed the doll back to Susan. "I promise that I will come back and see you."

Susan lowered her head as if she was going to start crying. "Okay, sir," she said. "I will be here waiting for you." She walked over and gave Cardinal Morrisey, who was still kneeling, a kiss on the cheek. "Sir, Mummy and I always went to church every Sunday; it didn't matter if we had nothing to eat. Mummy said the church and God would always be our salvation."

The expression on Cardinal Morrisey's face was one of total shame and humiliation as they left Susan and started toward the door. Suddenly the cardinal felt a tug on his pant leg. He looked down and saw Susan standing there, her eyes filled with water. "Sir," she said, "I would like Sheila to go home with you. I don't get to play with her very much and she says that she likes you a lot." Cardinal Morrisey paused for a moment, not knowing what to say. "Please, sir," she said, as she held the doll up as far as she could. "I know she'd be happy with you."

He knelt down and took the doll and held it close to his chest. She smiled as he took her hand in his, feeling nothing, of course, as it passed through his body. "You know what, Susan…," he said, "… if she is half as nice as you are, I am sure that I would love to have her as my friend." Then he leaned over and tried to kiss Susan on the forehead, as her face passed through him and by the time he pulled back, she was gone.

They walked through the door, through the torture chamber and into the hallway. Suddenly Cardinal Morrisey grabbed Stephen by the arm, stopping him in his tracks.

"How do we deal with this… all of this?" Cardinal Morrisey asked, as he looked at the paintings again. "My work has always been for the good of not only our Catholic parishioners, but for all of the community. I must admit I am finding this so horrific, I cannot cope with this. It is all far too painful. I am so ashamed. How did we let this continue? How could we have been so blind? How in the Lord's sacred name did this ever happen?" Stephen had been feeling this for a long time, so he had no answer. He just walked ahead of the cardinal and headed down the hallway and up the stairs to the theater above.

They walked through the theater. The cardinal put the doll on one of the seats and headed into the lobby with Stephen. All they saw were the two priests sitting there drinking a couple of Diet Cokes.

"Where is Jacques DuMond?" Stephen inquired immediately.

"He was here for a while," Bishop Duncan stated. "Then it looked like he just got bored and left."

"He got bored," Cardinal Morrisey asked. "Did you try talking to him?"

Yes, but he stated he had already taken enough insults from me, and, as Father Talbot was just an assistant to you, he just wasn't interested in anything further we had to say. You are right, Stephen, his ego is beyond words," Bishop Duncan replied.

Without saying anything further, Cardinal Morrisey walked around the lobby and called out for Father Jacques DuMond to appear.

"Father DuMond… this is Cardinal Morrisey. If you are here I would appreciate talking with you."

Once again a breeze blew through the lobby, and when it stopped, Father Jacques DuMond was standing directly in front of the cardinal.

"How may I serve you, Your Immanence?" he asked.

"I saw the way you worked and I was at first shocked, but then I understood what you are doing and understand your thinking and how to want to protect the church from all evil sinners," Cardinal Morrisey stated. "There has not been a parish priest in more than four hundred years who was as thorough as you have been. The Vatican definitely does not have many devout passionate priests like you."

Jacques DuMond's face lit up and his body seemed to puff up.

Wow, Stephen thought to himself, *I can't believe this bastard is falling for this shit. Something's going to happen… this is going too well.*

"Father DuMond, please allow me to take five minutes and place a call," Cardinal Morrisey said. "I will be right back." The cardinal walked out of the front door, putting his cell phone up to his ear. Five minutes later he was back. "Father DuMond, I was just talking to a friend at the Vatican and he told me of a parish that we would like you to take over as its parish priest. Would you be interested?"

"Where is it located?" Jacques DuMond inquired, his eyes lighting up at the prospect. His work was being appreciated by the Vatican for the first time.

"It is in a small town in France," Cardinal Morrisey informed him, as Bishop Duncan, Father Talbot and Stephen looked at each other with hope in their hearts of destroying this beast, but didn't say a word, leaving it all up to the cardinal..

"They are having a lot of trouble with stealing, damage and a lot of other really nasty stuff. They need someone like you to get things straight again," the cardinal stated.

Oh my fucking God, Stephen thought and from the looks of the two priests it was a thought that they were all sharing. *How could he be so stupid?*

Jacques DuMond looked like he was seriously thinking about the offer. He kept looking up, then glancing back toward the entrance to the basement and toward all four men. "Who would keep my work going here?" he asked.

"I was thinking about Bishop Duncan to replace you here," Cardinal Morrisey said. "He can see the work you did here and I am sure he would continue to keep your work intact."

Jacques DuMond hesitated for a few seconds and then agreed to have Bishop Duncan take his place and he also agreed to take over the parish in France. "It would be nice to get home again," he said. "It has been a few years since I was home and I miss the place."

"How many years has it been?" Cardinal Morrisey asked.

Jacques DuMond thought for a minute and did some counting and said that it had been 37 years since he'd been on French soil. "I left in the winter of 1869. Christmas week, I think. It has been so long," he said, with a tear in his eye.

Wrong answer, you idiot, it's been over 139 to be exact, Stephen thought, but of course he didn't say anything. *Holy shit, this fiend doesn't even realize how long he's been here.*

Cardinal Morrisey, Father Talbot and Bishop Duncan all had the same thought as Stephen, so they glanced at each other, as Cardinal Morrisey changed his approach just a little bit to adjust for DuMond's thinking of what year he was in.

Cardinal Morrisey looked at Father Jacques DuMond and told him that there was no time to lose, he had to leave immediately to make sure he wasn't late for the ship that would take him to France. "The tickets are waiting for you at the dock," Cardinal Morrisey informed the now excited Jacques DuMond. "We got you a stateroom on the main deck. There will be new clothes and vestments on the ship."

Father Jacques DuMond's entire attitude changed. He actually smiled and thanked all of the men in the room, especially Stephen. "Stephen," he said, "I want to thank you for everything. You brought these men to my church and you told them of my work and now I have a new parish to go to. Merci, my friend. Merci!"

Stephen didn't say anything. He just thought, *How can this fucking idiot be so fucking clueless? I really didn't think this was going to work.*

"We have to go," Cardinal Morrisey said, as he offered Father Jacques DuMond a ride to the ship. "I want to make sure you get to the dock in Erie on time. You can't be late or they'll sail without you."

He walked the satanic priest, to the door. As they reached it, Father Jacques. DuMond got a very frightened look on his face. No doubt the world had changed. He had not left the theater or even approached any of the windows to look out, and he wasn't sure what it was like. He could see through the glass, but that wasn't the same as experiencing it. Cardinal Morrisey opened the door and went out. Father Jacques DuMond continued to hesitate, suddenly paralyzed with fear.

"Come on, Father… we have to go. The Vatican will not, let me assure you, issue another ticket if you miss the ship. They need you in France as soon as possible. They are relying on you."

"Father, you cannot refuse such an offer," Stephen called out. "I am sure it has to be something special when the Vatican reverses its judgment on what you have done here, and actually wants you to take on a new church and rectify all that is wrong there." That one comment, called out in desperation by Stephen, was enough to push the defrocked priest enough to get him to leave.

Cardinal Morrisey was holding the door open when Father Jacques DuMond stepped through it. The minute he did, Cardinal Morrisey knew his mission had been accomplished, as a fire started to burn within Jacques DuMond's soul. It was all consuming and Cardinal Morrisey knew exactly what it was. Almost immediately, deep, festering rips started developing on Jacques DuMond's skin as the cardinal immediately slammed the door behind him. Then smoke, and lastly, flames began shooting from the rips.

"What on earth is happening?" Stephen asked.

"Have you ever read the Bible?" the cardinal asked, as he shielded his face from the heat, which was coming straight through the window. Not only the heat was increasing, but there was a noise that was louder, much louder than even the loudest jet engines.

"No!" Stephen yelled, trying to answer the question over the noise, but it was difficult.

"That is the fire of retribution!" Cardinal Morrisey yelled back. "It is the fire of the Ark of the Covenant; it is the fire of the anger of God!

Stephen Baker looked through the glass and saw that Jacques DuMond's skin was slowly melting from his body. His face showed a level of pain and torture that no one, not even evil Jacques DuMond, should ever have to endure.

"He is feeling all of the pain he inflicted upon others," said Cardinal Morrisey. "It is revenge for those 26 souls that he wrongly took. It is what was destined for him when he took that first life."

Flames of red, yellow, blue and black were turning the melting flesh to ash while Jacques DuMond was still "alive" to suffer through it. He pounded on the glass to get back in but Cardinal Morrisey had locked the door behind him and was holding it shut to make sure that there was no way for the priest to escape his punishment.

All present could hear Father Jacques DuMond's screams. Even though their hands were covering their ears, the sound was so terrifying, they could all still hear his agonizing screams even when it was all over.

The colored flames eventually died, but now what was left of Jacques DuMond was being devoured by flames that were nearly coal-like in color. It was dissolving the flesh and tissue, which had not already been burned, but Jacques DuMond was still there, reacting to the torturous pain. Then, suddenly, just as fast as it had started... the flames died, and when Stephen looked he observed to his horror the glass in the door was also starting to melt. There was nothing left of Father Jacques DuMond, not even ashes.

All four men looked through the glass. The three priests all made the sign of the cross as Cardinal Morrisey looked at what was outside and said, "Blessed is the power of the Father, the Son and the Holy Spirit". All of them, including Stephen, then said a united "Amen" before they started to head back into the lobby, but for some reason they all turned back to look at the glass door once again, as if looking for some sort of sign.

The glass had cooled very quickly, giving it a discolored tint. Then all three priests dropped to their knees and once again made the sign of the cross.

"Steven, look at that," Bishop Duncan whispered in awe as he pointed at the glass.

"It's a miracle," Cardinal Morrisey said in a barely audible whisper. "It's a true miracle."

Stephen looked and observed that the street lights outside the theater were just at the right angle, just the right brightness and the right color. There in the melted glass was a golden image... it was the image of Mary... the Virgin Mother of the Christ... the Sacred Feminine!

"What does that mean?" Stephen inquired, stunned at what he was seeing.

"I think it means that the evil that was Father Jacques DuMond has left this place and God has given His grace back to this land," Cardinal Morrisey said. "There will be no more death, no more pain or suffering in this place. He has shown His love and charity."

Stephen didn't wait to hear any more. He took off running through the theater with Cardinal Morrisey, Bishop Duncan and Father Talbot no more than ten feet behind him, asking him what was going on.

"Follow me!" he yelled back at them.

The four of them didn't slow their pace as they rushed through the theater and behind the stage, then down the steps into the basement. Nothing had changed except that the hallway, the torture chamber and the crypts were lit more than normal.

"Father, please do your thing," Stephen cried out, please save these poor captive souls.

The three priests dropped to their knees and Stephen lowered his eyes in respect as Cardinal Morrisey started with a prayer.

"Holy Father, Your grace has entered this building. On behalf of the souls captured here through years of torment, I beseech You to forgive them their sins and allow them all to enter the paradise that is Your kingdom," Cardinal Morrisey prayed, his eyes looked upward toward heaven.

At that moment the room lightened to a point where it was almost blinding to Stephen and the others. When the light dimmed Susan walked out of the crypt and right over to Cardinal Morrisey.

"Thank you, sir," she said, before she walked through the room and into the hallway. "I suddenly feel so safe and happy."

Stephen followed her out of the door. She stopped in the middle of the hall, right where Meghyn said that the veil between heaven and hell was. His eyes looked back at the door and across to the picture of Summerland.

"What should I do?" Little Susan asked Stephen, as she turned around to look at him, a confused look in her eyes.

"Susan, trust in God and I promise if you just take a step into Summerland," he stated softly, "for eternity there will be no more pain and you will find friends there to play with and…," Stephen looked into her thrilled eyes at all he was saying and immediately started to cry. "… Susan, you will at long last be at peace and you find your mommy and daddy there. I am quite sure that they are waiting for you."

Susan looked again, smiled back at Stephen and took a step across the veil. Stephen watched as white light enveloped her and took her into the painting. He looked and there she was. She had on a new white lace dress which had replaced the torn one she had always worn. Her hair was curly and held up with a pink ribbon and she was carrying a sweet little purse that matched the ribbon. The last thing he noticed was that she was smiling a smile that was the pure happiness that only a child can feel.

One by one, each of the other souls walked through the door, and, after being reassured by Stephen, they crossed through the veil and went from their hell into Summerland. As they did, each of their images faded from the one side of the hall and appeared on the other. Each one looked so different. The poor children, the ones who stole food, looked happy, well dressed and well fed. When the last of the souls crossed over, Stephen turned and saw what he didn't expect. The souls of Scott McClelland and William Jackson were coming down the steps, and even the reporter Jeff Davis. None of them said a word to Stephen; they just walked past him and into Summerland.

"I guess they were forgiven too," Stephen said with a laugh. Then he noticed that he hadn't seen Tina cross over. He looked carefully and she wasn't in the picture. He looked back at the painting on the opposite wall and saw that all of the people in the picture were gone. As a matter of fact, the painting was fading and the stone behind was coming though. It was a very short time, as Stephen watched, and suddenly the evil painting of hell was gone. At that moment Stephen felt his heart sink. Where was Tina? "Tina!" he cried out, "Sweet, dear, darling Tina, where have you gone? Why did I not see you crossing over? What has happened? Why, of all people, are you still being punished?" he cried out in despair and deep, deep sadness. "This is not fair! Tina, of all the captive souls here, you most deserve to go to Summerland."

"What is the problem, Stephen?" Bishop Duncan inquired.

"It's Tina... she didn't cross over with the rest. Where is she?

"I don't know," Cardinal Morrisey answered. "I am sure she was forgiven just like the rest."

"Then where is she?" Stephen yelled, as he grabbed Cardinal Morrisey by the collar and pushed him against the wall. His thoughts had gone from the pleasure of seeing all those happy people, suddenly to pure panic. With a lot of effort, he kept himself under control as much as possible, but deep inside he was in turmoil. He couldn't stand it anymore; he felt such utter despair. Of all who had been captive in the Strand Movie Theater, Tina was the one who most deserved to be saved. Feeling utterly helpless, he just collapsed in a nearby chair, and respectfully requested the fathers to leave him alone, or he would not be responsible for what might happen. Then he burst into tears.

Understanding that the girl Tina must have meant so much to Stephen, the three priests didn't say a word to try to comfort him... not that it would have done any good anyway. Stephen Baker was too upset and far too angry to hear anything from anyone... much less these three servants of God. The three priests walked down the hallway and up the stairs. A couple of minutes later Stephen heard Father Talbot yell down to him that there was something in the lobby that he must come up to see.

Stephen didn't care about what Father Talbot was saying. All he could think of was Tina, and, feeling so downhearted, Stephen ignored the priest. He stayed down in the basement, calling out for Tina but she never replied, and, in the end, he remained in the basement for more than an hour thinking, crying and cursing and praying he would one day see Tina's vision in Summerland. But apparently God had forsaken her. Why Tina of all people? He kept asking himself over and over again. After all the souls that had been saved, why was Tina not saved? Why, where Tina was concerned, why was God such an uncaring God?

Finally, with a broken heart, he walked up the stairs. The theater was dark except for the running lights on the edge of the risers. The room was silent... so silent that the only sound that Stephen could hear was his own breathing.

There were still tears in his eyes when he heard something. "What time does the movie start, please?" a voice said. "I have been sitting here for an hour and I can't even get a Coke. Is this any way to run a theater?"

His eyes adjusted to the light, or lack of light, and he saw a beautiful young woman sitting there. She was wearing a pink blouse with a black skirt. Her hair was down and covered her shoulders with soft auburn curls. Her eyes were fiery, full of life and she looked happy... extremely happy. "Tina, is that you?" Stephen asked in an awe struck whisper.

"Yes, Stephen, it really is me," she said, as she stood up and started walking toward him.

The moment she reached him Stephen wrapped his arms around her. She was real and he could feel her, and, as he held her tightly, he looked at her and smiled and then kissed her deeply. This time she wasn't a ghost. She was skin and bones. He could feel her breathing and even her heart beating through his chest.

"How?" he asked.

"I was ready to cross over," she said. "I was the last to die, so I was the last to cross over. When it came to be my turn something touched me on the shoulder and told me that it was not my time, and that I had some things I had to do in the Lord's name. The next thing I knew, I was sitting there waiting for you."

"Oh, my darling, darling Tina. I was in despair. I was so worried you were not going to be released."

"I don't know who it was, Stephen, but someone gave me my life back and I thank you for helping for making all this happen," she said, as she kissed him tenderly.

"What do you say we get the hell out of here?" Stephen suggested, as he took her by the hand and walked her through the lobby and to the front door.

"I think we already did! But I can't go outside, Stephen," Tina said, with a sudden look of fear on her face.

"Oh yes, you can, my darling," Stephen said, as he guided her through the door. "I am not going to let anything happen to you… not now… Not ever, my love."

She followed him through the door. She wanted to believe she was safe, but deep inside, despite her love for Stephen Baker, she was expecting to be killed the way Jacques DuMond had been. Instead, once outside, holding Stephen's hand tightly, she took a deep breath of fresh hair, smiled, and told Stephen that it was cold for her. He handed her his coat and they walked the two blocks over to the Steak & Eggs. He walked in ahead of her.

"Wait here, my darling. Wait here till I come and get you. All the others are inside and your appearance will make them all so happy."

As Stephen walked into the diner, Meghyn called out.

"How did it go?" she asked.

"It went extremely well," Stephen replied "Father Jacques DuMond is gone and it was great watching him burn. The souls have passed on to the other side…," He paused for a moment and opened the door. "… except, for one." He went out the door and returned, leading Tina into the room.

"May I introduce you to Miss Tina Dameron… the only survivor of the Church of the Sacred Feminine."

Jason, Laura and Meghyn all got up from the table in shock, then ran over to Tina, and, in turn, all gave Tina the warmest possible hug, as they immediately became aware she was not passing through them. She was still the same Tina, but this time very much alive, for the first time in 100 years.

Then they all sat back down, including Tina, and Jason ordered her a hamburger and chili fries. "Tina," he said, "I know that it has been quite a while since you've anything to eat, so we might as well get you into the 21st century with a good meal."

When the sun came up they were all still sitting there laughing, drinking coffee and Cokes and filling Tina in on how the world had changed in 104 years. Then, sometime around 8:00 in the morning, Stephen took Tina back to his house and they commenced their lives together.

EPILOGUE

The next day Stephen called the police and the county coroner about the bodies in the basement. They came and collected them all and performed autopsies on them. It took about four months to finish everything up. The causes of death ranged from blunt force trauma, to starvation to drowning and even a burning.

There was also a probe held within the Catholic Church. It was found that Father DuMond was decidedly crazy, but they decided that the proper thing to do, since the church was originally sanctioned, was for the diocese to handle the funerals for the deceased.

On August 21, 2008 all of the bodies from the Strand Theater were interred in a specially built mausoleum in a secluded part of an unidentified cemetery outside of Akron. There are no names, no dates on the tomb. It is just a plain white Greco-Roman building that no one would ever notice.

The only visitors to know the history of the occupants are Tina and Stephen, who, once a year, go and place 25 white roses in front of the gates of the tomb.

The theater is still open and showing two movies a night and four shows on the weekend. Meghyn was made assistant manager and loves spending time with her great-great grandmother. Jason still works as projectionist and Laura quit to run her own theater in Erie, Pennsylvania.

Tina and Stephen married in October 2008 and they had a set of twins nine months later. Tina named them Susan and Eleanor. They are still married and living happily in Cuyahoga Falls, Ohio and Tina, accompanied by her children, still goes to the movies, and sits in her regular seat, at least once a week.

ABOUT THE AUTHOR

R.E. Taylor, who turned 59 years old this year has devoted his life to writing the most interesting, vivid, entertaining stories his imagination can create. He enjoys the darker side of life because he says, "It gives me more freedom to create without the normal rules light side writers have. With "Captive Souls" he fills his promise to scare, elevate, entertain and make even the coolest person wonder.